Letters to Julius

Postmarked Palo Alto

Letters to Julius

Postmarked Palo Alto

Jodi Lynn Threat

Letters to Julius: Postmarked Palo Alto by Jodi Lynn Threat

Cover image by Rene Rauschenberger from Pixabay

ISBN: 978-1-0926288-5-3

Printed in the United States of America
First printing 2019

This culture
Predicts the future
Lives for the future
Wishes for shiny new
Always lives for the future
Forgets the past then again
Misses the past winds in the leaves
Remembers the soft air in the afternoons before dinners
No matter where you go, there you still are
Those memories emerge like idols
Where humorous elders rise
In order to tell the young
To listen to the creed
Honor the elders
Rise elders

Carol Lee Taylor

INTRODUCTION

In the mid-1800s San Francisco, California, was a city that attracted risk-takers, explorers, and the disenfranchised. It was a potpourri of individuals bent on starting their lives anew. Promises of wealth and adventure during the "Gold Rush" lured even the most common person to try to become a gold miner. Many of the newcomers who arrived at the ports didn't pack their trunks with refinement.

Nonetheless, the economy thrived due to the diverse groups of people who possessed talents and trades to build society and culture. Talents in culinary arts, gardening, painting, music, and theater. Avant-garde thinkers and writers.

Wealthy, established families who were enticed by the city's rich cultural opportunities needed tradesmen who were skilled in all facets of construction to build their homes, libraries, music halls, and theaters. These tradesmen came from all over the globe.

As San Francisco blossomed into a unique coastal hub of business and culture, smaller cities and bedroom communities sprang up in the Bay Area. By the late 1960s the upper middle-class town of Palo Alto, California, situated on the peninsula outside San Francisco, was well established as a center of education, technology, and business.

It would also become a hotbed of societal transformation during the era of the Vietnam War and social injustice.

The summer of 1967 became known as the "Summer of

1

Love," as the focus of the country was often on San Francisco and surrounding cities like Palo Alto, where teens and college-age "hippies" practiced "free love," accompanied by a soundtrack of psychedelic music and plenty of drugs. Young people grew up comparing their Age of Aquarius to their elders' stories of survival during the Great Depression and their own wars. Like the fictitious characters in this book, Palo Alto's youth had to come to terms with the contrast between their comfortable lives and what was happening in the world around them.

Although this is a work of fiction, it springs from my fond and still-vivid memories of growing up with a close circle of friends in "P.A."—our affectionate term for Palo Alto—during a turbulent time in our country's history.

This story is dedicated to the human experience of self-actualization, which opens in childhood, flowers during the coming-of-age years, and offers exploration in adulthood.

1 A BABY BOOMER BACK HOME
September 2015

Maggie awakens to the sounds of birds chirping and her heart wildly pounding. Her hairline and neck are sweaty, and from an elastic band her white and light brown hair unravels into damp tendrils over her eyes, occluding her vision.

"Where am I?" she mutters to herself before remembering she is back home in Palo Alto, California. She gives herself a moment to collect her thoughts and enjoy a bed to herself with no responsibilities.

"Okay, hop to it," she says out loud. "Make some coffee. Take a shower. You've got a mystery to solve."

She gets the coffee going before heading outside to the patio of her rented apartment. A perfect spot for her tai chi, Yang style, short form. First, she warms up with some gentle swaying movements, loosening her joints and muscles.

Next, she moves into stretching exercises that broaden her torso and limbs. Extending her lean arms overhead, she grasps her fingers together and moves into Salute to the Sun, a settling down for the continued stretches. Even at age sixty-two, her long, slender legs are her best feature.

The studio rental is the ideal place to indulge herself in a month-long, solo adventure far away from her troubled home life in Oregon. The residue of toxic living fades away like a trail of smoke in this bright and airy California refuge. The

San Francisco Bay area is where her life began. Hopefully, this is where she can find and free herself.

While the coffee is still dripping, Maggie makes her bed and opens the windows to let in a cool morning breeze. It's going to heat up today, reaching the upper eighties. Her plan is to explore Palo Alto on foot, so best to do so early in the day.

She thinks about calling home but decides against it. She checked in when she arrived yesterday. Now she just wants to bask in the relief of being away.

Back on the patio, coffee in hand, she contemplates nature. She loves the very air scented by piney juniper bushes and citrusy lantana flowers. She empties her mind of thoughts about alcoholism, conflict, and lingering grief to focus on her surroundings. Brightly ripened summer foliage surrounds the back yard. A fig tree in the middle of a red-bricked patio boasts fresh organic fruit. For a few moments, the only movement is that of a Cooper's hawk, gliding high above, swooping between redwoods, elms, and oaks.

Her mind eventually wanders back to why she is here in Palo Alto. She has a book to write, and she has a real-life mystery to solve. While her job in social services helps her pay the bills, Maggie's true passion is writing mysteries. It's essential to get the new novel off to a good start, she told her family and friends, and to do that she needs to be away from home for a month. She has enough vacation time accrued so that her absence from work won't be a problem. Her family is another story.

"But why Palo Alto?" her husband asked. "Why can't you write here?" her daughter chimed in.

"Because the main character is based on a guy I knew in Palo Alto," she replied. "A friend who disappeared. I need to be there for ... research. And my editor needs my first draft by Thanksgiving."

She doesn't share with her family her plan to find out what really happened to her old friend. And she doesn't share the anticipation that returning to Palo Alto will rekindle the joy she felt when she was young. Those barefooted summers, long-ago crushes, and first loves still linger in her mind like ghostly teenagers. To Maggie, Palo Alto is the land of enchanted memories.

A fluttering hummingbird evaluates a purple-flowered fuchsia bush and Maggie announces to him, "Today I'm going to try to find Julius's house. Oh, and wait, bird. That's not the only one. I want to find Olin's house, too. What's that you say, birdie? Yes, Julius and Olin were two of my boyfriends from 1968—my favorite year."

The hummingbird flies away, signaling his disinterest.

Julius Brownell and Olin Wolfe. They stole her heart for over a year. How often she has thought about them in the past forty years, especially when she feels disconnected from the grown-up world that a woman her age is expected to embrace.

And the girlfriends. Oh, how she misses them. They often laugh in a corner of her mind, even now. She has never had any trouble making friends, wherever she has found herself living, but her Palo Alto girls hold a special place in her heart. She is excited at the thought of connecting with them on this trip.

Even if they think she's a little crazy.

"Maggie, why does it matter where Julius is?"

"Maggie, of course we want to see you, but what do you hope to accomplish in Palo Alto?"

"You know, Maggie, I always thought you lived too much in the past. I love you, but Julius? Really? He's been gone for ages. Hasn't he?"

Maggie doesn't think her girlfriends fully understand her need to find Julius, but they are enthusiastic about spending time together during her visit. That's good enough for her.

Yesterday's drive from Oregon to Palo Alto was long and hot, so she heads for the shower before leaving her studio.

University Avenue is the heart of downtown Palo Alto. At one time parking was ample—and free—and the city buses were full. Now the streets and parking lots are packed with new sports cars and sport utility vehicles. It takes Maggie quite a while to find a decent parking spot.

She strolls familiar streets, and the aromas carried by the morning air arouse youthful memories. She recalls an article she read recently. "It's been scientifically proven that the brain's memory and scent regions are closely connected," the author asserted.

Little flower shops, coffee houses, home décor retail establishments. Brew pubs and wine bars. Some have been here since Maggie was a little girl, managing to survive somehow. She walks past several open-air restaurants, where servers carry trays of midday cocktails and sourdough bread. Maggie's relieved to see there are still many original Spanish-style buildings of stucco and wood with red-tiled roofs. Other, newer businesses are housed in original storefronts but magnificently renovated.

This is amazing and oh so refreshingly familiar. Maggie feels utterly contented. She stops at an outdoor tea shop.

"Good day, ma'am. Our special tea of the day is the herbal peppermint."

"That sounds wonderful," Maggie says, perusing the menu. Soon she is seated at a table along the sidewalk, savoring fresh fruit, molasses-ginger cookies, and tea as she contemplates her two mysteries.

The fictional mystery will be the third in her series of novels about missing people. Her old friend Julius is the inspiration for the new book. The real-life mystery is how and why Julius seemingly vanished fifteen years ago.

Maggie and Julius dated in 1968 and '69 and remained friends until they both left the Bay Area in the late 1970s. Julius headed to the redwoods of northern California and Maggie moved to the opposite side of the country, embarking on a new life in Connecticut. She seldom thought about Julius after that. She was distracted by exploring the East Coast, distracted by careers in journalism, medical assisting, and community health. And equally distracting ... domestic partnerships and motherhood.

It would be twenty years before Maggie reached out to Julius again. Divorced and raising three children, she was feeling lonely and nostalgic. For two years they exchanged letters and occasional phone calls. In 2000, though, he stopped writing and calling. He was living with his parents at the time, but when she finally phoned him after a few months of silence, his mother was of no help.

"I will tell him you called, dear," she said politely.

Another six months went by, and she tried calling again.

His father was curt. "Nope. He's not living here anymore. And he doesn't want anyone to bother him."

It was strange. Why had Julius stopped communicating and why were his parents being so secretive? Maggie felt abandoned. Eventually, though, she forgot about Julius and moved on with her life.

It was her foray into writing mysteries that brought Julius to mind again. This time Maggie sought out another old boyfriend, Olin Wolfe. If anyone would know where Julius was, it would be Olin. He and Julius had been good friends at one time.

Olin didn't sound pleased by her call. "Maggie, how in the hell did you find my phone number?"

"Is that any way to greet me?" she protested.

"It's been zillions of years since we've talked, Maggie. I go out of my way to keep my phone number private."

It took several minutes to divert Olin from the subject of how she tracked him down to the subject of Julius's disappearance. Finally, Maggie managed to get him to agree to join the reunion of Palo Alto friends during her visit. And perhaps more importantly, he had agreed to help look for Julius.

Maggie thinks about that conversation with Olin while sipping the last of her tea outside the University Avenue tea shop. She smiles at the thought that she has been able to retain her youthful powers of persuasion after all these years.

After teatime, Maggie explores downtown Palo Alto, looking for familiar landmarks. There's the Stanford Theater, built during Hollywood's heyday in the 1930s. Maggie and her friends had watched many a movie in this iconic theater.

Maggie is giddy as she peeks through the glass of the locked front door. A nostalgic bubble in her belly feels as if it's about to burst. She spies the original candy counter at the far side of the spacious lobby, which has been updated with new carpet and new chandeliers. She steps back and notices the marquee out front advertising a showing of *Gone with the Wind.*

Satisfied, Maggie heads north and meanders down a series of side streets until she reaches a neighborhood of old homes.

She remembers that Julius's house was close to the creek, but she cannot recall the address. No matter. It doesn't take her long to find it.

"Holy moly, there it is," she says out loud.

A single-story bungalow built during the Craftsman or Arts and Crafts period, Julius's house remains an oddity on its small suburban lot.

Large trees shade the property. The front porch spans the entire width of the house. Maggie notes that the wooden stairs and the floor of the porch have been painted white, but the wood is warped and the paint is chipped. Distressed, small, and shabby looking, the house brings back memories. How had Julius's large family fit in such a small house?

As a teenager, she was never permitted entrance. A knock on Julius's front door would sometimes be met by his mother opening it halfway, saying, "Oh, he isn't here." Other times, she would call Julius to the door and he would bound outside after giving his mother a quick thank you and a kiss. Returning to the house was similarly strange. Julius held Maggie's hand as they strolled downtown during their dates, but when they got to his house, he would drop her hand and make his way up the front steps, with no invitation to come inside and nary a look back at her as she stood on the sidewalk.

Maggie was only fifteen when she met eighteen-year-old Julius. She was drawn to his gentle nature, warmth, and friendliness. Such a contrast to the charming and extroverted Olin—the classic alpha dog. Julius had seemed harmless, a laid-back surfer with an untroubled laugh.

Yet something unusual had always stood between Maggie and Julius. She stands in front of his house now and realizes she still doesn't know what that was.

She struggles back into the present moment. Noisy little black squirrels are winding themselves in circles around the trunk of an oak tree in Julius's front yard. They chase each other around the lawn, speaking in tongues and skipping their way over to a picket fence, where they pirouette and posture.

"We did help each other come of age, though. Julius did that for me. Helped me trust."

Maggie notices the neighbor sitting on her front porch, staring at her. Maggie waves. The woman does not.

"Sorry, ma'am," Maggie calls out. "I have a habit of talking to myself."

Somewhere in this neighborhood is Olin Wolfe's home. The afternoon sun feels good on Maggie's shoulders as she moves on to her next destination.

Olin's neighborhood is a landmark on her map of 1968, featuring remarkable sidewalks that are unique to Palo Alto. When Maggie sees the familiar squares, she feels a tug in her heart. They signify an orderly, contained town where she felt safe.

Thirty-inch-by-thirty-inch squares, two columns wide, stretching block after block, winding from neighborhood to neighborhood. Just the right size for hopscotch, and Maggie gives in to the urge, paying no attention to how silly she might look to any onlookers as she hopscotches her way down the street. She is as much in love with the Palo Alto sidewalks as she is with her memories of Olin and Julius.

"There it is."

Her nostalgic ramble has led her to Olin's house. What was once a rather rundown, old white house—a perfect, magical, mysteriously vintage hangout for teenagers in 1968—is now a sequined beauty, renovated and repaired to enhance its architectural history. A fine lady because of her years.

It sits comfortably close to Palo Alto's longstanding Spanish, Victorian, and Craftsman homes and businesses, built between the mid-nineteenth century and the early twentieth century. Maggie's perception as a teenager was that

9

it was an enormous house. Actually, it's smaller than she remembers.

Forty-seven years ago, young Margaret Mayes kissed Olin Wolfe full on his lips in this very front yard while her nether regions glowed like a sunburn.

She stands here now, not a lovestruck slip of a girl but an older woman with many more pounds and many more wrinkles. She shrugs and sighs, then closes her eyes for a few minutes. She is beyond concerned if people see her. She likes to be in this state of mind—a vivid yet trance-like state.

She imagines entering a portal where the minutes fly out to the solar system and her breaths are measured in turquoise as if she is swimming with dolphins. The heat of the sun penetrates her closed eyelids. The backdrop of her vision fades into yellow. Black shadows squiggle across the canvas.

Maggie remembers experiencing teenage love as a heady brew, as transparent as glass, gliding like liquid, smoky and exotic as incense. She has never put boundaries around her feelings, believing that love appears like a player in a game of hide-and-seek in a garden. It crawls right up through the soil and finds you, grabbing you with curled fingers. Who, what, where, and how is love's prerogative.

Maggie lets her kaleidoscope of thoughts simmer until she feels refreshed.

She opens her eyes and focuses again on the house. Such a grand white house. Two stories tall, swathed in intricate spindle work, cross-gabling, fish-scale siding, and a side-wrapped porch. It was built in the late 1880s in the Queen Anne or Colonial Revival tradition. Restoration and order have replaced the threadbare chaos of Olin's time. Opulent gardens surround the front of the house—lacy English gardens where plants and flowers spill into each other alongside paths of stone and grass. Something is always blooming here, Maggie is sure of it. The colors must continually refresh the owners, she marvels.

A twinge of anxiety signals that the challenging transition between past and present is upon her. She dreads this internal, disorderly passage. It's nothing new. It's been with her forever, it seems—the melancholy, the gradual rise in panic, and sometimes even the nausea that precedes an emotional shutdown. She turns away from Olin's house, needing a distraction, something that will kick in and put her back in a good mood.

She thinks about calling one of her girlfriends. Her Palo Alto girlfriends are like comfortable old, soft, cotton sweatshirts she would never throw away. She seldom smokes anymore, but she feels on edge, so she pulls out a new pack of cigarettes from her purse. Inhaling steadies her nerves and diffuses her nausea. She needs to go home now, not to her family in Oregon but back to her temporary oasis where she can inhale the calming scent of jasmine.

In the car her thoughts turn back to Julius and their two years of communication fifteen years ago. His last letter had been handwritten, as usual, but it was full of mistakes, which was not usual. What had happened to Julius? Did he die? Become confined in an institution for the legally insane? Had the joyous folly of the man she once knew wound up hitchhiking in Bali or working in a tangerine orchard in Bakersfield? She could imagine him either way.

Of course, she knew it wasn't really her business. Julius was about fifty then and by now—goodness, he'd be sixty-five years old. If he wanted to vanish, it was his choice. Or was it?

Less than an hour later she pulls into the driveway of her landlord's two-story yellow farmhouse, a charming home with white trim and a wisteria-framed front porch. She parks in the spot assigned for short-term renters of the attached studio. A sudden calm comes over her when she sees the bougainvillea trained along a trellis that edges the property.

Hot pink flowers. My favorite. Reminds me of my mom's bougainvillea at home.

Standing for a moment outside the studio, Maggie starts to sway her hips to an old Aretha Franklin tune that is playing in her head as she allows the strong outdoor fragrances to stir pleasant memories. How she treasures this oasis from all the drama.

2 A PRETTY WHITE DRESS
WITH A PINK SASH
Spring 1968

Fifteen-year-old Margaret Mayes is preparing for her ninth-grade graduation from Jordan Junior High School.

Jordan—"Home of the Dolphins"—is one of three junior high schools in Palo Alto, California; and it is conveniently located only blocks away from Maggie's house, right next to her former elementary school.

She looks forward to September, even though she will lose the status she finally achieved as a ninth-grader when she becomes just another lowly sophomore at Palo Alto High School. "Paly," as it's called, has a reputation as the oldest and most established high school of the three high schools in town. Stanford University is located right across the street, and Paly reflects the influence of the collegiate culture.

Maggie loves her graduation dress for all its trendy white cotton and the way her slim waist is accentuated by its pale, pink satin sash. She preens in the mirror. *I am hip, fab.* The bodice of the dress is covered with white lace, and little white-laced buttons soldier up the front, leading from the waist to the mandarin-style Nehru collar. The long sleeves are sheer white tulle.

Then there is the skirt. Oh, that bitchen dirndl skirt! Full and sheer with a circular cut, gathered at the waist, featuring a white petticoat underneath, its outer fabric alternating with horizontal sheer tulle and polyester stripes all the way around. Stripe upon stripe of sheer white, falling above her knee.

"Get this, world," Maggie says as she twirls in front of a full-length mirror that reflects the pale pink leather, ballerina-inspired Capezio flats that perfectly match the sash around her waist.

Her mood turns anxious as she glances at the clock. Her father is supposed to drive her and her mom to the junior high's outdoor amphitheater, where the graduation ceremony will take place. They need to leave in twenty minutes in order to be on time. It's actually close enough to walk, but her dad wants to arrive in style in his new gold Pontiac Catalina, not on foot. An unpleasant thought comes to mind.

What is he doing back there in the master bedroom? How long does it take to put on some cuff links and splash on the Old Spice? Or is he busy drinking vodka from the bottle he hides in his closet?

She shakes off the feeling of dread and continues her self-appraisal. She washed her hair this morning with pink Breck shampoo and used their pink creme rinse. She believes what it says on the glass bottles: "Never overcleans your hair with detergents. Unlike the other shampoos, Breck uses natural ingredients that gently lather your hair and leave it soft and silky."

"Oh! I'm so silky," she pouts in the mirror. It's time-consuming to dry her hair without a hair dryer, so Maggie finds her own method of styling it. She combs her wet, naturally curly hair with a wide-toothed comb to force it straight. Then, when it's just a little damp, she wraps small sections of hair around empty frozen orange juice containers. The Donald Duck orange juice cylinders are just the right size.

An hour later, presto chango! Her hair is straight, soft, and full, hanging below her chin in a subdued "pageboy." The opposite of the pageboy is the "flip," the style where the ends of the hair turn up. Maggie lets her mood determine whether she should wear a sophisticated pageboy or a perky flip.

She wonders for a moment if she should have gone with the flip, but there's no time now. Or is there? No, her father will be out any minute now, ready to go.

At one time John Mayes wielded influence in the sales division at Campbell Soup, but once his revenues dried up, he fell into the subterranean vault where older, tanked-up employees resided. In spite of having adult-onset diabetes, he refused to give up his beer and vodka despite his doctor's warning that alcohol would affect his insulin levels. Nor would he stop smoking his unfiltered Pall Mall cigarettes. He seldom came home sober, let alone on time for dinner.

Maggie's mother regularly called all the dive bars in East Palo Alto's "Whiskey Gulch" neighborhood when her husband was late. "I know he's there. Go look for him." She slammed the phone receiver down in the cradle regardless of whether she talked to her husband or not.

"He cashed in all of our life insurance policies to buy... guess what? Vodka and jaunts to Whiskey Gulch, where he thinks people from work won't recognize him," her mother complained. Even though many of her friends' dads also frequented Whiskey Gulch, Maggie still thought her father was disgraceful for not taking care of them the way a father should.

When Maggie was fourteen, her dad "quit" work (his polite excuse for being fired). The summer after he "quit," he took the family camping at their usual spot, the Napa Valley Ranch Club at Lake Berryessa. As Maggie's mother stood by the Coleman stove, preparing to cook chicken for dinner, Maggie's father stood near the edge of their campsite, perched on an embankment above a creek. He began weaving, and a few moments later he collapsed and slipped down the hill into the creek. Maggie and her mother rushed down the hill and saw him lying on his back in the shallow water.

Maggie's mother figured he was just drunk, so she left him there. Eventually he managed to crawl his way back up to the campsite.

A week later in Palo Alto, Dr. Wagner gave them the bad

news. "John had a stroke. He has developed arteriosclerosis and heart disease. He hasn't been following my orders for managing diabetes."

After the stroke, her father talked funny. His left arm was limp and he never regained full use of it. Then he got really skinny and his complexion turned gray. His face was dotted with white stubbles that he never kept clean-shaven. His sunken eyes added to his skeletal appearance. *Leave it to good 'ol stupid Daddy to fall down a hill and get half-paralyzed because he wouldn't follow doctor's orders,* Maggie thought to herself.

He is still her father, but she hates him and blames him for his ruin. Her ruin. She is tremendously ashamed of him. She can barely look him in the eye.

Her mother, on the other hand, cultivates and nurtures her. She teaches Maggie how to plan and host a good party; how to shop for, wrap, and mail Christmas gifts for out-of-state relatives; how to cook, bake, vacuum; and even do yard work.

"Iron your own clothes, Margaret Pauline, if you insist on wearing cotton and silk. Those fabrics were all we had during the Great Depression. Why do you have to buck me on this? Wash and wear is far more attractive and easier to take care of."

A bond exists between them that excludes her father.

These days Maggie is the one who must bear the burden of her mother's anger and resentment toward her husband.

Maggie tries to push the intrusive thoughts away again. "Makeup, makeup, makeup. Where is my Yardley makeup?" A cosmetic company promoted by fashion models and idolized by pre-teen and adolescent girls, Yardley of London's pocketbook is full. The company spends oodles of money on colorful, slick magazine ads featuring famous models using their makeup.

"Black eyeliner—top and bottom. A hint of green eyeshadow. Follow with thick brown mascara. What more do I need to be any cuter?'

Whenever British model Twiggy wears Yardley, she looks dead-on foxy and pouty.

15

"Surely, any boy would kiss Twiggy," Maggie says coyly to her reflection.

She is growing increasingly anxious. Will she miss her graduation? She needs her ritual to calm down—tranquil walks through the house and the back yard.

She has a system. Placing one foot on a white, square linoleum tile at the farthest end of the kitchen, she steps on one tile at a time. No stepping on a crack. At the other end of the galley kitchen, she crosses into the foyer onto softened, brown, square cork tiles. A quick transition from the foyer and then to the other side of the house on gray and black, square linoleum tiles in the hallway leading to and past the three bedrooms and two bathrooms. One thousand square feet. She quickly completes the indoor circuit in under a minute. Keeping her time under a minute provides her with a feeling of power and mastery. She gives herself permission to transition outside.

She enters the backyard patio from the master bedroom. Stepping through a sliding glass door, she feels the June heat on her cheeks. The patio is made of concrete slabs that are arranged in very large rectangles and squares. Wooden strips serve as the grout between the concrete slabs.

Lushness prospers outside. Her mother's plants add color and fragrance to their small, tract-home back yard: a flowering pomegranate tree with bright orange blossoms and glossy, grass-green leaves; blue and pink balls of hydrangeas; lavender and pink, hummingbird-amorous fuchsias. The blood-red begonias are misty with pregnant water droplets from her mom's recent watering.

Maggie methodically paces each large slab of concrete around the patio, continuing down the narrower sidewalk squares next to the house and through to the back yard. The six-foot-high cedar fence, painted gray to match the house, provides privacy from the neighbors, unless you try to view them through the knot holes. The fence is lined with red, pink, and yellow hybrid tea roses; purple and hot-pink bougainvillea climbers with tissue-paper thin flowers and lethal thorns; poisonous red and pink oleander shrubs; and the benevolent apricot tree. The birds love to eat the small red and orange berries that grow on the pyracantha bushes, even though the fruit makes them drunk and causes them to fly crookedly into the windows of the house.

The backyard circuit takes Maggie ninety seconds. Time to start again. She repeats the indoor/outdoor circuit a few more times, but it doesn't do much to curb her anxiety. She heads out a side gate to the front of the house and sidewalk. Back and forth she marches carefully in front of her house. Stepping on lines is strictly forbidden outside as well as inside.

Finally weary of walking the desolate street alone, she sits on the curb at the end of the driveway like a crab on the shore. There's not even a whisper of a breeze. It is too quiet in her neighborhood of small, modern homes.

Nobody is outside. Only Maggie, the little crustacean, scrambling and looking for the next wave. She cannot wait to see her friends tonight. After graduation there's a dance in the gym. A San Francisco band called The People is going to play.

She knows every one of her classmates—if not by name, then at least by face. Shy by nature, she comes out of her shell when she's around very close friends. To earn their admiration, she transforms herself into an amusing performer who's not above silly antics and wild dares.

Her reverie is broken by the sound of the garage door opening. Finally. *Okay, okay, okay, right on. Let's go.* Her dad backs the car out of the garage. Maggie's "I-hate-to-drive" mother is in the front passenger seat. Both of them are frowning.

Her parents used to work so well together, back in those Campbell Soup glory days. At home they danced the foxtrot and the cha, cha, cha. In those days they held each other close and laughed.

"Your mother is my Hollywood blonde," her father would boast.

Maggie gets in the back seat and buckles up. She doesn't even want to know why they're frowning. She'd rather concentrate on the fact that her latest crush will be in the audience at the graduation tonight: a sixteen-year-old boy named Don.

Her inner chest feels wounded, wiggly, and liquefied all at once. Don is so cute. His profile resembles Adonis with his foxy Roman nose and full lips. He has casual, blondish "surfer hair," much of it combed to one side with bangs that almost cover his right eye. He looks good with a cigarette hanging from his bottom lip. She likes to call him Donnie; and man, can he wear a pair of tight jeans and a white T-shirt like no other boy she knows. He is genuinely kind, fine, and bitchen. She likes to relax on her bed, listening to her 45-rpm record of "Love is All Around Me" by the Troggs. She dreams of kissing Donnie.

There's just one complication. Don happens to be going steady with her good friend, Rhonda.

Rhonda lives right around the corner from Maggie, and they've been friends since fourth grade. Her parents make a lot of money but her dad—like Maggie's dad—is an alcoholic. When Maggie visits, she never knows what to expect. Usually Rhonda's parents don't even notice her. They maintain their sullen, slack-jawed expressions as they sit in club chairs opposite one another in the family room, smoking their cigarettes, holding their glasses of bourbon on the rocks, and watching golf on television.

Maggie's happy just to slip by the dirty dishes, cluttered and trashed rooms, and dog poop on the carpet on her way to Rhonda's room. "At least they give you tons of clothes and makeup," she tells her friend.

Rhonda generously trades clothes with Maggie and confides that she wants to be an airline stewardess. Maggie can easily see her in that job, given her trim figure and perfect makeup, which takes her a full hour to apply every day.

Rhonda is loyal, but she's also opinionated and edgy. It's tiresome to try to convince her that there are other ways of doing things, but, damn, she puts up a good sales pitch.

Besides the fact that Maggie's crush, foxy Don, is going steady with Rhonda, there is another complication. Rhonda is only going steady with Don because she has a major crush on Don's best friend, Pat. Maggie thinks Pat's just a slippery ladies' man and doesn't care for his quiet, tight-lipped smirk. "Don't forget, he's dating Spider Eyes," she cautions Rhonda. Spider Eyes is a hard-looking older girl who drives a souped-up black Mustang and layers on the black eyeliner.

That is not the whole enchilada.

The biggest complication in Maggie's obsession with Rhonda's boyfriend Don is the fact that she is actually going steady with Don's younger brother, Chuck. Chuck isn't very cute; in fact, he's shorter than Maggie and he's only an eighth grader. He writes her never-ending love letters and kisses her in public. She endures all the embarrassment only because she's willing to suffer to be closer to Don. At least Chuck has a band—a small consolation.

Tonight all three boys—Don, Pat, and Chuck—will be in the audience watching Rhonda and Maggie graduate from Jordan Junior High School.

There will be so many more boys in her high school this fall—older boys. She can leave Chuck behind. Forget the young ones. And who knows? Maybe Rhonda and Don will get tired of each other, leaving Don to Maggie.

Maggie feels a sense of freedom when she crosses the stage to receive her junior high school diploma. Her anxiety disappears, at least for now.

3   ONE TIME WE GOT A LITTLE DRUNK
Spring 1968

Palo Alto is known for attracting a rich variety of individuals: the thinkers at Stanford University; the doers at Stanford Medical Center: the students of humanities, bravura, and Romanesque football; and the brains of technology, invention, and science.

Stanford University and Palo Alto are twins that share an umbilical cord connected to the freedoms in San Francisco and Berkeley, just across the Bay Bridge. The entire Bay Area basks in the glow of music clubs, concert theaters, and dance parlors.

Just thirty miles south of San Francisco, the farmlands of Palo Alto over time turned into middle-class and upper-middle-class suburbs. Maggie and her friends never lack for creature comforts, and they are slow to discover some folks have more than others. Discrimination and hatred are dormant in their comfortable houses until the boats rock and dissension arises.

In 1968 Palo Alto is a breeding ground for activism, art, music, potent poetry, and performances borne of a new freedom. Creativity also leads to spontaneous sex and alcohol consumption.

And then there are the drugs. So many mind-altering drugs.

Drugs have been on Maggie's radar since the ninth grade.

She hears whispers about the easy availability of drugs in Palo Alto and is curious about the great highs that are promised. But she's also consumed by the physical changes that are taking place, as she and her girlfriends try to deal with hormones that are making them feel crazy.

"Why do we sweat so much? It's unbelievable."

Maggie is with two of her closest friends, Anne Ayres and Deb Hamilton. Sitting around a brown card table set up in Anne's den, the three are putting together a puzzle and listening to pop songs on AM radio. They keep jumping up to go to the kitchen and refill their glasses with Mrs. Ayres' homemade lemonade.

They try to make the best of their physical discomfort by laughing away embarrassing underarm sweat stains. At fifteen it's so much easier to laugh when suffering is shared with friends. Shirts are off at the slightest damp collar or underarm stain and replaced by clean ones.

"You know, we have an enemy other than sweat glands," says Maggie. "Greasy hair."

"Got any cure for zits? Look at my oily chin. Look at it!" Deb points to some whiteheads about to pop.

"It's Murphy's Law: My zits erupt when I have to give an oral report in English."

"Erupt! Ha! Erupt sounds like a burp." Anne belches, surprising everyone, even herself. "My hair is just limping along and drenched in grease. Look at my hair today!"

Maggie makes an announcement with great gusto. "We are badass, bitchen broads. A hip trio, bound together. I present to you the legendary blonde, Miss Anne Ayers; the boss brunette, Miss Margaret Mayes; and Miss Deborah Hamilton, the fiery redhead."

"Well, this legendary blonde has to wash her hair every day. It needs to be washed every day! Why me, god? Why this cruel and unusual punishment? Alas, if I skip a day, I never leave the house."

The girls create a code name for themselves: the GP Trio. G for grease. P for perspiration. This is one of their constant sources of childish humor. They obsess about their bodily functions and speculate about boys' bodily functions.

Sitting at the card table, Maggie declares, "If drugs are so accessible, I want to find them." Anne and Deb nod their heads in agreement.

Deb has long, red hair and freckles. Although petite, she is "stacked," which probably helps when she's flirting with boys. Maggie thinks her flirtations are more intentional than innocent, but in spite of that, she's thoughtful and friendly. A hint of sadness lurks in her eyes, though.

Anne is also petite and stacked. She is the perfect sun-worshipping California girl, with her blonde hair, dark tan, white teeth, and dazzling smile. Not one to rely on her looks, she gets straight As in school. Maggie loves her slapstick sense of humor and sharp mind—sharp enough to lie to her parents and convince them she is an angel.

Maggie feels less attractive when around her friends with big boobs. For shit's sake, her own mother sews falsies into her bikini tops. Maggie struggles with the mixed messages her mother sends. *It's kind of odd how she wants me to be stacked, but then she struts around like a nun ready to wash my mouth out with soap if I mention sex.*

Maggie avoids talking to her mom about sex. Or drugs. Even when the drugs are right under her mother's nose—like during the ninth-grade mid-winter experiment.

The mid-winter experiment sprang from the rumors circulating around the Jordan Junior High grapevine that mixing Coke, aspirin, and cough syrup produces a high. At the time Palo Alto households were receiving small promotional bottles of Romilar cough syrup in the mail. The cough syrup's active ingredients were dextromethorphan and codeine.

The GP Trio made a plan. Just before school on a cold February morning, the three girls were each supposed to drink a bottle of Romilar, take two aspirin, and chug a bottle of Coke.

At seven-thirty Maggie gagged the cocktail down in the bathroom. Vomit rose in her throat, chunks lowered and stayed, then she brushed her teeth. Jordan was only a three-block walk from her home. She talked to herself on the way to school. "I'd better not barf ... Guy! Oh, yeah ... this is so tough." Supposedly, it would take about twenty minutes for the high to kick in. Maggie was filled with anticipation. During roll call in her homeroom and math class, Maggie had a Cheshire cat smile plastered on her face. It was beginning to fade when the bell rang. During second period, the GP Trio felt dizzy, lightheaded, and goofy. They exchanged notes in the hallways between classes, reporting every new sensation and experience—like tripping over nothing. Maggie deliberately exaggerated her "high" around Deb and Anne.

By the time she made it to Spanish lab, Maggie found herself with her head on her desk, dozing off and on, drooling on notebook paper while the voice in her headphones chattered away about ordering food in a Mexican cafe.

The GP Trio's amateur foray into mind-altering substances produced an unexpected revelation for Maggie. When she was high, her nervousness and sadness disappeared. They fueled her self-worth and self-esteem. She was perched, saucy and pert, on a towering, rebel passion, ready to dive.

Maggie decided to keep this revelation a secret.

Months later, Maggie is sorting her laundry after school, her mind racing with thoughts about her father's drinking and her parents' fights. Why does she keep overhearing her name during their arguments?

Out of restlessness, she quiets her mind by switching to another activity: changing purses. She empties one purse and a note falls out. It's from Deb Hamilton, written just before their experiment with aspirin, cough syrup, and Coke. Maggie has a dim memory of Deb slipping her a note under the cutting table during sewing class.

Maggie,

Did Alan or anyone raise their hand in your science class when the teacher asked if they smoked pot? Did you raise your hand to the question about who would smoke it if it was legalized? Anne and I did. So did everyone else.

So, our friend, Tina, is on this thing she took yesterday and she won't get off of it till Thursday!!! It's something like you take half a pill and you might become blind. If you take two, you might DIE!! Oh no!! I think Joan is going to get some, too. And, you know, she almost took opium. Don't worry, I'm not thinking of doing it.

If you keep going around with Don's brother, Chuck, he might get you started on drugs. He's in a band. You know band members have access to drugs.

Speaking of Tina, did you know that the guy she is going steady with, Alan, has a lot of nerve because he almost slapped her? What's the biz? It was because Tina made out with that seventh grader, Andy. And Alan was jealous. You know Andy? The guy who rides his Stingray bike to school— the one with peace symbols all over the seat. He gives bennies to Tina.

I wonder where you can get downers. They are supposed to mellow you out.

Later, Deb

Maggie laughs as she returns to sorting clothes, separating the lights from the darks. The note is a brief distraction from laundry and troubling thoughts.

For one thing, why do I look so different from my parents? I'm all gangly. They aren't. I have a small nose and freckles. They don't. I get tan real easy. Their skin is so pale, no matter what they do. Maybe I'm adopted.

There are secrets in her house. Maggie is sure of it.

She keeps her own secrets, even those a parent should know about. Especially secrets about sex and shocking behavior by men.

When Maggie was five, she was playing in the rain puddles at the end of her driveway one winter day when a car slowly drove past her. It stopped in the middle of the street and a man got out. He was naked from the waist down as he stood, staring at her. This had been an important day for Maggie, the first time her mother let her play outside alone. Then, the naked man. She froze in disbelief when she saw something frightening and foreign to her—something between his legs she had never seen before. She ran back to the house and didn't tell her mother.

When she was nine, her grandmother took her to San Francisco's Playland at the Beach. She was standing at the fun house near the merry-go-round when a man with a camera beckoned her to come closer. Her grandmother was distracted by Maggie's cousins and didn't notice what was going on. Maggie inched herself closer to the outside wall of the fun house, feeling fear and confusion. Her grandmother reappeared, the man slinked away, and Maggie said nothing—although her mind was racing. It was a different feeling from the disgust she felt when her father stumbled around the house, naked and drunk.

My fault, my fault. Somehow what they did was my fault.

How about those precocious feelings of pleasure she explored with school-aged girls? How about that desire at age nine for the boy she had a crush on to be her brother and sleep in her bed?

What a sicko I am, Maggie thought to herself.

Maggie's mother arrives to find Maggie parked in front of the television set in the living room, piles of laundry in a circle around her. Maggie pushes her secrets back into the locked room in her mind.

"Mom! Hi. See, I'm doin' the laundry."

"You look surprised to see me. Everything alright?"

Maggie nods. Her mom sheds her blue polyester coat, drops her brown vinyl handbag with the extra-long strap on a kitchen chair, and asks Maggie about chores, homework, and laundry. She seems happy, and when she smiles, her blue eyes shine.

She calls out a hello to her husband, who's been in bed reading most of the day, still wearing his pajamas and robe. The dog—a fat Dalmatian who spends most of her time with Maggie's father—waddles down the hall, tail wagging.

"Well, Miss Margaret Pauline Mayes, how many shirts have you worn today?"

"That's cute, Mom. You rhymed."

"What is going on with your laundry? I haven't had time to get to the washing."

"I'm already on it, Miss Scarlett," says Maggie.

"Aren't you the clever one? *Gone with the Wind*. Prissy."

Maggie and her mother share a love of movies. Movies draw them close, but other things keep them apart. Her mother thinks she knows her daughter and judges her behavior harshly. Maggie is afraid of her mom's wrath when she frowns, narrows her red-lipsticked mouth into a slash, and squints her blue eyes. She is especially judgmental when it comes to sex, which Maggie finds confusing as her mother can be so accepting in other areas.

Maggie lies to her parents to avoid embarrassment and disappointment. Survival in this house means putting on a good front.

Maggie feels her parents can't possibly understand what is happening all around her. What was known by her parents is shifting and moving, making room for what can be known by Maggie's generation. Chatter and shock are a way of life. The news is full of scorched suffering. Police spray black folks with fire hoses in the Deep South and in Los Angeles. Bras and American flags are burned in the streets. The Vietnam War is televised on a daily basis as young men resist the involuntary military draft. The assassinations of Martin Luther King, Jr., and Bobby Kennedy rock the nation. There is rampant anger over racism, sexism, the war machine, and other hallmarks of "the establishment." Once-trusted institutions are no longer believed or respected.

The music scene is a crucial part of the shift that is happening. Even without the help of drugs, people feel high and enlightened by an explosion of new music that churns in their bellies and makes them sway and smile for the future.

In addition to sports events and educational fairs, Stanford University sponsors the musical concerts that Maggie loves. This spring a concert is coming to the university's Stanford Laurence Frost Amphitheater, featuring Sons of Champlin, Quicksilver Messenger Service, and Jefferson Airplane. Maggie can think of nothing else for days.

Frost (also known as the Grass Steps) is an outdoor amphitheater with rows of wide steps sweeping like an arc from the top down to a bandstand. The grass steps are sharply edged with wooden strips. Surrounding the grass steps are large oak trees and dirt paths that wind around dense foliage. For suburban kids, this is a forest. When not in use for a concert or other event, parents often sit on the steps in the bowl-shaped arena and wait for the young children up in the woods to wear themselves out exploring.

Frost offers a place to escape convention as people of all ages share these woods with an eclectic array of musicians. The sounds of drums, guitars, electric flutes, and keyboards fill the air on any given day.

Two days before Maggie's concert, Anne Ayers slips a note to Maggie in history class.

I hear you and another girl want to ride your bikes to Frost. One of our friends might get "it" for you. If you want it. At Frost, I hear that people sit in the trees and smoke it and nobody cares. I am so jealous. I want to go too. I'll ask my mom.

School is boring today. Do you have any pep pills? I sure need some.

Anyhoo, back to this weekend. Don't make out with any boys. We found out in science today that you can get VD just from making out. Be careful because you can also get it from a toilet seat. About two million people get VD a year. Right now they are saying that it's an epidemic.

One day before the concert, Maggie tells her parents she will be riding her bike over to Don and Chuck's on Sunday for a swim.

The next day, she bikes to the Frost Amphitheater and falls into a no-worry zone. Surrounded by dancing friends and strangers and exotic, heavy scents of patchouli oil and skunky marijuana, she listens to the little birds singing in her ears as the music takes her home.

4 GET YOUR MOTOR RUNNING
June 1968

Maggie sits at the kitchen table while her mother reviews a stack of papers she received in the mail from Maggie's grandfather.

"I'm not putting your dad's name as a beneficiary."

"What's a beneficiary?"

"A person who inherits someone's money and property after they die."

"So who's the beneficiary if not Daddy?"

"You are, Maggie."

Maggie doesn't know what to say. When it comes to her dad, she mostly feels angry. Her father is sick and drawing closer to death every week. He practically lives in the master bedroom, his only company being Lil, the Dalmatian. His infirm body is clearly losing its battle with alcoholism, diabetes, the effects of his stroke last year, and heart trouble.

According to her mom, her father cashed in their joint life insurance policy after he exhausted his paychecks and personal savings.

"All to buy more vodka, Maggie. So I'm going back to work part time to bring in some money for us—you and me. Thank god my father said he's willing my portion of his estate just to me. And then you are the beneficiary after I die."

So now her mom is away from home more often, working at her secretarial job for a schoolbook publishing company.

Maggie embraces her independence. She has just graduated from the ninth grade and her freedom is as spontaneous and freewheeling as diving into a pool and soundlessly swimming underwater. She ignores her anger toward her father and supplants it with camaraderie and exploration of Palo Alto by foot, bike, and city bus. She can always count on at least a few of her girlfriends for an adventure, so one summer day can spread out like marmalade on a hot, concrete sidewalk. A full week's worth of notions, dares, and double dares can be had between daybreak and darkness.

"Maggie, Elizabeth and I are taking the bus to Round Table in about a half an hour." Maggie's friend Skipper sounds urgent over the phone.

"Okie dokie. That's great."

"And I just called Anne and Deb. They're meeting you at your house. It's so exciting!"

"What's the story, Skipper?"

"Not gonna tell you 'til you get to Round Table. The one in Midtown."

It doesn't take Maggie, Deb, and Anne too long to ride their bikes about two miles to the pizza parlor in Midtown. The GP Trio arrive at Round Table, lock their bikes, and find Skipper and Elizabeth waiting inside. The two girls look unusually animated, although with Elizabeth it's difficult to tell. To Maggie she always seems nervous, fidgeting all the time—short bursts of legs untangling, hands telling a story, fingers tapping on a table. Elizabeth is dressed simply in faded cut-off denim shorts and a white T-shirt, which nearly matches her pale skin. Unlike the other girls, Elizabeth embraces a minimalist style—no makeup, no fussing with her straight, light brown hair, and no interest in wearing any shoes other than her beloved leather sandals. As the GP Trio arrives, Elizabeth covers a giggle with her hand as she watches high-energy Skipper bouncing around in the booth, her big boobs bouncing, too.

Maggie is relieved she had the foresight to stuff her bra with tissues because all these girls are well-endowed. She hates being so thin and flat-chested, and she never understood why it took her until age fourteen-and-a-half to get her period when every other girl in the world seemed to be on the rag by twelve or thirteen. She confessed her frustration about her slow development once to Anne, who had the opposite problem—big boobs and a lot of pubic hair. In a moment of silliness and bonding, Anne told Maggie she once took a pair of scissors and tried to cut off her pubic hair. Overcome by paralyzing laughter, Maggie in turn confessed she once cut some hair from her head and tried to glue it to her private parts. From that point on, turning everything from serious to silly was key to their friendship. The memory of that incident springs to Maggie's mind as she enters the pizza parlor and notices Skipper's bouncing chest. For a moment her thoughts distract her from the present—a common occurrence.

"Wake up, Maggie!" chides Skipper. "That's better, girly girl. Sit down and listen up. Here's the deal. Elizabeth and I met these two guys downtown yesterday at Swenson's Ice Cream Parlor. They're going to be seniors. Elizabeth and I were just standing outside with our cones when these two guys on a motorcycle pull up next to us."

Maggie isn't surprised by the way Skipper's story is starting. She thinks Skipper is a wild child. She finds a boy around every corner and doesn't mind using her boobs to get attention. Outgoing and fearless, she's like a flame that never goes out.

If there is an adventure, Skipper will be there. Booze or drugs? She'll partake. And if there is a cute boy, she'll go after him. Maggie thinks Skipper ought to be more careful because her parents are threatening to send her away to a private girls' school.

Still, Skipper manages to persuade Maggie and her other girlfriends to follow her down paths of indiscretion. With a sly look she whispers, "I know of a party where there's going to be a lot of boys. This kid has a private party space in his pool house. C'mon," she encourages them, "think about it."

If they hesitate, she adds, "I'll be right with you. We'll stick together."

But oh, ho! What does she do? Disappear with some boy and forget her friends.

"Snap out of it, Maggie. Where's your head? Elizabeth, you tell them the rest."

Elizabeth chows down on a slice of extra cheesy pizza. "Ha, ha...wai... mou full. Okay. Very hot pizza. Anyway, these guys are pretty cute, I guess. One has a motorcycle."

"They drove up to the curb at Swenson's. Voila! There we were: sophomores chatting with seniors," says Skipper.

"Olin, he's the talkative one and Steve, he's got the motorcycle," adds Elizabeth.

"You just have to meet them! They wanna meet you," Skipper insists, her voice rising.

"Yeah, you have to!" Elizabeth chimes in, goaded into enthusiasm by Skipper.

Skipper says a rendezvous with Olin and Steve has already been set for Thursday. No one argues with her. Of course they'll follow her lead.

Maggie, Deb, Anne, Elizabeth, and Skipper board the city bus at one o'clock on Thursday afternoon to meet up with Olin and Steve at the Poppycock in downtown Palo Alto. The Poppycock is popular with the young crowd because as long as they buy some food or drinks, the owner will let them stay as long as they want.

The girls are all wearing the uniform of the summer— cut-off jeans and either halter tops or boys' T-shirts.

They spot the boys waiting for them outside.

"There they are," whispers Elizabeth.

"Oh my god, they are so foxy," Maggie whispers back.

A short, stocky young man with red hair laughs as he sees the girls approaching.

"Steve, quick, look. Look at those chicks."

Steve is smoking and leaning against the building. He looks nothing like his friend Olin. Tall, dark-haired, and slender, he's wearing blue jeans and a white T-shirt. Maggie appraises him quickly and decides his moustache makes him look mature.

"Hi. I'm Steve," he says quietly.

His friend is more talkative. "Well, looky looky here. Pleasure to meet you ladies. I'm Olin."

After introductions, Skipper and Olin immediately start doing most of the talking. Skipper gives Olin a few flirty, playful shoves to his upper arm. He smiles back at her and laughs, hearty and deep.

Maggie stares at Olin and feels like her legs suddenly can't move, like she's walking through water or something. Olin has one of those surfer hairstyles, his straight, thick red hair sweeping down over one eye, and his face is dotted with freckles. Maggie never thought of freckles on the positive side, but on Olin they look less childish and more attractive. Funny how he and redheaded Deb Hamilton look like they could be siblings. Olin is tough-looking, with a crafty half-smile and a cigarette clamped in the corner of his mouth. He is wearing a black leather jacket, striped bell bottoms, and black combat boots. When he looks at Maggie, she thinks she sees a suggestion in his unwavering stare.

She tries to decode it. *Does he think I'm cute?*

Quiet Steve watches the girls and Olin as they chatter away, his deep-set brown eyes not revealing his thoughts. Maggie doesn't know what to think about him.

Maybe he's just shy, like me. Boring. That's what it is when no one talks. He's kind of rough around the edges. Hmm. Mysterious. And then again, maybe he's doing just what I'm doing. Watching everyone and sizing 'em up.

She notices Steve has his eyes on Anne's white teeth and giggly smile. Blonde, tan, and blue-eyed, she draws a lot of attention.

After an hour or so of talking out on the sidewalk, Steve asks if the girls want to take turns riding on his Kawasaki. When it's Maggie's turn, Steve turns his head back to her before they drive off and shouts, "Hold on to me so you won't fall off. I want you to get back home later today safely."

She places her hands gingerly on his back as he accelerates slowly.

"I'm gonna hang a Louie up here. Hold me tighter and lean

with my body. It's all about leaning into the bike."

Holding a boy around his waist as they spin around town is a whole new ballgame. Maggie hopes some of the kids she knows from junior high see her riding a Kawasaki with an older boy. Steve's body and hers are so close. They are like one person with her arms around his white cotton T-shirted torso. His tanned, muscular arms look like stout ropes as his hands grip the handles of the bike. Maggie presses against his warm back, clinging like she belongs to his body. His long brown hair with its golden streaks blows back against her cheeks and she can smell his shampoo.

The only other time Maggie felt such freedom was when she went horseback riding long ago. This feels even better.

With motorcycle rides complete, the two senior boys and the five sophomore girls saunter around town, chatting about the downtown stores. Eventually Olin steers them toward his house, which is just a couple of blocks from downtown. He wants the girls to see the house but doesn't suggest they go inside. Instead, they go back to the Poppycock, where steam from the kitchen blows in the fragrance of battered fish and salty fries.

They order root beer and the guys get a couple baskets of fish and chips to share all around. The back room of the restaurant has redwood picnic tables, a pool table, and a jukebox. Quarters feed the jukebox and Maggie selects her current faves, "Born to be Wild" by Steppenwolf and "Jumpin' Jack Flash" by the Rolling Stones. Wailing guitar licks, percussion booms, and rebellious male vocals fill the room.

At home many hours later, Maggie cannot sleep. Her head is filled with echoes of the afternoon's laughter and freedom. A full moon fills her bedroom window and a quiet breeze blows on her head and shoulders, but rest eludes her.

She hates her sorry little family and their alcohol-fueled arguments, but today has been a shift and a promise.

Maybe I can ignore my loneliness because things change. Maybe life doesn't stay the same.

She thinks about her neighbors, some of them even worse

33

than her dad. The couple next door who scream and break glass during their physical fights. Maggie's mom says they drink a lot. One time the man staggered across the neighborhood lawns, blood running down his forehead, because his wife hit him with an iron.

Around that time Maggie's mother frequently kept one of her little playmates, Janie, at the house because Janie's mother liked to drink all morning and then pass out on her bed.

On the occasions when Maggie's mom and dad stop arguing, there's too much quiet. How did Agatha Christie put it in her latest book? Oh yeah. "Tragically quiet."

Maggie flings about in bed in the darkened room and revisits the incongruity of her perfect day downtown and her chronic anxiety and sadness. She relishes this day like a shot of energy into her bloodstream. Steve and Olin are a welcome addition to her life. Eventually, she calms down as she replays in her mind a conversation with Olin. She can remember every word.

He was looking directly into her eyes, his mouth close to her ear. "I really like you, Maggie. You aren't like your girlfriends. You're quiet, but you think about stuff. I like you 'cuz you talk when it's important, not just to talk." Maggie was almost holding her breath as he continued. "And you don't giggle all the time like Anne, over nothing. I can tell she thinks she's cute. But I think you're the cute one."

She stumbled over her response. "Well, I don't know. Yeah, I guess. Thanks."

Swift, real swift, she thought. The real truth was he was making her sweat. He was so different from the younger guys, who couldn't say anything without acting goofy.

Olin walked away and whispered something to Steve. When Steve nodded his head, Olin returned. "I'm borrowing Steve's bike. Let's take a spin."

"What about the others?" Maggie was embarrassed at being singled out. She wondered if her friends would be mad at her.

"Will you be kind enough to do me the honor of riding with me, Maggie? After all, you went with Steve. Please.

Pretty please."

"I suppose so," she said. Screw her friends. She's into something new.

5 A MONTH AWAY FROM HOME
September 2015

Maggie stands at a darkened window inside her rented studio apartment, looking up at the sky. Where is the moon?

This trip to Palo Alto is more than a distraction from problems at home. It is more than a search to find a friend or write a book.

I just want to find the boys of summer again. The summer of 1968.

That was the summer she first felt perfectly alive. Life was at its best. The year exists in her head like a comforting mother, a mother that swaddled and held her close to a vibrating and pulsating heartbeat.

I try to be my own comforting mother for solace. But I can't make it happen. Maybe I should call the family and see if they are okay.

A cloud moves and the moon is revealed at last. "How do I do it?" she says to the moon. "How do I find the right words to make my husband and daughters see what I see? They might stop being so angry. They might even thank me."

She is suffocating under the weight of trying to help an actively drinking husband and daughters who are making the wrong choices. She remembers her own youth and learning process but is troubled nonetheless by her children's decisions. Her failure to change them prompts her to try to save others.

She turns to community health, where she encourages healthy living for those who desperately need support. Regrettably, she discovers it's just as hard to fix people outside her family, but she finds it easier to understand their choices than those of her family.

I could so easily be one of them if I turn a bad corner, down a dark street. Assaulted by the unknowns of life. I see myself in them.

Stepping away from the window and the moon, she grabs some sorbet from the freezer.

A familiar chorus of voices fills her head.

You're not good enough. Lazy, more like it. Look at all the garbage you carry around. Yes, garbage. You're way beyond carrying baggage. What a messy bunch of feelings you have, my dear.

"Shut up!" Maggie recites the Serenity Prayer and smooths out the wrinkles of doubt with some tai chi, but she's still restless. Now what? She wants a friend to talk to. Rhonda works from home, writing jingles for commercials. It's late but she's probably available. Maggie calls her on her landline since Rhonda doesn't own a cell phone. "It's just not for me," she told her friends.

Rhonda answers the phone with a long, husky sigh into Maggie's ear.

"Oh god! There you are, Maggie! I've been thinking about you all day!"

Rhonda is still as loyal a friend as ever. Maggie realizes she had just assumed Rhonda would drop everything for her. She catches herself. *Where do I get off thinking Rhonda will jump through my hoops?*

"I hope I'm not interrupting your dinner or anything, Rhonda. I thought I'd better call you and let you know I'm in Palo Alto now."

"God! No! Me and hubby and kids don't eat dinner together anymore. I am so glad you are here! Did you hear from Olin yet? He's supposed to be coming to the Bay Area ... right? You were kind of nervous he would just blow you off."

"Yeah, yeah. He is fairly like that," agrees Maggie. "He's coming at the end of next week."

"What have you been doing since you got here? Do you want company? I can just leave the house now and be there pretty soon."

"Aww, no, no, Rhonda."

Maggie scolds herself. *Why did I say no when I thought I needed a friend?* She suddenly feels overwhelmed.

"I'm dead tired, Rhonda. Beat. Really."

"Well, you know, you put a lot of effort into this trip. I can't wait to hear about your book. And it'll be good to see old friends."

"Well, yeah. It was a long drive here …"

"You seem to have a lot of useful and devoted friends, Maggie."

Maggie wonders what, if anything, Rhonda means by that. "So do you."

"I don't, actually. See, you set people in motion. You go and try to find Julius and the next thing you know, you've been able to get all these people to help you. You probably won't have time for me."

Maggie twists her neck and hears groaning sinew. She changes the subject.

"Hey, Rhonda, how are the kids? Did your son find a job after college graduation? Is your daughter in high school or is it college by now?"

"I don't want to talk about them right now. They hang out exclusively with their dad. They don't ask me to join them. Anyway, take my advice and don't trust anybody. Even so-called best friends of mine keep calling me and complaining on and on about their families and all the stress they have. But, when I try to ask questions and try to help them, they won't talk to me long enough to figure out what's going on with them. Shit.

"For instance, just the other day Don calls me to talk, but he won't take my advice. Why do you think he does that? Doesn't that mean he must not understand? I'm worried his lifestyle is affecting his health. Wouldn't you be worried, Maggie?"

Indeed, Maggie is worried about Don, Rhonda's first love, but she thinks Rhonda's lucky to even have a friendship with Don after all these years. A nasty criticism looms near and she doesn't want to hurt Rhonda's feelings. She puts down the phone and lets Rhonda talk while she goes into the bathroom to pee. Her eyes wander to the toiletries she's placed on the rental unit's shelves. She's marked her territory. She takes time to brush her teeth, but even so, when she picks up the phone again, Rhonda is still talking about Don. Maggie risks a provocation.

"I don't know. I think it's really none of my business. I better go now. It's getting late."

"Yeah, yeah, Maggie, but first I just need to say, I don't understand what he was trying to say. He would not finish his story."

"I don't think it really matters to Don if you have an answer, Rhonda. He just wants to talk."

"Okay. So I guess I could do that. Maybe I won't talk so much next time and let him talk."

"Give him some space for a few days and call him again. Well, I'll talk to you later."

Her conversation with Rhonda was pretty meaningless, but Maggie feels better after contact with another human. She feels safe now.

She loves the studio apartment. Everything she could want is visible just by turning around. Admiring the feeling of space, she twirls around a few times under a spacious, soaring, white cathedral ceiling with white wooden beams. A tall, white, wicker screen separates the sleeping area from the living room, filled with white wicker furniture that doesn't quite go with the modern, flat-screen TV that's attached to a swivel arm bolted to the wall. The cozy kitchen and small bathroom are big enough for Maggie.

"It's all for me," she said when she first arrived. "No sharing."

Maggie's husband said he was okay with her going away

to work on her book. He planned to do a lot of yard work. Her husband has no idea about her plans to find Julius or meet up with Olin and Steve, let alone any clue about her obsession with the "boys of summer." She doesn't want to reveal this part of herself to him.

In spite of telling Rhonda she was tired, Maggie feels restless. *A night walk will do you good, ol' girl.* She laughs to herself. *I'm right behind you, Ancient One.*

She's been walking many a night street for many a year. But none so often as the streets of Palo Alto.

The wind is still and the salty air, damp. The town is situated on the San Francisco Bay, so the afternoon winds blow in off the bay until night falls. Maggie feels secure when she's outdoors, where nature serves as an umbilical cord, feeding and soothing her. Therapy and medication have kept her fairly well-adjusted for years, but it's just not enough sometimes. Sometimes it takes alcohol and a few harmless drugs. But not tonight. Nature whispers in her ear, "Just let it go."

Sleep comes easy.

The next morning Maggie awakens to doves coo, coo, cooing. White cotton curtains billow in the breeze coming through an open window.

Her head is surprisingly clear, and she has a desire to bound out of bed. Adventure awaits.

6 SECRET AGENT MAN
September 2015

Olin Wolfe dreams he's in a hammock that is stretched over a canyon. He sways back and forth in the hammock, which is held securely in place by strong ropes. Sweet. Without warning the hammock starts swirling round and round, twisting and encasing Olin in the canvas like a sausage. Then it spits him out, and he falls to the ground.

"Shit, man! What a harsh dream!" Half-awake, he has hazy thoughts about going back to sleep, but he hears faint bird chatter in the dark. "Uh oh. I'm not supposed to be in bed. I'm supposed to be in a taxi, heading to the airport."

Bird chatter again. But, no; it's a voice. A velvety female voice calls out, "Sir? Mr. Wolfe? Are you okay?"

He fully opens his eyes and lifts his white-haired head off his chest. "What?" He sees darkness and dancing white and yellow lights in the dark. His body is restrained by something. Of course, a seat belt. He is in a taxi, just like he's supposed to be.

"You were talking in your sleep, Mr. Wolfe. Good news. We are only twenty-five minutes from the Boise Airport."

Olin is still foggy-headed. Maybe that bowl of G13 weed he smoked was a bit too much.

"Oh, yeah. Thank you, ma'am. Thanks. It is kind of you to ask."

It's true, then. G13 is so potent that it warped his sense of time and place.

"First time using Uber?" the driver asks.

"Uber, oh, yeah, no, I use it all the time." *When did I call for Uber? Man, how much did I smoke?*

Olin straightens up and tries to clear his head. *Yeah, I've got a flight to San Jose that leaves about 7:30 a.m. Way too early. Palo Alto. His old girlfriend Maggie needs him in Palo Alto. Yeah, that's it.*

Olin lives near the foothills of Boise, Idaho, in a modest house situated on nine acres of land. After many years of working as a private investigator, he decided to retire and raise goats. He valued his privacy, so when Maggie called him, he was upset at first. They had not been in touch for more than forty years. Back then she was living in California and he was living … hell, he didn't remember where he lived then. Maybe Palo Alto as well.

"Hello?" he had half-coughed, half-snarled into the phone.

"Olin? Olin Wolfe? Oh, my god! Your voice is one I just will never forget!" Maggie squeaked gleefully.

"Listen, Olin, Julius is missing and I need to find him. We were writing letters for a while and then he wouldn't return my phone calls and his parents were so secretive when I talked to them … "

Olin was of two minds. It was kind of a blast to hear from Maggie, but he didn't like being found. It made him angry. Especially when Maggie told him she found him through their old friend Elizabeth's drug-dealing brother. He and Julius used to buy and sell acid and mushrooms.

"Oh, yeah, Maggie, well, it's a coincidence you called me, considering the line of work I got into. Do you remember once upon a time I wanted to go into private investigation with Steve? While he was with the police department and I wanted to be a source for the cops? Yeah, well, I did it. I worked as a private detective in the San Francisco Bay area. Then I got involved in this other government shit and I can't tell you more than that. I had to disappear for years."

"Well, that's cool, Olin. But Elizabeth's brother knows

where you live now, so you haven't disappeared completely."

"Yeah, well, I just came out of hiding," he added. "I was under cover."

"Sounds very hush hush, Olin. That brings me back to why I called. I need your help."

After that initial contact, Maggie and Olin talked frequently. Olin enjoyed their conversations, so much so that he started recording them. He told himself it was because he didn't trust his memory anymore.

At first he couldn't understand Maggie's motivation. "See, I'm not only still looking for Julius," she explained. "I'm writing my new mystery novel, based on a character who goes missing. That's why I'm taking some time off. To write, you know?"

"You're a writer? You have books published? I'm flabbergasted. But in a good way."

"I'd like to bring you into the search. I can share what I know of Julius so far."

"Okay, Maggie. I'll see what I can do. What's your next step?"

"I'm renting a studio apartment on Cowper Street for four weeks in September. To work on my new mystery and to look into what happened to Julius. Olin, I think foul play is at hand with Julius's disappearance."

"Jeez, you used to say I was the dramatic one. So what do you want to do, Maggie?"

"Well, for one thing, when I get there, I want a reunion. All of us. You, Steve, me, all the girls ... I like keeping the adhesive with all my friends and it's been way too long. Plus we really need to find out what happened to Julius. At least I do."

Olin is silent for a moment. *Is she crazy or high? I'm not sure.*

"Well, I am retired, Maggie, so I guess I'll think about it."

Later he speculates about Julius while he's feeding his goats. He thinks about the last time he saw him. Hey, maybe the guy just wanted to disappear. Find a quiet place to close his eyes. Dream. Smile. Find some harmony. Die. Yeah, he could see his old friend doing that. Olin always thought he knew more about Julius than anyone else. His family was so messed up. Lots of secrets. Maggie has no idea.

By the time Olin boards his flight to California, his mind is clear but there's still enough G13 in his system to make him feel pretty relaxed. He's got time and money and the goats are being tended to by a neighbor, so no worries, man. He feels a boost, a little kick out of remembering bygone youthful pursuits in Palo Alto. He will be in his hometown this afternoon, which makes him long for the sensual way his body felt when he used to look at teenaged girls and they used to look at him. The present day melts away as he recollects that hot summer of 1968.

The girls were so damn tan. They wore blue jeans or shorts and boys' T-shirts. Bare feet, white teeth … he remembered how they would tilt their heads, just looking at him or each other, and laugh.

Olin pouts and visibly blushes as he passes his left hand over his bald head. Old age and chemotherapy. He is sure he has shrunk in height and positive his belly is never going to be flat and muscular again. He thinks he will tell Maggie he had bladder cancer. That sounds more dignified than prostate cancer.

His buddy and boyhood friend, Steve, will meet him at the San Jose airport. He's glad they never lost touch. Their friendship is always uplifting, strengthened against any and all ups and downs because they accept each other as they are.

Steve is retired from law enforcement, but he's still pretty busy with part-time security and loss-prevention work, not to mention all his family obligations. He still owns motorcycles. A Triumph and a Harley.

Steve agreed to go to Palo Alto, too. "Yeah, Olin, they were the girls of summer, weren't they?"

"Anne, Maggie, and Deb—the blonde, the brunette, and the redhead," Olin reminds him. "Should be an interesting trip."

7 SOMETHING IN THE WAY THEY MOVE
July 1968

Maggie has been in love with Olin for three weeks. It all began when she discovered a damn fine kiss in a coat closet at Deb's house.

Olin said, "It's a contest." He wanted to take Maggie, Deb, and Anne into the closet "for privacy." Sensible Elizabeth wanted nothing to do with it; instead, she sat outside on the patio, telling Steve how dumb it was. Steve didn't want to gossip, but Elizabeth sensed he knew something about his best friend Olin's actions. She pressed him for information.

"Ya know, Elizabeth, he's telling each one that he likes them best."

"It's crazy," she sighed.

After that kiss in the closet three weeks ago, Maggie finds herself obsessed with Olin. The bite mark of love is thrilling and exhausting. Maggie is now a devotee of Olin's warm skin when they hold hands, the brush of his lips against her cheek, and even the scent of his Aqua Velva cologne.

Her make-out sessions with Olin are getting very creative. She practices the art of making her mouth, lips, tongue, and teeth tease and reward his ardor. He tells her she is the best kisser of any girl. He's got this whisper—a convincing explanation of her lips exciting his lips.

In *Seventeen Magazine* she reads about "chemistry," and how it causes a simmering sexual desire. It must be chemistry that makes her want to get close enough to catch his scent, touch him, and kiss him.

Rhonda's boyfriend Don and his younger brother Chuck are around less and less. Don is noticing Rhonda's sappy eye contact with his best friend, Pat. The best thing to happen to Rhonda is when Don sees them making out in Pat's garage one Sunday afternoon.

"Maggie, you should have heard Don screaming at us. I've never seen his eyes so dark and spit coming out of his mouth. It went something like this: 'Shit man! Go on! Go ahead! Take her, Pat! I'll take your other chick, Spider Eyes.'"

Sitting at the picnic table on Maggie's patio, Rhonda starts drawing pictures of Pat while she tells her story. Maggie pops a grape in her mouth and pours some lemonade.

"Maggie, you spend hardly any time with Chuck."

"Yeah, and he shows zero acknowledgment. He isn't getting any of the usual hints. I'm scarce, rude, and indifferent."

"You don't even love Donnie anymore, do you? You're just gaga over Olin Wolfe."

"I don't get it, Rhonda. I was so in love with Donnie just this spring."

"Can't you just be honest with Chuck?"

"I don't know how."

"It's pretty obvious, ya know. To everyone, Maggie."

"Yeah?"

"Yeah. Making out with Olin in front of Chuck pretty much sealed a breakup."

"You think so? Is that what they mean by passive-aggressive?" Maggie likes being flip and smart.

She also likes time to herself to write poetry about love, and she writes best when outdoors. One favorite spot is next to the train station in downtown Palo Alto. She finds inspiration on the expansive lawn, away from her small, suffocating house. Outside, she can express her heart-wrenching adoration for Olin, that redheaded bad boy who continues to string along not only Maggie but the rest of the GP Trio, Deb and Anne.

The train station and adjacent lawn sit high atop an underpass connecting downtown Palo Alto's University Avenue to Stanford University's Palm Drive. As she writes, Maggie can see a palm tree-lined street ending near the campus's massive, Spanish-style buildings. Looking the other way, she can see downtown shops and businesses. She imagines she's atop a mountain retreat in her own hometown.

Olin brings some new friends around to meet the girls. Chris is a swarthy seventeen-year-old with average looks. He drives a white, four-on-the-floor, 1962 Humpback Volvo. He's generous with his car, money, and patience. At first the girls can't quite figure out if his constant smiling is because he's a little goofy, high, or lecherous.

He falls madly in love with Anne from the start. He adores her sense of humor, vulnerability, and Hollywood-style blonde and tan beauty. Anne smiles at his attention and lets him sweep her off her feet, even though Steve has been lazily wooing her.

It is unclear how Chris effectively inserts himself between Anne's and Steve's flirtations, but Steve is no dummy. His good manners prompt him to step aside.

Chris soon becomes Anne's caretaker of sorts and she becomes rather needy when he isn't around. Without Chris's over-the-top affection, she looks for appreciation from other guys. Maggie doesn't like it, but she doesn't judge her.

I'm not really so different from Anne. Am I?

Maggie thinks she is different in one way: She never cancels plans with her girlfriends just because a boy enters the scene.

She sees how a lot of girls her age quickly toss aside loyalty and friendship for guys, and she hates it.

It turns out Chris's goofy smile is related to drugs, after all. Steve and Olin keep it to themselves that Chris is a heroin user. If he shows any sign of wanting to give heroin to Anne or any of the girls, they vow to intervene. For now, they watch.

The other new friend Olin introduces is named Julius Brownell. Julius is nothing like Chris. He speaks of a joyful world with honesty and candor.

Julius is over six feet tall with a slender build. He sports a deep, dark tan. He appears to have confidence and comfort in his own skin by the way he purposefully strides into a room. He's a born storyteller, waving his arms when he talks, sometimes jumping around to make a point. His facial expressions are delightfully exaggerated and listeners are drawn to his large, inquisitive brown eyes.

Maggie is immediately attracted to Julius and his authenticity. Right away, she trusts him. She believes he could never be hurtful.

Gaining confidence from Julius's encouragement and acceptance, over the summer Maggie discovers a new way of talking with boys. She finds that she feels particularly comfortable with older boys. They don't act goofy like boys her age. They take time to listen to her and when she listens to them, she can tell they enjoy her attention. Boys let it all hang out when she is in the mix. They stop talking about cars and surfing and switch to opinions, debates, feelings, and music. Maggie revels in her male audience. As she soaks in their deep voices, she feels her skin tingling.

Of all the boys, Julius has perfected letting it all hang out. No topic is off limits. His dark eyes make direct contact, locking Maggie into his world, during their intense conversations.

When not with the guys, the girls get around by bus, bike, or foot. It is mostly the fathers who drive them around at night to the movies. Most days they ride their bicycles around Stanford University's 8,100-plus acres. There are a multitude of bike paths that wind through the campus and surrounding tracts of outdoor spaces dotted with eucalyptus groves and dry, flat, savannah-type terrain. Closer to the historical buildings, the land becomes lush with palm trees and gardens. At the western edge of campus lies the university's man-made lake, Lake Lagunita, and its perimeter of trails.

Anne and Maggie often hike the two miles to the main library on Newell Road and search the shelves for mysteries—fiction and nonfiction. Maggie also loves books about true crime and the paranormal. True crime has been a passion since she was nine years old, when she found her mother's pulp magazines, complete with color photos of crime scenes.

One time Maggie woke up in the middle of the night to feel a woman's hand holding hers. She couldn't see it in the dark, but she could feel it. It wasn't a menacing hand but rather kind and reassuring. Her interest in the paranormal was kindled.

An alternative to the quiet library is a noisy shopping mall. Maggie has three favorites in Palo Alto: Stanford Shopping Center, Mayfield Mall, and Town and Country.

The girls spend a lot of time trying on clothes, but Maggie's favorite thing to do at the mall is watch people. Especially when there's conflict, which triggers both fear and curiosity.

Why are those people yelling? Is there going to be a fight? I want to watch. I'm so embarrassed for them.

Maggie watches not just because she is a voyeur. She wants to figure people out in hopes of figuring herself out. She feels strange inside. In public, it's all an act to make people think she is normal.

I wish I could vomit out the real me. Maybe there's someone else inside me.

For years she's examined her high cheekbones and dark hair in the mirror. Her skin browns easily during the summer. She grows her hair long, paints her eyes, and makes her own cotton clothing, especially from those tapestries made in India.

Maybe I'm really a Cherokee. Maybe a poor Irish peasant. I feel tortured inside.

Every night before bed she asks the bathroom mirror, "Where do I come from?"

Even John Lennon is tortured. I can hear it in his voice.

In his lyrics. It's the broken people I understand. It's the broken who rise up in their music and take back what is stolen.

That's me. Maybe I was stolen in the night.

Friday morning the phone rings just as Maggie is waking up. She reaches for the phone on the dresser and topples out of bed onto the floor, landing painfully on her left hip.

"What the hell?" Crawling to her feet and laughing at herself, she picks up the receiver.

"Hello?"

"Is Maggie there?" It's a guy. Could it be … ?

"This is Maggie."

"It's me. Julius. Remember me?"

"Of course. Thought it sounded like your voice."

"You know my voice. Righteous, man. God. That's great."

"How ya doin', Julius?"

"Really good. Hey! There's this movie theater in Redwood City that only charges a dollar and that movie with Audrey Hepburn, *Wait Until Dark*, is playing. I don't have a car, but if you wanna go, we can find someone to drive."

"Oh, yeah. I want to see it. Don't know if my dad will drive us tonight, but I'll ask. He's kind of sick a lot. If not, do you know anyone else who can drive?"

The movie turns into a group date, and Olin ends up driving. In the theater he silently fumes as the lights go dim. This is not what he had in mind when he offered to drive. *So I'm here sitting not next to Maggie, but stuck between Deb and Rhonda. Maggie is sitting next to Julius. And not me! What the fuck.*

"What the hell are you staring at, Olin?" snarls Deb.

"Shush!" the others say in unison.

Two-thirds of the way through the movie, the madman

character plunges the lead female character into darkness by shutting off the power to her apartment. What the bad guy doesn't know is that the woman is blind and isn't affected by darkness. The movie screen goes black, but the audience can still hear ominous sounds.

Maggie and her friends whisper to each other. "This is maddening."

"This is scary."

Julius grabs Maggie's hand. He screams. She jumps. They both laugh.

Maggie replays everything in her head that night in bed. What a perfect evening she had. Complacent. That's the word that springs to mind. It was all so complacent. With Julius she can be herself. He understands her vision, her intelligence, and he never tells her she's too young to understand things. Around other people she fakes what she thinks others consider normal. It takes a toll, not showing how crazy she really is. Alcohol and weed help quiet her mind. But with Julius, she doesn't need them.

I can breathe when I'm with him, she realizes. I can be light and free.

She smiles as sleep drops.

8 OLIN AND HIS HURT
July 1968

Elizabeth and Maggie stand across the street from Howell's Chevron gas station in downtown Palo Alto. They want cigarettes, and they know they can get them at Howell's even though they're minors.

"Okay. Let's do it, Maggie. I'll talk to Howell while you stand outside the office. The cigarette machine's in there."

"Righto."

Elizabeth strolls across the street, her generous hips swaying inside her faded jeans and her sandals flip-flopping on the asphalt. Maggie follows her to the Spanish-style, gold, stucco building. In Palo Alto even the gas stations are attractive.

Elizabeth knows Mr. Howell. In fact, Elizabeth knows a lot of people in Palo Alto because her parents introduce her to all the old-timers, the folks who have been working in town for decades. Her parents work in the local schools, giving Elizabeth and her three brothers a sense they have connections in this town.

Mr. Howell is in his office, so Elizabeth strides right through the arched doorway toward the old man, who is wearing greasy work clothes. Through the glass Maggie sees a smile light up Mr. Howell's weathered face as her friend starts talking to him. Elizabeth is a schmoozer like her parents and is good at getting what she wants.

Maggie envies Elizabeth's family. She's got brothers to talk to and her parents aren't alcoholics. If Maggie had siblings, she would have someone else to talk to about her dad. She tells none of her friends about his sloppy addiction and barely mentions his health issues.

Elizabeth hurries out of Mr. Howell's office. "Okay, a pack for me. A pack for you. Virginia Slims menthol, just like you asked. Let's go somewhere else."

They walk two blocks west toward the railroad tracks on the other side of busy Alma Street. Originally, during the early 1900s, there was only a dirt pathway along the tracks before it became a paved road for vehicles skirting the perimeter of the western side of the city.

They cross the street. There is no fence. Instead, there's a landscape barrier of nine-foot-tall evergreen oleander bushes. Their dark green, thick, and leather-like leaves embellish abundant clusters of pink, white, and red buds and flowers; and they serve as a barrier between the street and the tracks, reducing some of the noise from the iron railroad engines. It never crosses the girls' minds to think about safety. Who would put themselves into the path of a moving train?

"Now watch, Maggie. Concentrate real hard on your feet and only your feet. Balance on the rail behind me. And ... go!"

Maggie lights her cigarette from Elizabeth's and steps up behind her on the rail. Watching their feet, they slowly pace the burnished smooth rail, listening for an oncoming train as they smoke their cigs.

"Whoa. I'm so dizzy. I think this cigarette made me high," Elizabeth laughs.

"Oh my god, this is so cool," says Maggie. "Me too!"

"My head is spinning ... I must be high. Remember the first time you and I smoked weed? A joint my brother gave me? In my back yard?"

"Yeah, the very first time. Yeah, your brother told us the first time you smoke grass, you don't even get stoned."

"He was right, wasn't he? We didn't get stoned that first time."

"This cigarette high is kinda like the second time we smoked grass."

"Yeah. Or, kinda like I felt after we took those bennies and yellow jackets before the Vietnam riot at Lytton Plaza."

That night Maggie woke her social consciousness.

Lytton Plaza was created in 1964 by a banker. Located downtown on University Avenue, it was a privately owned, open-air square, designed as a gathering place for Palo Alto residents and visitors. Since it was not part of the city park system, trespassing laws did not apply. People regularly enjoyed the sunshine while sitting on the benches under the trees. It also drew community and university crowds for dialogue and free-speech events.

The Free Speech Movement at UC Berkeley began October 1, 1964. Berkeley's sister/rival college, Stanford, paralleled the movement. In 1965 alternative educational opportunities sprang up: the Free University of Berkeley and the Experimental College at San Francisco State University. In January 1966, classes began at the Experiment at Stanford University and at the Free University of Palo Alto. A year-and-a-half later they merged to become one: the Midpeninsula Free University (MFU). Free universities cropped up at or near campuses all over the country.

Teach-Ins were popular. They were educational meetings in forum fashion on college campuses designed to be participatory and oriented toward action. Instructors and outside experts lectured and invited the audience to take part.

The Vietnam anti-war movement at Stanford attracted the MFU. It took advantage of Lytton Plaza's free space by staging anti-war demonstrations, political rallies, and music concerts. Some resulted in police intervention. The local paper, the *Palo Alto Times*, reported business owners disliked the hippies who hung out at the new MFU scene at the plaza.

Maggie and her friends were hearing rumors that a protest against the Vietnam War was scheduled to take place in Lytton Plaza. Their parents warned them about the danger.

"Stay away from the plaza at night." "This is a serious warning with great consequences!" "There's supposed to be dangerous rioting." "Police will be there." "It'll be a madhouse." "I don't want you to get hurt."

Ignoring the warnings, Maggie had a plan. She invited a few girlfriends to spend the night at her house, a cover for sneaking out to go to the plaza. A protest sounded intriguing. Like something in the news. It didn't happen every day.

They slept in a tent trailer set up in Maggie's garage. Her parents had done a really nice thing for her so she could have more space to hang out with friends. They helped her put up their pop-up, canvas tent trailer in the oversized two-car garage, which had a tall, cathedral ceiling. There was room for the car on one side and the tent trailer on the other. They never considered how easy it would be to sneak out of the garage at night.

Elizabeth brought some prescription drugs from her parents' medicine cabinet. Pills and alcohol were the easiest things to sneak. Once they took the pills, the girls waited until it was quiet inside Maggie's house.

"I think your parents must be asleep."
"They sure go to bed early!"
"Is this a good time to go?"

Then they snuck out a side door in the garage and grabbed a city bus headed for downtown.

Their parents had been right. Cops were everywhere and red lights spun from the roofs of their cars. People shouted through bullhorns. The plaza was packed full of young people. Maggie and her friends kept a safe distance from the melee, watching from across the street while hiding behind or blending into trees. They were high on bennies and yellow jackets but shrewd enough to stay invisible.

Maggie, especially, was thrilled to watch huge plate glass windows shatter and cops and civilians shouting at each other. She almost peed her pants as she watched anti-war protesters make history while she hadn't the maturity or the foresight to know it would be history.

It was a memorable night, one that Maggie would recall for years afterwards.

Back on the railroad tracks, Maggie tilts her head back and blows cigarette smoke up into the sky. She promptly loses her balance yet manages to land on her feet beside the track.

Elizabeth is still jabbering. "And the cig high is kinda like the Romilar, Coke, and aspirin experiment. Buzzing. That's it, Maggie! I am buzzed. Buzzzed. Maggie, where's Julius these days? I kind of like his being around."

Maggie chuckles. "Yeah, he's a funny guy and has loads of oomph."

"Oomph! Hah! Maggie, only you would say 'oomph.' Anyhoo, Julius isn't conceited like Olin, ya know. Are you still hung up on Olin?"

Maggie pretends not to hear Elizabeth's question because Elizabeth already knows the answer. *Sometimes she likes to needle me and I'm gonna ignore her.*

"Hey," Maggie says. "We are supposed to meet Anne, Deb, Rhonda, and Skipper at the underpass in about fifteen minutes."

They fall into step on their way to the Alma Street underpass.

Inside the cavernous tunnels of stucco and cement, the other four girls are waving at Elizabeth and Maggie. They walk up an incline, through an arched doorway that leads them outdoors on El Camino Real. It's only a few minutes away from the Stanford Shopping Center. At Woolworth's lunch counter they plunk themselves down on swivel stools in front of the counter and order Hot Fudge Tulip sundaes. Anything served in a tulip-shaped glass goblet is worth the indulgence of spending a dollar. Skipper pauses as she's about to bring a spoonful of whipped cream and a maraschino cherry up to her lips. She's just remembered some important gossip.

"Olin's girlfriend from high school broke up with him just

before summer vacation. He's still so sad he wants to die!"

"Hey. He never told us he had a girlfriend," Elizabeth and Anne say in unison.

Skipper smiles. "Yeah, well, she lives on my street. Her mom told my mom Olin's a sex pervert."

Rhonda squints in disapproval, making her narrow blue eyes even narrower.

"I never trusted him. Always trying to kiss you all, all the time. All of you! Oh, but not me! I knew. He has beady little eyes!"

"Yeah, it's true," says Deb. "He told me this morning on the phone how sad he is and he took a bottle of aspirin to somehow end it all. He's relieved he doesn't have a gun. I think he's home alone."

"So, Deb, you knew about this babe?" Anne sneers.

"His mom's at work," Skipper chimes in. "I was with Deb when she talked to him."

"She spent the night at my house," says Deb.

Anne changes the subject. "Did you sneak out when your parents went to bed?"

Deb shakes her long red hair until it practically covers her freckled face. "What's that got to do with anything? But, if you must know, we fell asleep watching Peter Sellers in *The World of Henry Orient*. C'mon. Finish up. Let's go see how Olin is."

Maggie remains quiet while her friends talk about Olin, but now she's intoxicated by the prospect of drama going down at Olin's house. "Are you going to call him first?"

"Why?" asks Skipper.

"Well, what if he gets mad that we just show up?" says Maggie.

"Come on. Let's go already. He'll love it if we show up."

Anne casts her eyes down at her half-eaten ice cream. "Well, I'll go, but I'm gonna hide behind a bush while I watch you guys knock on the door."

"I'll wait there with you," says Rhonda. "We'll come in if he's not mad."

"Yeah. If he's mad, I'm running for the hills. Or the

Stanford Theater," Anne jokes. "I'll sneak in and watch *Chitty Chitty Bang Bang* with the little kids!"

Olin's house isn't far from the mall. It only takes about fifteen minutes for the girls to reach it, especially since they decide to run most of the way. There it is. The big, white house with the weathered paint. The players take their positions: Elizabeth and Deb in the front yard, Anne and Rhonda behind bushes; and Maggie and Skipper on the porch. Skipper is known not only for having the biggest boobs but the biggest balls. She marches to the door and rings the doorbell. No sound.

"Maybe it doesn't work. I don't hear anything. And I don't hear anyone coming to the door."

"Knock," whispers Maggie.

Skipper knocks loudly. After a few moments, Olin opens the door.

His sad eyes lock on Maggie's. The stretched-out neckline of his stained navy T-shirt exposes his pale, freckled chest. She suddenly wants to kiss him. Whoever this old girlfriend is, well, she cannot possibly be a better kisser than her.

Anne and Rhonda creep out from behind the bushes and join the others inside, where they take their places on seriously worn out, scarlet velvet club chairs. Maggie is in a daze. She feels hopelessly naïve as she takes in her surroundings. *Try to look like you know what you're doing here, Maggie. Don't look stupid. What else am I supposed to do now?*

Lace curtains, pulled back from the big front window, frame the two huge oak trees growing out of a rectangle of dirt close to the street. Their great gnarled surface roots crack and buckle the concrete squares of the two-columned sidewalk. The crown sends out thick limbs that shoot over the street, draping chilly shadows under the clear blue, heat-wilted sky.

Maggie has no idea what it takes to lift a guy out of depression. Bizarre thoughts about what to do for a lovesick, suicidal boy come to mind. Some of them involve the removal of clothing. She only knows what she sees and hears from her friends and the media, which perpetuates a culture of unrestricted sex.

She remembers her reaction when she discovered, at age twelve, how babies are made. She told her friends, "That's crazy. It can't be the only way to have children. I'll have to turn out the lights and close my eyes."

Her mother taught her to work, not how to keep a guy happy. It is more complicated than weeding and watering garden beds, mowing the lawn, and painting a fence. Her impure thoughts about Olin scare her, so she stuffs her fear in one of those locked rooms in her brain and returns to the present moment, trying to appear composed and sophisticated.

She studies the flowered, threadbare carpet in the living room, waiting to hear what Olin will say next.

"Oh, God, you guys. How sweet. I don't deserve this."

Olin sheds a single tear, which he dramatically brushes away. He swoons over them as they chatter sympathetically, then he pulls out the Rolling Stones' *Flowers* album. The music and his many nursemaids soon restore his self-worth.

A clamor is heard from the second floor.

Olin's motorcycle-riding friend Steve saunters down the stairs, languidly dragging a girl by the hand. She has expensive threads and wears a disparaging expression under her long, straight bangs. This is not the first time Maggie has seen her with Steve at Olin's house. She never says hello. Coming down the stairs, she keeps her fingers locked around Steve's.

"Look who's here, Steve. My, my. How cute." She laughs and tosses her flip over her shoulder. Maggie interprets this as a sign of superiority and imagines the girl's thoughts: *What have I got to be jealous about? After all, I'm his, aren't I? The girl who hangs out with foxy Steve in a spare upstairs bedroom on hot summer afternoons.*

Steve shakes his head and smiles, a change from his usual brooding expression.

"Man, Olin. You got it goin' on. Shit man. Right on."

He laughs and turns to push the girlfriend back up the stairs.

Maggie is humiliated. Steve must think she's a real nothing. He's so good-looking, and he's with one of the rich, popular Paly girls. How dare that girl give her such a public middle finger.

Maggie doesn't know what to do with her embarrassment, so she quietly slips out the front door and stands on the porch, biting her nails.

9 OBSESSIVE RUMINATIONS
September 2015

September is Maggie's favorite month because the air is still. Traffic noise is less audible. Skies are bluer. Heat and humidity dissipate. The leaves begin changing color and shake from warm afternoon winds.

The woods in September are as still as an empty cathedral. Little animals traipse across fallen leaves. The beach fog lifts and the ocean is crystal. Dogs chase the coastal birds.

Nesting in her bed in her Palo Alto apartment, she whispers, "This is real. Not a dream."

After a breakfast of hazelnut-flavored coffee, scrambled eggs, and orange juice, Maggie sets out to enjoy the neighborhoods and parks surrounding the studio. After about forty-five minutes, she returns with a fresh mind, ready to work on solving the mystery of Julius's whereabouts.

Several months earlier, Maggie had found three possible locations for Julius on the internet—all in California. She sent a note to him at each location, but all mail was returned to her: "Return to sender." "Attempted. Not known." "Unable to forward."

The telephone numbers that were listed were all disconnected. There was no digital footprint for his parents, either.

Before leaving Oregon, Maggie had sorted through many years' worth of mementos to find everything that related to

Julius. Now she pulls out a picture Julius drew and a poem he wrote for her in 1977. The profile of a serious-faced woman wearing a turban is drawn with colored pencils. One arm is stretched out and her hand reaches for a potted plant. Beyond the plant is a star and the woman's gaze is steady.

To Maggie

Like a little spark
It bursts to flame
And then fire and
It heats our minds
And makes us feel
Warm with human
Compassion, makes us
Care for and stand
In protection for a
Fellow human, and
Each time it's out
It leaves its mark
Like the coals in
The fireplace. Full
Of memories so
Strong they can
Burst into flame
With a remembered memory.

By Julius Brownell

Maggie remembers his exceptional artistic talent. He once told her he gave most of his high school drawings and paintings to Olin for safekeeping.

Inspired to write, she spends the next three hours working on her mystery novel. The desk in the main living area of the studio is big enough for her laptop, her piles of old letters from Julius, and her many draft manuscripts. The window above the desk also affords her a lovely view of the trees and gardens surrounding the apartment.

After a few hours she feels drained. She brings a chair outside to sit on the patio, closing her eyes and letting the breeze coax her into a feeling of contentment.

But she wants more.

She lights up a joint and waits. Not enough. She grabs a Saint Pauli Girl from the refrigerator and takes a drink.

Once thoroughly stoned, she develops a sharp sensation in her chest like a seashell inside her shoe. It rubs and moves about, never once letting its presence go unknown. It begs to be found. It wants attention. When she takes it out, she sees that the sensation requesting attention is her sixth sense—her extrasensory perception—and in these moments she feels closer to divine love and her god. Her sixth sense is her open spiritual path to whatever dimensions are out there.

She's been on this path her whole life. No one ever knew—not her mother, not even her Paly friends.

Her childhood and teenage years were populated by shiny, new explorations suspended in the blue twilight of golden stars where the unbelievable lived. The world was full of jungles and marvels, prairies and pavement tethered by parental umbilical cords. She found independence and the nerve to experience it all, pushing every obstacle away.

Breaking into Stanford University's stables at midnight and riding horses bareback. Winter camping in the coastal mountains. Cutting class to drive to neighboring high schools and stroll nonchalantly down the halls while kids sent puzzled looks her way.

At age sixty-two Maggie's rebelliousness is mundane: driving without a seat belt, sitting on public toilets without a paper shield, and wearing pajamas to walk the dog.

In her youth her need to explore extends to sex. By age nine she experiences intense desire and by age ten she has her first sexual climax.

The first object of her desire is Tony, a boy in her third-grade class. She wishes he was her brother and at the same time imagines sharing a bed with him. Just sleeping, of course. While still in elementary school, she has several sexual experiences with other girls.

"Remember Maggie?" "Who could forget?"

Maggie carefully placed those thrills into a bundle of memories, a package that stayed wrapped until she had children. Then, lo and behold, her daughters and son surprise her with their own explorations and she unwraps her package of memories.

Santa was real again. Every street was a new street. Every butterfly more colorful. Strawberries warmer in the sun-blessed sweetness. Every vacation was a time of abandonment. To hold her young children and smell their clean hair created a bond she had with no other.

By the time she is feeling the perfect high, it is ten o'clock at night. She turns on the TV and gets into bed. The soothing drone of the actors' voices puts her to sleep.

The next thing she knows, a bell is ringing.

A chime? A song? Where is that? Her cell phone? It's dark and she scrambles to the end of her bed where the ringing is coming from. Christ! It's Olin's phone number.

"Well, Miss Maggie! I finally got to San Jose. I kinda missed my flight and took another flight. You sound groggy. Oh, God! Did I wake you? Oh, shit! Yeah, I see it's midnight."

"Olin, I was starting to think asking you to come here was a mistake."

"Oh, no. No, honey. God, no. I'm behind you on this journey."

"I feel so alone right now, Olin."

"Alone? You? Never."

"Alone? I didn't say I was alone."

"Yes, honey. You did."

"I said I'm tired."

"No, you ... Nevermind. I'd better let you go back to sleep. I'll call you tomorrow."

For God's sake! Now she has insomnia. The clock says 2:47 a.m. Did she go back to sleep after Olin's call? *Try to sleep. Try to sleep. Try to sleep now.*

Incessant thoughts are roaring in her head. A repetitious loop plays all the scenarios where she could have been a better person. All those guys. All the escapes. All the mistakes she made with her children.

She tries to soothe her restless body by swaddling herself in the comforter and hushing the barrage of thoughts. Rumination is a devil. Why did Olin have to stir everything up? She never said she felt alone. He misunderstood her. She would never tell him that.

The morning light fills the studio as Maggie sits up, tangled in the maroon cotton bedsheets, pillows strewn around her bed. A fleeting dream of dining with her mother, who passed away sixteen years earlier, still hangs over her perception of reality versus hallucination.

Ringing. Ringing. Ringing in the air. The phone again. She manages to answer even though she's still visualizing the restaurant where she sat with her mother.

"What is missing? The check receipt?" Someone is talking. The voice in her ear suddenly becomes louder, accompanied by coughing and sputtering.

"Maggie! I'm sorry! I've woken you again."

"Olin? Again? What time is it now? Eight a.m. It's impolite to call this early. Are you still smoking? What receipt are you talking about?"

"Sorry, I was talking to Steve. Hey, you remembered I smoke. Or I used to, rather. Not anymore. This is just my old-man voice. What are you doing?"

"Absolutely nothing, Olin. Not even sleeping, thanks to you. Are you here, in Palo Alto?"

"Yes, of course! Well, sort of. I'm in Steven's car headed for my niece's house. You remember. She's near San Jose."

Somewhere in her foggy brain, she remembers he told her that the guys would be staying with Olin's niece while in town.

"Well, that's progress."

"So Maggie, do you want to tell me what you've uncovered since you've been in Palo Alto? You've been here over a week, right?"

"Yes. And to your first question, no. It's too early and I've had no coffee."

"I gather Julius isn't dead. That's good. Do you remember that time in 1968 when you and Anne and Deb and Rhonda thought I was trying to kill myself when I took too much aspirin? Wait … what? Oh, Steve just told me to shut up."

"Good. He can read my mind. Oh … wait … Anne sent a text last night. Let's see if I can read it and not hang up on you."

"I don't know. You might hang up on me, but just call me back. I think—well, two or three different things. Deb and Anne might not want to see me. I've tried calling Anne, but she never takes my calls or phones back. I've talked to Deb, though. She's kinda mean to me over the phone. She has a problem, not just with me, but with her whole family. It seems she might be into drugs."

Maggie can hear Steve in the background. "God, Olin! You sound like a soap opera. If you can't make sense, give the phone to me and I'll talk to her!"

"I know the law pretty well and you should too, Steve. No driving and talking on your cell," yells Olin.

"You might know the back of my hand. Now shut up, hang up, and call her later."

Maggie can't deal with Olin and Steve's disjointed interactions on top of her own. "Olin, you're making me horribly confused. Goodbye."

She tries to find her bearings in the silence.

The phone rings again.

"I really think you need to know a secret about Julius's family," Olin whispers.

"What secret?" Maggie asks wearily, but Olin ends the call.

She groans and burrows into the nest of tangled bedclothes and feather pillows, ruminating about why she ever fell for Olin and his drama. It seems so obvious now: He had a foxy smile. He said sweet nothings. He craved attention and knew how to use his sad eyes to get it. She was young and inexperienced. He still says sweet nothings, as if time had stood still and they were still teenagers instead of sexagenarians.

Sex-agenarians.

How apropos. Is sex why she had so many boyfriends?

She thinks about her many relationships. They started out as candles burning brightly, but sooner or later the wax melted and the candles dimmed. She would dig and dig, frantically trying to find the wick buried under all the wax, but the wax always won. She could never get the wick to keep from going out, to keep burning for her.

Burying her head deeper under the bedclothes, she mutters, "Don't tell me. I've heard it before. Emotional abandonment." She tried to be honest once. Early in their relationship, she approached her current husband with an intention to reveal her secrets. She told him of the memories swept behind closed, locked doors. There were so many rooms holding her troubles and secrets that she couldn't even count them. It felt good to be candid. She wanted to tell him more about what lay behind the closed doors, but his response spooked her.

"Well, don't you think everybody is like that? I wouldn't let it bother you. You just need to let it all go."

She knew then that he couldn't understand. She put a smile on her face and shrugged.

"Well, I don't know if I can let it go, but I'll try."

"No, sorry, if you want to talk, go ahead."

"It's all kind of fading now. Maybe another time. When I remember."

"Well, I'm always here if you need me. Good talk."

Her husband's family experience was one of ease and love. How could he ever understand her secrets and loneliness?

The comforter atop her is too hot and heavy. It's keeping her awake. She throws it off the bed onto the floor, but not before it knocks a water glass over and the clock, too.

"What is wrong with me? And I was almost asleep! Now

67

where was I before that? Oh, yeah."

She falls back asleep, waking up gently at ten o'clock, feeling refreshed.

She looks up at the white rafters and tall, white ceiling. She knows she should get up, but she finds herself thinking about her early childhood, the days before Olin and Julius came along. She felt unusual at a very young age. A savior spoke to her early, an inner voice that told her all humans were equal; they just did some stupid things sometimes. She listened to the savior inside her. "You are special, Margaret Pauline Mayes. Believe me."

Her parents and grandmother told her *Little Margaret Pauline* stories. Charming. Adventurous. Pretty. Even ornery, but she loved all the stories.

"Do you remember the time you were roller-skating in the back yard?" her mother asked. "You were pretending that the patio was an ice rink and you were a figure skater. It was summertime and you had on your red corduroy ice-skating dress that Grandmommy made you, the one with long sleeves and gold satin lining under the short, flared skirt. Topper, our Dalmatian, was outside with you and he was racing up and down the yard. You pretended he was your skating partner. Well, I should have watched you more closely because that dog ran pell mell right into you and you fell face down on the concrete patio and got a concussion. I felt so awful. So mortified. I let you get a concussion!"

"You fell down a lot," said her father. "Your knees were skinned and you cried and cried when Mommy set you on the kitchen counter, washed your knees, put that stinging iodine on your boo-boos, and then finished with a nice Band-Aid on each knee."

"Ooh, Margaret Pauline. You got in such trouble that time you ran away from your mother and me over at that playground in Golden Gate Park," Grandmommy said. "For some reason you got so mad at us that you took off and ran all the way back to my apartment on Cole Street. We couldn't keep up with you, us two old ladies running, purses swinging from our arms. Hah! You even waited at the stoplight at that busy Haight Street and then crossed all by yourself!

"I loved you so much I could hardly be mad. You were only five years old and independent as the dickens. When we caught up to you at my apartment, your mother slapped you in the face. I yelled at her. Then she slapped me in the face. I never forgave her for that. I never told your father, either. I was just glad she wasn't my daughter. Your father would have been furious."

Maggie distinctly remembers the power and freedom of that runaway day. She had never strayed so far away from them—the adults. Yet, she could. And she did. No slap in the world could ever take away that exaltation, that exhilaration she felt from being free.

10 REMEMBER THE TWIST?
September 2015

The clock says eight-thirty. In the morning. Not Maggie's favorite time of day. She's a night owl. Stepping out of bedsheets, she burps right out loud because she can. She decides to go for a walk while the coffee is brewing.

Her little apartment is attached to a yellow farmhouse on Cowper Street. Many of the houses originally built along Cowper Street have been either renovated or torn down and replaced by bungalows, ranches, or two-story McMansions. There's every style of house one could imagine. Architecture has long been one of Maggie's passions, and even in Oregon, she still follows Palo Alto's real estate market religiously.

It isn't unusual to find grandiose Spanish, Mediterranean, Craftsman, Colonial revival, Victorian, or uber-modernist villas and mansions erected on tiny lots that were once ample size for the modest homes of Maggie's parents' generation. Maggie's favorite homes are those original bungalows that have been kept up with new plaster, paint, and new tiled- or wood-shingled roofs; garnished with wrought-iron fences and gardens; and enhanced with grand front doors and cottage-style, white wicker furniture on the front porches.

Another clear, blue-skied California day. A few cars mosey down the street.

A quarter mile from her rental studio, Maggie strolls into a community park. Black squirrels and crows mingle, daintily stepping and searching for food in the grass. Three men practice their tai chi on a basketball court. A dirt path winds through the sandboxes, playground, tennis courts, dog park, and picnic benches. She follows it until she reaches the other side of the park.

She remembers running through these streets with Deb on a dark Halloween night when they were fourteen. They stopped to catch their breath and give their aching legs a rest. Hearing fast footsteps behind them, they turned around to see a group of teenage boys getting ready to pelt them with tomatoes and eggs. Within minutes, they are both anointed with a headful of shaving cream. Squealing girls, shouting boys ... the shadowy sway of bodies was like that of spirits awakening.

"What was that song?" Maggie asks herself. She feels a pulse in her neck like a beat. She touches her wrist and feels a beat there, too. "Oh ho! Yes! Revolution. John Lennon."

Her phone rings. It is Deb. Which one of them has ESP?

"Hey! What's up?"

"What are you doing, Maggie?"

"Taking a walk. Just went by your old house."

Maggie hears a few breaths.

"Deb, you still there?"

"Yeah, sorry, just lit up a cig. Hey, Olin called me this morning and he started up with 'honey' this and 'honey' that ... "

"Did he wake you up? He has a habit of waking me up."

"Yeah, he woke me up. Listen, I've been talking to him on the phone and through emails for five years now. He used to say 'we belong together, girl.' Not once has he followed through on visiting me. We just talk. And he just talks, talks, talks. I am suspicious he would make this trip to P.A. all of a sudden. And isn't it convenient. He gets to see not just one old girlfriend, but three at the same time!"

Maggie really does not want to hear any bad news.

"Damn. I haven't talked to him since yesterday. What's he up to now?"

"Steve dropped him off at his niece's house near San Jose. Steve couldn't stay with him. He had to go back to his house because of some family deal. I'm fuming."

"So, now what?"

"I don't know. Olin is stuck at his niece's until he can get a car to drive to P.A. Or, until Steve picks him up. Whenever that will be."

"That little shit!" says Maggie. "Why am I getting the feeling he's giving us the runaround?" She has her suspicions. He probably isn't that cool-looking dude anymore, the one with a full head of hair and a leather jacket. He's probably shrunk and has stringy hair and a paunch belly. Not charming and foxy like he once was.

"What now? What do you and Anne want to do?" Maggie asks.

"Well, both Anne and I are taking this week as vacation time from work. We don't have a whole month like you do."

Deb works at a bank in the human resources department. Anne owns a pottery studio and volunteers at a nursing home.

"I think all the girls should hang out. We can still have the reunion with Olin and Steve later."

"Do you have coffee at your studio? I can round up Rhonda and Elizabeth. And some donuts."

"Okay. Yes. Yum, donuts. I'll give you some highlights from my book-in-progress. It will be fun to talk about Julius, right?"

"Sure, whatever. See you soon."

It's all Maggie could ever ask for. Her friends are coming to see her. Hoping no one is watching her, she skips a little, just to see if she remembers how.

Sixty-year-old women can easily slip right back into the sleepover culture they learned so many years ago. They never forget how to party. Ghost stories in the dark. Gobs of Fritos and cake. *The Man from U.N.C.L.E.* Mad Libs.

The world can unravel, yet girls can gather, ignore it all, and have fun.

"Let's twist again," Maggie shouts as she stands up and

starts doing the twist in the studio. "Chubby Checker!"

Deb gets up and joins her. "Like we did last summer," she sings.

"I never danced," Anne says to Elizabeth.

"Look, Anne. Rhonda's doin' the swim."

"I liked the pony and the monkey, too. Couldn't figure out the bugaloo."

The studio is lively all day. Three pots of coffee, a dozen donuts, and fresh figs from the tree out on the patio make up the perfect breakfast.

"Rhonda, it's good to see you," Elizabeth says. "You're lookin' good. How can you get your hair to grow that long? It's almost to your butt. Amazing. What's up with your songwriting?"

"I'm on my fourth agent in twenty years. This one seems adequate. He gets me lots of work. Almost too much, sometimes."

"What percent does the agent get from you?"

"I never discuss the money end of things. I'm having fun, though. Let's just say my college education in business and music has paid off."

Maggie cannot interest anyone in talking about Julius yet. She just has to wait for the right moment.

The women take a ninety-minute walk in the afternoon sunshine, enjoying the breeze.

"Deb, I'm delighted to see how fit and trim you are," says Anne. "At the last Paly reunion, you said you'd been homebound due to some medical issues."

"Yeah. The last two years have been rough. It was one thing after another: broken arm, pneumonia, and an icky intestinal bout. But look! I can do a little hop, skip, and jump." And she does.

Maggie loves listening to her friends talk. It means everything is copacetic. She appreciates that Anne is as caring as ever, always so concerned about everyone's health.

It's four o'clock in the afternoon and they are hungry and thirsty. Back at the studio Maggie attempts to talk about her book and the mystery of the vanishing Julius. Deb is slightly interested, but Maggie loses control over the rest of them. Probably not in the cards today.

They consume four bottles of spring water; two bottles of an old-vine zinfandel from Amador County, California; one bottle of chardonnay from Anderson Valley, California, which tastes like butter; a cheese and fruit plate; sourdough bread and sweet, local butter; and salted, organic, sweet potato chips.

Anne and Maggie demonstrate yoga moves. It's impossible to stay on track as they go off on ridiculous tangents. "Focus!" someone says every fifteen minutes.

"On what?"

"Olin. And Steve. Isn't he supposed to be here, too?"

"Olin is such a loser," Rhonda cackles.

Deb and Anne are in the kitchen, making martinis.

"I don't drink! This is crazy to watch. You've had too much to drink. None of you can focus," says Elizabeth.

Rhonda stops laughing and turns serious. "Do you guys remember that party at my house in the garage when you girls invited all these guys from Paly and Cubberley high schools? And do you remember you forgot to invite any girls? There were too many guys. They were bummed. So I invited some neighbor girls over and the guys were all gaga over one because she won a beauty pageant. I will never forget."

"We gotta get out of this place," Maggie announces.

"If it's the last thing we ever do," chimes in Deb.

They take another walk at dusk. Laughing and loud.

"Shush. Everybody inside is gonna hear you guys."

Rhonda says, "C'mon, just give up this silly idea of finding Julius. What's the big deal anyway? Also, I'm not getting sober. I'm gonna have to crash with you, Maggie. I can't drive."

A great opportunity to take command falls into Elizabeth's lap. "You guys can leave your car here. I'll drive you home. And we better do it soon 'cuz I've gotta work tomorrow."

Elizabeth is still the same good girl she was in 1968. Abstainer of drugs and alcohol, punctual, reliable, well-ordered, inviting, and accommodating. Her personality suits her part-time job in parole and probations, although these days, she's mostly pushing paper.

Maggie watches them pull away from the curb, waving at her always-and-forever best friends and feeling a tug on her heart.

Back on the quiet patio and yard behind the studio, she thinks about how temporary their lives are. She wants to stay outside and measure her good fortune. In the darkening night, she recites the Serenity Prayer:

God grant me the serenity
To accept the things I cannot change,
Courage to change the things I can,
And wisdom to know the difference.

"I think I've been self-centered," she whispers. "Does Julius even know I cared for him?"

What kind of friend would be willing to spread his letters out for others to read? And disrespect his confidentiality? Thank god the girls weren't interested.

A manipulator, that's the kind of person who would do that. A coward. Selfish. Demanding. No wonder he disappeared.

It's with shame that she ponders Julius's humble naïveté. It is entirely possible he may have been the only person capable of accepting her imperfections. She didn't pretend with him.

Good people do not lie or cheat or steal. They do not wish ill upon others. They do not spy on other people. They do not read their mail or private journals. They do not mix alcohol and drugs. They also do not attempt suicide.

Sixty-two years suddenly seems like far too long a time for such intolerable games. "I've been a bad girl," she chides herself as she pinches her skin. "Wake up!"

As she sits on the patio under the fig tree, she gazes at the stars and moon and ponders the fact that she's sitting on a patch of land stolen from First-People inhabitants. She feels shame for her European ancestors who changed it all. It hurts her heart to imagine Native residents having to watch their hills and valleys being sculpted into forts and trading posts and muddy streets for commercial greed. To see their lands swollen with Mexican and European peoples as they were pushed into a world where all respect was lost.

"This is getting too heavy." Maggie goes back into the studio and pops a Xanax. "Jesus loves me. Yes, he does," she sings softly as she locks the door, draws all the curtains, turns off the lights, and turns on the TV. Maybe it doesn't matter if she finds Julius. The maroon pillows on the bed feel good under her tense neck. She turns on her side and waits for the Xanax to kick in.

She drifts into a dream while a 1940 Ray Milland movie plays on the flat-screen TV. In her dream men and women take turns looking through the eyes of Buddha and Jesus statues. She's hosting a dinner party and one table is reserved for the folks wearing masks.

A phone rings. The clock says midnight. The dinner party dissolves into thin air.

Olin's voice says "Maggie."

"What?" Maggie struggles to sit up. "Olin, it's midnight! Why the hell do you keep calling me in the middle of the night? What is it now?"

"Listen, honey, I think Steve and I can find Julius through good old-fashioned investigative work. Remember, me and Steve used to be private eyes. Hey, are you alone? Am I on speaker-phone?"

"Of course you aren't. No one's here but me."

"You know, Maggie, there were years when I worked for the government. I was called in on special assignments and was gone for months at a time. People literally could not reach me and I was instructed not to contact anyone."

Maggie is a little dizzy in the dark. Is Olin not making sense or is it the Xanax?

"I will get you some answers about Julius. I promise. How about tomorrow? Steve will drive us to Palo Alto. How about all of us meet at Round Table Pizza on University? For nostalgia's sake. Since the Poppycock is gone."

"Us meaning who?"

"Whoever you want."

"Okay. Okay. But just lay off the melodramatics, Olin. Okay? You're giving me a headache."

11 ACCEPTANCE
August 1968

Maggie won't even consider going to second base with Olin for fear he will discover just how flat she is. At five feet, seven inches tall, she weighs just one hundred eighteen pounds and her small boobs are in the spotlight. There's something there, but not enough. This morning, her mother hands her one of her bikini tops. Maggie notices that she sewed falsies into it.

"Jeez, Mom. You know, I didn't ask you to do this."

"I know, honey. I just thought this would help."

Since she's not "stacked" like most of her girlfriends, Maggie decides to focus on her straight, white teeth, long legs, and tanned skin.

In the afternoon she steps in stride with Julius as they lead Anne, Deb, Elizabeth, Olin, and Steve down University Avenue to listen to the jukebox at the Poppycock. It's become a habit. It's a happening place. Joy to the world.

Olin steers Steve behind everyone so he can talk privately.

"Every time I turn around, there's Julius with Maggie."

"What does that mean for you, Olin?"

"She's my girlfriend."

"I don't think she knows that. And besides … you tell lots of girls that they're your girlfriend."

"Okay, man. I admit it. I'm kinda jealous."

"Kinda? I've never seen you this jealous before. If you

want her as an exclusive girlfriend, you better say something fast. She and Julius look happy. You know?"

Julius is talking to Maggie about surfing, which she thinks is fascinating. He is the first person she's met who surfs. He also takes time to ask her what she's been reading this summer and then he listens to her.

It's a moment of sweet, warm, taffy-like lark. Maggie is part of a crowd. It's one of those perpetually sunny, kind of dry, summer days. Purple-flowering Jacaranda and lemon-scented, white-blooming magnolia trees line the street and stretch out canopies of shade.

She loves her friends, her gang. She proposes to crown them "mystical." They not only exist in this moment, but in the starlight cosmos where their pretty faces are held by some god's favorite hand.

Walking next to Julius, Maggie loses herself in thoughts of her place in the universe and a future where she travels through time. "Wake up, Maggie. You look kinda goofy. Take my hand. What's up?"

"Aww, Julius. Your choice. I'm just a daydreamer. Hey! Do you know Anne and I like to check out books at the library about strange stuff? I think about spooky stuff and true crime stories. Do you know that?"

"Yeah. I know. Is that good for you?"

"Maybe. And maybe not. You know my house is haunted; or at least I'm being haunted. You know that, right?"

"I'm a little surprised."

Once they are seated at the Poppycock and drinking their root beers, Anne tells everyone about the library books she's been pouring over.

"One of them is by this guy, the famous paranormal investigator, Hans Holzer. His book is about true-life, ghostly accounts. One chapter is about a World War II veteran who lives in Palo Alto. Holzer found out this guy saw an Army buddy on Cowper Street in the late '40s. Just walking along. But the buddy had been killed in the war!"

"Yeah," says Maggie. "I read it, too. I know this story."

Anne continues. "See, the war was over and he came back home to Palo Alto. He was taking a walk one summer day down Cowper Street. Under the shady trees. He sees a man coming toward him down the sidewalk. The guy looks familiar. He politely nods at the man and they pass. Then! He remembers who this guy is!" Anne, in her enthusiasm, is unaware of a spittle of drool running down her chin. "This guy was another soldier and his close friend during the war. He immediately turns around to look and the guy is gone! That old friend, the soldier, he died in combat!"

"Let's go to your house, Anne. Let's all look at the story. Anybody game?" Maggie asks.

"Yeah, man, but I don't like ghost stories. They scare me." Julius recalls how he screamed in the theater when watching *Wait Until Dark* with Audrey Hepburn.

"Yeah, I remember that," says Maggie.

She's very disappointed Julius doesn't share her interest in ghosts and the unknown.

"You are a rare one, Maggie Mayes. I never know what you will say next." This time it's Steve chiming in.

"Yeah, but hey … Remember that story I told about the doll dress raising up above my bed?"

"I'll never forget it," Steve answers. "Who are you really, girl?"

Maggie is pleased that Steve recognizes her complexity. "Okay then. Anybody else interested in going to Anne's?"

Only Olin agrees to go with Anne and Maggie. Once at Anne's house, they search through Holzer's book.

"Look. This guy's address is here. Well, his street. Let's look him up in the phone book," says Olin.

Sure enough, the man's name is listed on the same street as mentioned in Holzer's book.

"I want to talk to him," says Anne.

"Me, too," says Maggie. "Let's call him!"

"I'll call him," offers Olin. "Let's pretend the three of us are researching ghost stories for a summer school project. We'll ask if we can interview him."

Olin acts self-assured when the man answers. Good ol'

confident Olin. The fellow verifies he is the man in the book and his story is accurate. Indeed, he is the man who saw a ghost. The author, Hans Holzer, reached out to him when he was writing a book.

The man believes Olin's explanation about a school project. "Sure, you can come over right now if you want."

Olin drives them over in his faded aqua VW bug. The man meets them in the front yard of his small white ranch-style house. It's awkward at first.

Anne surveys the front lawn. "My dad's hobby is gardening. He'd tell you this grass is lush. Well-kept."

The man smiles pleasantly and the kids begin to relax as he recalls numerous images of the ghost on Cowper Street. His respectful attitude towards them makes them realize that the least they can do is to take some actual notes. They aren't about to confess that the school project is only a stunt.

"You must wonder what it was like to see a guy in 3D but realize he was a dead man. Well, I wasn't the least bit frightened at the time, only puzzled."

So puzzled that eventually he told the story to anyone who would listen.

"Word got around somehow or other and this Holzer fellow contacts me. I said, 'Sure. You can put my story in a book,' I tell him."

The experience of meeting this man has a positive effect on Maggie. He treats the three of them as if he is their equal, despite their age difference. A man's true story is as good a victory as any three teenagers could have expected.

They wind up talking about human connections. Maggie talks as she's never talked before. It's a rare opportunity to chat this way with an adult. The initial brazen request for an interview no longer feels deceitful or selfish. She experiences a vital human need: sharing stories.

Maggie is in love with Olin; in love with Anne; in love with the man and his ghost story; in love with humanity; in love with Palo Alto. She thinks she is on a spacious frontier.

What can this mean? Anything's possible? With all this

love, maybe I can be in love with Julius, too. Can I? How about Steve?

"To be us is exhilarating, isn't it?" Maggie asks Olin and Anne back in the car.

Back at home that evening, Maggie's father makes a rare appearance at the dinner table. He's even clean-shaven and dressed in slacks and a shirt. Maggie tells her parents about the man and his ghost. They listen and ask her questions. Her dad shares some World War II stories. He had been in England for three years and had actually met a spy in a pub who he turned in to the military police. It feels so normal tonight, sitting around the table, talking. Maggie remembers what it was like when she didn't hate her father.

At bedtime, she remembers a magazine article she saved about the "hippie culture." She reads it again with a new perspective.

Flooded by the attractions of alcohol, drugs, and rock and roll music, they simmer in their generation's newly found, immature, experimental sex, revolving around each other into an inseparable embrace slowly morphing into chaos.

Feeling the exhilaration of freedom, they do not know yet that idols eventually become nature's mammals: carnivorous animals, animals in traps. Wild animals, like teenagers, are difficult to domesticate. They chew off their own decency. They turn play into fight. They outgrow their suckling and seek separate nutrients. Inevitably, their claws and teeth bring each other down for the kill. Even in demise and dishonor, they explore and couple with fervor and cling to their twin limbs. It's nature.

The end is never clean and the end of one teenage infatuation is the beginning of sporadic cravings for a new crush – for the taste of another's heart of blood.

12   GOT ME A TICKET FOR AN AEROPLANE
August 1968

A s the plane begins its ascent, Maggie closes her eyes and hears Cream singing "Strange Brew" in her head. She is flying alone to visit her mom's family in Iowa. When her mother planned this trip back in March, Maggie was thrilled because she loves all her Iowa relatives. As an only child, she craves the extended family of cousins, grandfather, and aunts and uncles. Now that the time to travel is here, she is torn between Iowa and her Palo Alto friends.

Deb is off to visit family in Florida. Anne, sadly, is stuck at home. The GP Trio is to be separated for three weeks. They promise to write.

Olin yearns for Deb and Maggie equally and tells them both he will write them letters. There's power in their affection; it makes him feel like a big deal.

Julius does not offer to write and neither does Maggie. There's no tension in their developing friendship. He handles her absence in his usual laid-back fashion. He'll miss her, but for him, everything is copacetic.

Maggie's grandfather lives in a tiny town (population: sixty) in Danish-settled western Iowa. His small, cedar-shake home sits on a large plot of land surrounded by farmlands on the prairie. Winds blow the wheat and corn tassels in a swishing motion under a wide blue sky that seems bigger than California's. Maggie's aunts and uncles and cousins are spread between farmlands and the state capital of Des Moines. They all love to talk about family history. They don't say much about Maggie's dad in her presence, so she wonders if they know he is an alcoholic. Maggie's mom gave her a warning before the trip. "Don't be fooled by your aunts and uncles. Some aren't so picture-perfect."

Maggie's grandparents emigrated from Denmark to Iowa in the early 20th century. Her grandfather was a blacksmith by trade, but he also became a successful businessman. He purchased farms and paid tenants to work the fields and livestock. When automobiles and trucks made their debut, he turned the blacksmith business into a truck repair shop.

Maggie's grandmother was a petite and pretty woman. Unlike her husband, she never learned to read, write, or speak English. She found prairie life to be harsh and missed her family back in refined Denmark.

After graduating from school, Maggie's mother Greta and her sisters worked in secretarial jobs in Des Moines. The two boys quit school after eighth grade and either worked the farmlands owned by their father or helped out in his repair shop. One later served in World War II, and all the siblings remained in Iowa when they became adults.

One hot summer day, Maggie's Danish grandmother put on a winter fur coat and went outside. She was found stumbling down the dirt road through town, and her husband had her committed to a nursing home with a diagnosis of schizophrenia. Maggie's mom told her that her mother hadn't been acting right for a long time. Her troubles may have started when she lost a baby girl in infancy.

Maggie's mother and father had very different childhood experiences. Her father, John Mayes, was an only child, living first in Des Moines, then Highland Park, Illinois. Only a few miles away, the mob-controlled city of Chicago was battling violence and corruption during Prohibition. John's father worked for the narcotics and firearms division of the FBI, a dangerous job that got him killed.

Maggie's paternal grandmother was completely unhinged

by her husband's death. She tried to commit suicide by throwing herself down a flight of stairs. She broke her neck, but quickly recovered and announced Jesus had saved her life. She became a Christian Scientist and started a new life, working in the cosmetics department of a large Des Moines department store.

She doted on her son John. Later their bond proved to be a challenge for her strong-willed daughter-in-law, Greta. Maggie's mother and her paternal grandmother became visible competitors for control over Maggie's father—and eventually Maggie, too.

Maggie's father was working as a dance instructor when he met Greta, a secretary. Right after the Great Depression, they left Des Moines for San Francisco, where jobs were plentiful. It would be nearly twenty years before "Grandmommy" would leave the Midwest for sophisticated San Francisco so she could be near her son John and baby Maggie, her first grandchild.

Maggie's trips to Iowa haven't always been alone. A few times her father drove them all cross-country in his Pontiac Catalina, and on occasion they flew in style from San Francisco.

Maggie experiences her Iowa summers as still-life paintings. Such vivid colors everywhere. Green and golden cornfields surrounding small wooden houses and vegetable gardens. White sheets hang on the clothesline while untethered dogs roam between the houses. When there is a sound, it is a rush of prairie grass and corn. Mostly it's postcard still.

When she was little, "Granddaddy" would spend time with her in his garden. He'd point out the strawberries, bend down to pick one, and give it to her to eat. Sunshine and sweetness. On to the carrots. Again, he bent down, pulled one from the ground, brushed off the dirt, and said in his lilting, Danish-accented English, "Try. Eat. Is good right out of the soil? Yes?"

Granddaddy's carrots tasted like cotton candy.

Maggie's not a little girl anymore, and although her relatives haven't changed, she no longer feels like part of a tribe when she visits. Her tribe is back in Palo Alto.

Hi Maggie,
Deb here. Things are great in Florida. This was my first plane trip without parents. You too, right? Wow! It's pretty hot here in Miami. Constantly dealing with wet pits.
Did you see any of the guys before you left for Iowa? Meet any guys on the plane?
Olin left your albums over at my house the night before my flight. I didn't know he borrowed those from you. Julius is soooo cute. He was at my house then, too. He told me he really likes all of us girls! He was dancing again and wanted to wear a hat when I took his picture.
Hey, did you say goodbye to Chuck? Does he know how much you've been hanging out with all these older guys? Does his brother Don know? Does Chuck know you don't like him anymore? How come you don't just break up with him?
Oh, I forgot. Olin kissed me goodbye. Did he kiss you?
Olin's got a new girlfriend. I hear she's German. I'm glad I'm here in Florida. Well, gotta go. We are going to a drive-in tonight.
I don't know if I want to stay here forever or go home tomorrow. And, get this, one of the latest tidbits: Anne said Olin is trying to decide between you and me. What? Boys are too much trouble.
Bye, Luv ya, Deb

Howdy Kid!
Annie here. Here's the biz. Right after we finished din-din a few days ago, Olin came over. He brought me some bright orange flowers. Imagine that. Rhonda came over, too. I thought she hated me. I never thought she would come to my house. Besides, she's so busy with Smooth Operator Pat.

NO ONE came over today or called. All day I sat home and cleaned my closet and drawers. Everyone (including Steven and Olin) is at a Frost Amphitheater concert wingding. My mom made me stay home because she thinks I've been too busy.

I think I'm getting ESP. One night I woke up suddenly and started singing "2 + 2." You know, the Bob Seeger song. I had the urge to turn on KYA. Guess what was playing? 2 + 2! Isn't that amazing?

Well, Julius is going to Lake Tahoe. He left Olin here and Olin's sad 'cuz he expected to go and now he won't go anywhere for vacation this summer. My mom thinks Olin is a smooth sex maniac. Isn't that dumb?

Steve is trying to convince me to stop seeing Olin and says he treats me like dirt. And Olin is going around telling everyone that I can't live without him. It all makes me extremely ill!

I was going to wind up this letter yesterday, but so much has happened. Hope you hear it from me first. Flash ... are you ready for this bulletin ... Now Olin isn't going to see us or call us or nothing! The big, bad bastard! Excuse the language, but this is the last straw. What's bizarre is how he changes all the time. I just went to a movie with him the other night. And the night before last, my dad saw Olin's arm around me. After he drove everyone home, he told me that if he ever catches Olin with his arm around me again, I will be forbidden to see him.

So, here's a doozy from Saturday night. Olin called me at 11:30. Too late for my parents. My mom comes running into the hall with hardly anything on and tells me to get off the phone and go to my room. She grabs the phone, pushes me in my room, and leans on the door so I can't get out.

Also, Olin has the idea you are really hung up on him. My good, old plump mom says, "Don't make the boy think you like him." That's the kind of advice she gives me. Did you know my parents met on a blind date? Look who my dad got stuck with.

Have you ever heard Steven say the word "pickles?" He

cracks me up. Sometimes he just says pickles over and over again.

This is stupid. I'm going to watch the Smothers Brothers.

I'm such a bad friend. I didn't mail this letter yet, but maybe that's a good thing because there's more news to tell you. Olin called me and said he misses you and Deb. He also misses an old girlfriend. All he does is cry and is in all sorts of bad moods.

Maggie, this is going to be very sad news. Olin stabbed himself in the stomach today! I am not kidding either! Remember that girlfriend who broke up with Olin? Well, he called her and she finally told him she will never go back with him and she wants him to stop calling. Olin told her, "Fine. You never have to see me again." Then he hung up on her. Then he stabbed himself. Steve called and told me all this because he and Olin were supposed to come over tonight.

Update. Guess who just called? I wrestled the phone from my mother. It was Olin himself. He said he did stab himself. Steve called an ambulance for him, but he wouldn't take it. He says he is going to be alright. Suddenly, I want to forget it all. The Doors are coming here. Do you think our parents will let us go?

Bye for now, Anne

Hi Maggie,

It's me. Sad Olin. Got your letter, it sounds like you're having fun. Don't get too hung up over some guy. I still want you to be free for me. You've been gone for five days now and I already miss ya! Wish you were here. I would like to meet you at the airport when you come home if it's alright with your parents. (Hope so!) Steve says he might come along, too.

I went surfing. The waves were big. I was kind of chicken, but I went out. I caught one wave, but it didn't last long. Then I caught another wave and it was big, so I was on top of the wave and it broke and I fell right to the bottom. Fifty million tons of water fell on me.

I am friends with Rhonda now. She's funny to be with because she is so mean to everyone. She asked me to go horseback riding with her, but I went swimming. By the way, when are you going swimming with me? If you can swim in a lake there in Iowa, you can swim with me. I've been having a drag since you've been gone. All I do is think about you everywhere I go. (Isn't that cute?) I am watching the Johnny Carson show. Rhonda is still going to call. Do you have any boyfriends there? Hope not. I liked your letter. I got asked to play bass in another band with one of the guys I went surfing with. Yesterday I walked to Rhonda's with Anne. Uh oh! I hung up on Annie three different times yesterday. I am getting to be a bore, so I'll let you go now.

Love you, Olin

Hi Maggie,

Hey thanks. I just got another letter from you. How have you been? You know you never answered my question about meeting you at the airport. That was a very nice poem you sent and I enjoyed it a lot. I hope you are having fun on vacation because I'm not. I just sit around doing nothing. When are you coming home? Hope it's before Aug 21 because Aug 21 is my birthday. Not much of a reason, but I want you to come home. Please!

You know I really miss you. Wish you were here. I am having such a drag with nothing to do, but I walk a lot at night. From about 10 to 12. I have lost 10 pounds in three days. Bad, huh? Everybody's parents are starting to hate me. Anne's parents are not letting me see her anymore.

That idea on killing myself is a bad idea. I'm getting so many people in trouble.

Oh are you still going to Sea World with me? I hope you still want to. Ok?

I sure wish you were here. I am running out of things to write. I hope you still like me because I like you and I hope you come home soon or write me again. But be home by Aug 21! That's an order. Got it? Good. Please come home.

Love ya, Olin

13 ROUND TABLE PIZZA
September 2015

Maggie expects her girlfriends to arrive at the rental studio any time now. At four-thirty she finally hears a gentle tapping at the door. It's Elizabeth, who volunteered to be the chauffeur for their outing to Round Table Pizza Parlor. Anne and Deb are already in the car. Rhonda has chosen to stay at home because her husband is yelling at her, her kids are swearing at her, and her dog is sick. "I'm gonna lock myself in my bedroom with my flat-screen TV and a bottle of wine. Have fun."

Olin has promised that he and Steve will meet the girls at Round Table. Five o'clock on the dot. Olin's been in California for a few days now and Steve is his chauffeur.

The pizza parlor is only about fifteen minutes away. Five o' clock comes in friendly. Anne, Deb, Elizabeth, and Maggie wait at a round table.

At five-fifteen Anne says, "Oh, the guys are running a little late."

At five-thirty they look at the clock again.

"God knows what Olin's up to." Anne shakes her head.

"This so rude." Deb stands, hands on her hips, and shouts to Elizabeth. "Call Olin. Find out where he is."

"No," Elizabeth answers. "You call him."

"No. You call him."

"No. I never call him."

Maggie says, "I'll call him."

She steps away and calls Olin. When he doesn't answer, she leaves a low-voiced message.

"It went to voicemail," she reports.

Finally, they decide to order pizza.

Olin's rudeness has them fuming, but they manage to choke down a few slices of melted cheese and hot dough. The phone rings.

"Olin?" Maggie answers.

"Maggie? Hello?" The coughing confirms it's him.

"Yeah, it's me." She puts the call on speaker.

"Aww, honey ... You just won't believe it. Steve and I were on our way. Swear to god. We were on our way."

Anne speaks up. "You're right about one thing. We don't believe it. Lemme talk to Steve."

"Who was that? Annie? Am I on speaker-phone? Well, yeah, that's not gonna happen. Steve's leavin' this up to me. He says he's reluctant."

Deb can't restrain herself. "Wow! Olin. You don't have to call me or any one of us 'honey' and you don't have to act like you're leading a pack. It isn't 1968 and we won't take such bullcrap."

"Olin, you were going to tell us about Julius's family. Remember?" Maggie tries to salvage the conversation.

"This is a shit show," laughs Elizabeth.

The line goes dead.

By 7:45 it's obvious the "reunion" is off. Maggie is soon back in her studio, alone. Her heart feels empty. Instead of seeing all her friends, everyone is upset. Elizabeth was right. The whole thing was just a shit show. Feeling the need for a little buzz, she finds a pain pill and a benzo. Soon she smooths out.

The phone rings the next morning. It's Deb.

"Listen to this, Maggie. Olin called me and said Steve's car broke down and they had cell phone trouble last night. He said it was too late to push for Round Table. I'm so done with him."

Maggie feels herself being drawn into drama as Deb keeps

hammering away about Olin and the way he hasn't changed since 1968.

"Listen, Maggie, this is too bizarre."

"I know, Deb. What is he doing this time?"

"I say, skip a reunion with him and let's salvage this vacation with just the girls. I don't think anything is gonna develop with Julius, either."

Maggie feels as if cobwebs are descending over her and she can't seem to mentally brush them away.

"I have to go, Deb. I have some writing to do."

A blank page stares at her all day. She can't concentrate. How can Olin not have changed in forty years? In life things happen that change everyone. Did he never have his world shaken to the core even once?

She gets up and adds a joint to her "remedy" to quiet the hamster wheel that is getting ready to spin. Wandering out to the patio, she settles into a chaise lounge and puts her earbuds in. The first song that plays on her iPod is "Shock the Monkey" by Coal Chamber. Ozzy Osbourne has lead vocals.

Her son used to play this version for her. She would play the original version that was written and sung by Peter Gabriel and then they'd laugh and talk about which version was best.

Their good-natured arguments over "Shock the Monkey" ended when her son died from a heroin overdose. Maggie still can't believe it's been nine years.

She cranks the music up and closes her eyes.

Peter, Paul, and Mary are harmonizing in her ears when Maggie gasps awake to find she's sitting in darkness outside her studio apartment.

I've been out here for hours. God, I'm so cold. Gotta get to bed before the hamster wheel starts again.

Cozying into the bed, Maggie shuts her eyes. The gentle release of her tense muscles signals sleep is near. But it's a ruse. Her heart feels like it's bursting and her left arm hurts. Signs of a heart attack. No, that's a ruse, too. It's a panic attack. She takes another Xanax and lets thoughts of home drift into her mind. She had just as much trouble getting to sleep at home as she was having now. In fact, back home it was often much worse.

She recalls all the nights in Oregon when rest seemed to be elusive, no matter what she did. Her after-work tai chi classes were a mindful and pleasant distraction from her troubles. She treasured the sacred peace tai chi provided as she drove home at dusk while the western skies shone over the coastal mountains. Even the lumber yards and train tracks, which skirted her route home, looked beautiful under the rays of the pink setting sun.

Maggie's husband was partial to vodka and tonics, a lot of them, so she made it a habit to go to bed several hours after he fell asleep. All the sacredness and peace dissolved, however, as soon as she lay next to her husband. His snoring, alcohol-fueled grunts, and rancid breath turned her off. Their shared bed had long been empty of amity yet bursting of blame. She felt trapped in her marriage and unable to still the shaking in her chest—a cocktail of grief and anger, constantly being stirred.

Maggie felt guilty if she didn't at least try to sleep next to her husband, but inevitably, she would flee to one of the two guest rooms down the hall. She preferred the one decorated with Grandmommy's favorite pictures on the wall.

One night she was plagued with unpleasant dreams, even after seeking refuge in Grandmommy's quiet and peaceful room. In the first dream something huge was trying to crawl out of her belly, a beast with an unquenchable thirst to break her down. She pleaded for an exorcism, an intervention— anything to liberate her from this beast. Half-awake, a gurgled, guttural sob erupted from her in the quietness of the guest room.

In the second dream she was in a bed. A strange bed. As she sat up, the Arctic moved inside her skin; the Sahara traveled to her cheeks and tongue. She was alone yet surrounded by a room full of people. She saw their mouths move. She couldn't hear their words, only the sound of a body bag being zipped up.

Then: "Don't come in here, ma'am. You don't want to see this. Let the mortuary handle this." A police officer held her hand at a kitchen table.

A neighbor wandered up in his white bikini underwear. "You vomited into the climbing, purple clematis outside your front porch. That is what you did."

"That can't be true, Rodney," she protested to her neighbor. "I don't have any climbing clematis. There is no clematis. There is no front porch. I've had too much whiskey and heroin. I can't remember so I'm locking you all away."

When Maggie awoke the second time, a sliver of light was coming through the window. The dream was still vivid in her mind, as vivid as the purple gauze curtains that billowed next to the open window in Grandmommy's guest room.

Lying in bed in her studio apartment, Maggie stares at the ceiling, trying not to think about anything that might cause her turmoil. Not Olin, not Julius, not home. Like the tai chi classes, this trip to Palo Alto was supposed to bring her sacred peace. Where is her sacred peace?

14   A DEATH
August 1968

O n a typical languid summer day, all seems static and safe. Not the kind of day for a tragedy. But when does tragedy make an appointment?

Maggie wakes up to the sound of the phone ringing. Deb's voice is in her ear and foggy morning brain, delivering the news. A teenage girl has died from a drug overdose in Palo Alto.

"And, the story is all over the *Palo Alto Times* as well as the *San Francisco Chronicle*," Deb reports.

Drug use is fairly common in the San Francisco Bay area. A drug overdose in Palo Alto, though, is not. This is new territory.

"Some of the gang—whoever can make it—are going to meet under the largest redwood tree at Rinconada Park. Five o' clock after Steve and Olin get off work. Let's go over together."

Rinconada is a public park that sits on a large city block. It has expansive lawns, dotted with shady redwoods and oaks.

Julius, Steve, Olin, Anne, Rhonda, Deb, and Maggie meet as planned. A typical late afternoon summer breeze brings the temperature down to a pleasant seventy degrees.

"She was only sixteen. She was going to be a junior this fall."

"Do you think her parents knew what was going on with her?"

"Maybe they couldn't relate."

"Shouldn't a parent know if their daughter was this bad off?"

"What kind of party do you think it was? What part of town? Does anyone know?"

They piece together what they've heard. A sixteen-year-old girl died of an apparent cocaine overdose after being found unconscious at a party over the weekend. The party was at another Paly student's house in one of the swankier parts of town. The girl's boyfriend found her and took her to the hospital, where she was pronounced dead on arrival.

Police found puncture wounds on her arms and cocaine, other drugs, needles, and drug paraphernalia in the bedroom of the house where the girl had collapsed. Their statement was brief. "She had been at a wild hard drug party in a sedate neighborhood of the University town. Several young men and underage teens were taken to the city jail for booking and questioning."

Police also found vials, tablets, and drug paraphernalia in the trunk of one of the cars parked at the party home, and they are linking them to a Menlo Park pharmacy robbery last week.

"This girl went to our elementary school, Maggie," says Rhonda.

"Yeah, that's right. I remember her. She's from our neighborhood. She's so pretty."

"She was in a couple of my classes at Jordan," says Steve.

An outburst from Julius surprises them all. "That cocaine is hard-core stuff. No way, man! That's insane. You can't trust it."

He has definite ideas about drugs. *I like my acid and grass, but not heroin or cocaine. Cocaine's a demon alright. Like a goddamned, black Mastiff with hooded eyes and long jowls staring me in the eyes.*

"I won't let you go to any of those parties or take any hard drugs." Olin breathes fire into that proclamation.

"You won't 'LET' us?" Deb raises her eyebrows and her

voice. "You don't own us, ya know, Olin."

Olin stops making a show of himself, but he is remembering all too clearly that he and Steve introduced their friend Chris—the same Chris who has the hots for Anne—to some girls in Redwood City about a year ago.

Olin and Steve know that Chris does heroin and sometimes he gives it to other people. In fact, he gave heroin to one of the Redwood City girls, who later overdosed. Olin feels obligated to protect Anne and the other girls, but he doesn't want to throw a huge bummer on an already bad day, so he drops the subject. He glances over at Steve, who gives him a knowing wink.

"Anyone want to go across the street to the library?" says Anne. "I want to get some books."

"What the hell, Anne! We've got a death in our town. We gotta talk about this and you want to go to the library?" Rhonda's tone is derisive.

"Actually, I think I'm going home. My mom said something about needing me for a sewing project."

"I'll give you a ride home on my motorcycle, okay, Anne?" says Steve softly.

"Thanks," she answers.

"No way! Not yet. You have to stay here," pesters Rhonda.

"Lay off," says Steve.

"I can take you home, Annie, in my V-dub," says Olin.

"I said I got it," snarls the usually even-keeled, quiet Steven.

"Holy shit." Julius jumps to his feet. "It's a showdown at the OK Corral."

"I'll call you after dinner, Anne," says Deb.

Maggie sees tears in Anne's eyes and says, "I'll call you, too." She worries about her sensitive friend.

Anne feels sick to her stomach over the Palo Alto girl's death. She feels like she is losing something—all the little-girl stuff. To be replaced by what? If this is maturity, she doesn't want it. She wants to get back the goodness of childhood.

Over the last few summers, she introduced Maggie to catching baby frogs in the San Francisquito Creek. They had a super time down in the wide creek with its steep banks. It was a child's paradise, just a bike ride away from the 'burbs.

The creek forms part of the boundary between two counties: San Mateo County (the city of Menlo Park at the northern side of the creek) and Santa Clara County (Palo Alto at the southern side).

Generally, the creek is about a hundred feet wide, but in some places it's as wide as two hundred fifty feet. It supports Mother Earth's garden: willows, bay laurels, redwoods, alders, cottonwoods, dogwoods, valley oaks, and coast live oaks.

Winter rains can fill the creek to flooding. Significant portions of the creek and its tributaries dry up by mid-summer. Still, water seeps through the gravel and shallow pools form.

Baby frogs are abundant in the shallow pools in late spring and early summer. Anne and Maggie sometimes collect dozens of them and take them home. It was just a few weeks ago that Anne found an albino baby frog and brought it into her house in a cardboard box while the other frogs were placed in her front and back yards.

The albino frog escaped its captivity. Anne never found it, dead or alive; and the baby frog pops into her head when she opens her front door. Suddenly she feels queasy as she says goodbye to Steve and thanks him for the ride. At this moment, San Francisquito Creek is for little kids and she doesn't feel like a kid right now. A girl her age is dead. As much as she fights with her mother, Anne feels safer at home, surrounded by tan stucco walls and bone china vases full of roses.

15 LETTERS TO JULIUS
1998-2002

June 1, 1998

Dear Julius,

Thank you for the postcard you sent me in May. I like that you bought it from the de Young Art Museum in San Francisco. It brought back fond memories of all the visits I made there, even as a young child when my grandmother and I roamed the spacious halls. Now that you are a studio artist, the picture on the card of "The Broken Pitcher" by the French artist William-Adolphe Bouguereau in 1891 must have some significance to you. Is the young, barefoot girl sitting so demurely by the water pump someone you feel a connection with?

When you and I talked on the phone last month, you told me you had gone back to college when you were thirty-six to pursue a dream: a degree in studio art. Sometimes, it is so hard being an adult. I am looking for a place within myself where the child and the adult can enjoy life together, savoring the nectar and trashing the heavy weights of stress. Art, artists, they can find that joining of the two, can't they?

Here we are after thirty years of first meeting, and a good twenty since we've even seen each other or spoken. Again, thanks for accepting my out-of-the-blue phone call last month. It's nice to communicate again. I am looking forward to your letter. I will also write, but I think I'll type mine on the computer. I can write almost as fast as I think, and my atrocious handwriting gets in the way.

Till then. Maggie

June 17, 1998

Dear Julius,

In honor of your birthday, I got you this card. The poet pictured on the front was also an artist. Do you like his poem?

I am sitting on a bench on a sidewalk in the quaint little college town of Amherst, Massachusetts. Diminutive shops, restaurants, coffee houses, juice bars, musicians, patchouli oil scent drifting. Summer humidity clings to every molecule. Such is the trademark of a New England summer: hot and sunny, then rain showers and thunder.

A rose quartz crystal rests in my left hand. Its task is to unleash energies of the heart, soul, and creativity. Walking through the doors of the past, I am young and you are sitting on this bench here with me. I imagine we are laughing at the collage of people, squinting at the sun, and slapping our bare feet on the damp cement.

Why do I imagine? Remember that birthday cake I made you and brought to your house on a hot summer day? It was either your 19th or 20th birthday. You were not home and your mother smiled at me and the melting frosting and accepted the cake.

Did you eat it?

Whatever cake you eat this 48th birthday, I hope it tastes good.

Maggie

June 17, 1998

Dear Maggie,

Well, if you only knew how many letters I have started to you in my mind and on paper ... Writer's block is child's play compared to basic illiteracy in terms of writing.

I think that since first grade my biggest handicaps have been a seeming insurmountable inability to grasp basic spelling and writing. I'm sure I could be a PhD candidate if nature had blessed me with a much better memory, and if I could remember all the words I've learned and had the ability to bring them out in an intelligent way on paper and in speech. I have to agree with you, using a computer is an easier method of writing. The delete and spell check world might take some of the fear out of my communication process. Maggie, it may seem that I'm going on and on about this composition issue. If you only knew how many times I have let possible friendships slip by because I didn't want to expose my "dark secret of functional illiteracy." I'm going to face it in your case not only because I think you will be accepting, but because I want to communicate with you!

So much has happened since we last saw each other in '77. In fact, everything we have experienced in our lives outside of our time together could become communication topics. It's scary in a way.

The weather has been so wet this past winter … it seems as if there wasn't a spring, really, it seems as if the sun came out just last weekend. I was in San Francisco. There is a Borders Bookstore with a second story coffee shop overlooking Union Square. I spent some time there sitting in a window seat flipping through magazines and watching the crowd below.

On Monday, I hitchhiked home. It was so warm I put on a baggy, bright blue, short-sleeved silk shirt over some black shorts and soaked up the warm breeze, in no hurry for my next ride.

I've been going down to the city often in the last two months because I've tore a ligament in my shoulder and I've been getting treatment at the VA hospital there. I hope my last appointment will be June 24th. But we'll see.

Speaking of seeing, can you see Long Island, New York, across Long Island Sound from Connecticut? Is the water in the ocean warm enough to swim in without a wet suit? Do you do it? You are within two hours of New York City. What is its influence on you? Did you like Seinfeld? Do you still go to the movies?

Maggie, you are looking for a place within yourself where the child and the adult can enjoy life together, savoring the nectar and trashing the heavy weights of stress. I can identify with you! What are some of your nectars? I guess to be fair I should be able to ask you what some of your stresses are.

Maggie, reveal yourself at your own pace ... I am interested in what you'd like to write about or talk about and look forward to sharing with you.

Your Friend, Julius

June 28, 1998

Maggie,

It's funny that my letter to you and your birthday card to me crossed paths. They were written on the same day; did you notice?

Thank you for inviting me to share a bench with you in Amherst, Massachusetts, even if only in your imagination. Your description made me feel as if I were there enjoying the place, the people, and the environment—the summer humidity clinging to every molecule, the showers and clanging thunder. Then the clouds left and the sun was shining and you described yourself sitting on that bench barefooted, dipping your toes into a puddle of water. I was comfortable in your company.

The only cake I received on my 48th birthday was your description of the cake you made me on my 19th birthday. I cannot distinctly remember it, but can, by your description, imagine me enjoying it, melted frosting and all. Thank you!

I will remember, however, how happy your card made me on my 48th birthday. I appreciate your attention.

Julius

July 10, 1998

Dear Julius,

Finally, your letter takes shape in front of me on my

computer screen. I do not know what has taken me so long, since my short note and birthday card came so easy. Guess there was less to reveal, less to commit.

This letter began while I was on vacation, and saw its beginning in scribbles on a note pad. I was in New Hampshire with the kids and the dog at a "family-type resort" the brochure says. But it was so rustic that 'resort it ain't.' I am not the fancy resort kind of person, but there was a brown spider the size of a baby goat in the shower and the only way to take the deep chill off those mountain mornings was to light a fire in the fireplace where there were no instructions about flues in this chimney.

Look at a map: I was in Lyme, New Hampshire, near Hanover, in between the Green Mountains and the White Mountains, two miles from Vermont. Vermont means "Green Mountain" in Latin. The motto in New Hampshire is "Live Free or Die."

Two dozen rustic cottages set above a spring-fed lake, a main lodge that used to be a farmhouse, and a big old red barn. It was very clean and quiet in this part of northern New England. We could swim, canoe, kayak, hike, play tennis, or just lay back.

We did some college shopping for my older daughter. (In September she'll start her senior year of high school.) We went to a drive-in movie, made some new friends, went to an old-fashioned church supper, and drove around a lot in this minivan I rented. Now I am home. Ho hum. Life goes on ...

I started a new job at a visiting nurse association as an administrative assistant to the director of community services. In other words, she and I coordinate the programs offered to the community, such as clinics for infants and children, flu and pneumonia shots, support groups, wellness seminars, and a health fair. It's full time; I have an office and many perks I haven't seen for years. I have a desk, phone, computer, typewriter, bulletin board, bookshelf, window, and door. Yeah, I've got all the toys, but it is scary being so committed and responsible. Sometimes the clock hands move real slow and I'd like to get up and go to the beach or a movie with the kids or take a nap. Sometimes I want to take my shoes off and walk around the building barefoot. However, that behavior will not pay the bills.

It is 11:00 p.m. The kids are all gone for the night. I went to a wake for an elderly woman who was a neighbor. Then I watched a movie at home: *Torch Song Trilogy*, rented from the library. The screenplay writer and lead actor is Harvey Fierstein, who happens to live in my town. I read a manual on how to hook up to the internet. I got confused.

What is scary about communicating with each other? You said that.

Ok, I'll answer your questions:

I can see Long Island and the Sound from an elevated point on my street. The beaches on the Sound aren't like the West Coast beaches. The sand is browner in color, the water is warmer, and there are no waves. Of course, we see the sunrise on the East Coast instead of the sunset.

New York City is a big, dirty, noisy city with so much to do that its first impression of ugliness disappears. It has enormous influence on Fairfield County—my county and the one closest to New York. We become an extension of the city's sophistication, yet we escape the majority of its violence. I live in a little pocket of small-town America.

I like to go to New York with friends or my kids. Sometimes we go to a museum, or to a concert or sporting event, or maybe to a Broadway play. It is fairly expensive to get there and the traffic is heavy. The train is fun to take, but, again, rather expensive. I do not watch people in New York because they do not want to be looked at.

Nectars and stresses. Okay. Nectars first. Using my senses to listen, watch, feel, touch, smell, taste. Sand, water, wind, birds, flowers, clouds, music, seafood, mountains, trees, sun, sex. (Oops! Did I say that?) Read, write, laugh, watch movies, a mug of coffee or a glass of red wine on my back porch, sing, sleep late, rise early to walk, swim, boat, ride my bike.

Stresses next. Bills. Yard and housework. My children. My mother is very ill and living in a nursing home. She appears senile.

Thanks for being so open about your fears of writing. Despite your opinions of yourself, I find you to be quite sophisticated in your communication. You can trust me and I believe you can write anything. I am pleased to hear from you. I hate to think you are so hard on yourself because I find you extremely bright, original, and honest. I still believe you are one of the few people I know or have met who is comfortable in his own skin.

Yes, I still love going to the movies. Remember when you screamed in the movie theater when a group of us went to see *Wait Until Dark*? Remember all the drive-in movies you and I went to with other couples? I cannot remember what we saw. I recall there were more make-out sessions than movie watching.

What are your stresses? Your nectars? Do you read novels? What did you want to be when you were a child, then an adolescent? What did you become? Who are you now?

First, I wanted to be a fashion model and a June Taylor dancer. Then I wanted to be an oceanographer with Jacques Cousteau. I always wanted to be a writer. Later, after getting my bachelor's in journalism, I wanted to be a movie reviewer. I also like the paranormal, crime, and forensics.

Looking forward to hearing from you, Maggie

August 19, 1998

Dear Maggie,

Thank you for the card with a picture of those little old ladies. They look like the reputable three monkeys: see no evil, hear no evil, and speak no evil. You called it a "wake-up card" because you wonder where I am, perhaps. I am not avoiding you. I was on the verge of writing you a letter when an out-of-town friend called and asked me to help him on a patio construction project. I have been at his house and not even home since July 11th. I will sit down and write you a "real" letter sometime before the end of the month.

But feel free to write me anytime. I don't feel there is a need for tit-for-tat. A note, a thought, a pretty picture, a poem, a short story, or even a novel! Anytime either of us want to reach out. Relaxed is the key.

Julius

September 1, 1998

Dear Maggie,

Well, here I am … What a summer. It was foggy almost all day long until mid-July. A few days were clear.

I've got a habit of sitting out in nature every day. Today, right now, I'm sitting by a slough. It's about twenty feet across to the opposite bank. I'll describe it for you. My view, top to bottom. A huge line of large birds are flying in a blue sky. The blue changes to a white blur below and a fog bank is a quarter mile away.

I'm about half a mile from the beach looking northwest. I can hear the waves. I can even hear the surf from my room at home. Anyway, the fog bank is kind of a billowing orange/white/gray. Then, a green multilayer of bushes blending into light green in the succulent marsh grasses. Then a band of dark green mud. Finally, the blue ocean's waters.

You will not believe it. I just went down to the shore's edge and a little fish jumped out of the water, disturbing the perfect reflection of the sky. I have moved back six feet from the shore, sitting cross-legged, and you are on my mind.

The mountains behind Arcata are tree covered. Redwoods are common. Founders Hall, the dominant feature of Humboldt State University, crowns Arcata. I live at the south end of Manila, a far-flung area of Arcata and a one-thousand-person community about six miles west of Arcata. Between Arcata and Manila there is a coastal plain out about four miles. I live out on a split about half a mile wide and eleven miles long. It separates the Pacific Ocean from Humboldt Bay.

I am surrounded by water and the shore life of the split. The air is fresh and clear if it is not foggy. I'm not sure what the future holds, but I've enjoyed the last ten years here on the northern California coast. I can identify with the small-town feeling you speak of. It is like a favorite piece of china you see every holiday for years and years.

Congratulations on your new job! Having your own office sounds good. Sounds like a good gig. Bennies and all. Plus you must be able to dress comfortably there. Rockports seem to be comfortable shoes. I've had many pairs and have found them comfortable if you have to wear shoes. It's interesting, but I get the impression that you identify not wearing shoes with comfort. I remember when you sent me a note telling me you were sitting at a bench with your shoes off. I have been taking your comments to heart and cherishing my barefoot times.

You are on the Internet? You have a computer. Pretty high tech. Let's see ... you have a car, a job, a house, kids, and a computer. You are back into the world.

There are lots of college students in Arcata now that summer vacation is over. Seven thousand kids at Humboldt State in a town of 15,000. I saw a mother showing her daughter how to withdraw money from the bank and I thought of you and your daughter looking at colleges. I hope you are handling it okay. I know I've left home many times in the past. Your oldest kid is your witness for the whole thing, at least most of it. I know, as oldest kid in my family, I have a very strong connection to my mom.

I like the train. I used to go down to San Luis Obispo quite often by train. I've also been to Reno by train in the winter, and down the San Joaquin Line to Hanford. One year, I jumped a boxcar in Denver and rode down to Pueblo and then jumped a flatbed across the Colorado Rockies to Rifle.

Nectars. The "Oops!" sounds like fun! I can identify with experiencing one's senses. Life is big. The birds, the flowers. The kids. The sky. Books. Mountains. The seas. Dance frenzies. A good night's sleep. Peace.

Stresses. Bills. Other people. I'm very sorry to hear about your mother's health. I enjoyed talking to your mom. I think she is the only mom I ever felt comfortable visiting.

I've had some stresses in the last few years. My mom broke her back twice. Three of my siblings went crazy. The twins were institutionalized for years. My sister moved into my parents' home and started physically and emotionally abusing us. Eventually, she moved out and got her own place, but she still calls a lot and comes over to make trouble. Another brother, Willy, is doing well and has held a sheltered job for a few years. He still has problems, but has managed to hang in there. I hope he can keep it up. It's very painful to experience someone you love losing their mind. People are trying to help him make it. He's got big problems. My dad is emotionally abusive toward my mom and me. My mom is very overweight and the doctors tell her she is a ticking time bomb. I love everyone but my sister. I hate her for what she puts me and my parents through.

To be fair, my brother Joel, the next oldest after me, has his own pad and job in San Francisco. He made it out somehow.

My stresses are complexities beyond my control. And, being a big brother in a crazy world. Oh, also, being an adult when I'd like to play.

Yes, I like to read. Many of my favorite reads are on saltwater sport fishing. I read newspapers, magazines, and journals. I am going to send you a copy of a book I like, *Eva Luna*.

When I was a kid, I wanted to be a mountaineer. Later I wanted to run a cultural center. Be a farmer. Grow fruit trees. Work with aqua culture. Be a cook. A teacher. Help tourists. Sell something internationally. Be a dancer, singer, and artist. Lead tours of the Rockies. Run a coffee house somewhere in the middle of nowhere; a place with good pastries and gourmet coffees for tired travelers.

So you will know more about me, I am going to send you a bunch of papers that represent the official Julius. You might be interested. It's all there is.

You wanted to be a dancer, fashion model, writer, oceanographer, and movie reviewer. Well, you'd be a good dancer, I'll bet. Funny, I don't think we ever danced together. I love to dance when the band is so good that you don't even have to try. I traveled once with some women dancers who I thought were great!

You know, fashion model sounds like fun. That reminds me. Do you remember when the cops checked in with us? When you and I and Anne and Chris were hanging out in Chris's Volvo near Foothill Park? One of them said you and Anne were a couple of good-lookers.

Take care. Your friend, Julius

p.s. Books I read:

Russian, Hindi, and Pakistani short stories

The Oxford Book of Exile

How the Other Third Lives (3rd World Lit)

The Pushcart Prize: '98 Best of the Small Presses

The Three Musketeers by Dumas

September 7, 1998

Dear Julius,

Thanks for calling this morning. Good conversation.

I had a blast discovering page after page of the official you! One thing I like about you, Julius, is that you make me smile. I'll cherish each and every page.

Your high school diploma. United States Seventh Fleet Navy citation of outstanding performance. Navy training records. Foothill college transcripts. Performance reviews as a sheet metal specialist. San Jose City College transcripts. Certificate of achievement in machine technology. Personnel transactions from the parks department. Peace Corps papers from Botswana. Humboldt State transcripts, student I.D.s, and diploma. Performance reviews from the Canyon Lodge in Wyoming. Resume and employment history.

Your mother seems like such a sweet lady. I suppose it isn't easy to face your sister's and father's abuse. I'd like to talk to you more about how this affects you.

Thank you again for *Eva Luna*. I discovered little surprises inside the book: a tiny bouquet of local, dried wild flowers and a postcard of the Northern California coast.

Back to this morning, I like to hear your voice and to exchange ideas quickly through conversation. You know something, though? No, of course you don't. So, I will tell you (and I want to be honest so that you know I tell you the truth). I felt so good that I got scared.

I question my morals, values, strength, integrity, and loyalty. I don't feel strong because I depend on people for financial security and companionship when panic attacks are overwhelming. I've made so many mistakes in my life I'm afraid that I will never again be able to sustain a good feeling about myself. I tend to be enthusiastic and then fall short on commitment. Maybe I am not as good a friend for you.

What if truly I am an evil person while you are a good person? What did you say on the phone this morning? Did you say that you want to be careful to keep our friendship? Did you say you don't want to do or not do something; or say or not say something? The texture of your voice was veiled in protective skeins of soft woolen mittens.

It sounds as if your family has been through an ordeal. Is it so overwhelming you are prevented from settling the loose ends of your life? Julius, I'd like to see you become independent and put some distance between yourself and your family. If there is nothing hindering you from taking care of yourself, how about getting a full-time job, buying a car, and getting your own place? If your mother needs you, you can live within easy driving distance. Let's say you have thirty to forty years left to live and seventeen of them you can devote to work before you hit age sixty-five; you will be pretty secure. You can still provide some support for your mother.

If you get angry with me, then tell me. Another thing, don't ever be afraid of me. I don't need that kind of power.

Love, Maggie

p.s. My hardly intellectual book list:

A time travel, science fiction novel about a man in 2362 who goes back to the dinosaur age

The Ann Rice trilogy *The Witching Hour, Lasher,* and *Taltos*

Suspense/mystery/crime novels

Two nonfiction books: *Indian Country* by Peter Matthiessen and *The Over-40 Job Guide*

September 10, 1998

Dear Maggie,

After talking with you I realized that I've been reading a detective, espionage novel just for the fun of it: *Smiley's People*. It was in my backpack as we spoke. Then I remembered a novel that really kept me on the edge of my seat when I read it. I would run to the kitchen, gobble my food, and get back to my bedroom to continue reading. Back and forth I went. My parents asked me if something was wrong. I said, No, I was just reading a very exciting novel. Well, I decided to go buy it for you: *The Magus*.

I hope you don't mind me sending you these novels and I hope that they bring you some enjoyment during the coming winter. They are yours and there is no obligation to return the favor. Send me a book sometime.

Your Friend, Julius

p.s. (Sept. 19) O.K. On equal footing. Despite our imperfections. Enclosed are stickers of two amphibians. You can choose if you want to be the frog and me the salamander or vice versa!

With Love,

Your Friend, Julius

September 16, 1998

Dear Julius,

I had a dream about you last night. I'm writing it down now, as I just woke up. I don't want to forget it.

You and I planned to meet on a boulevard. You were in a restored 1940s or '50s car, a pale yellow car with tail fins. I was walking and said I would have to take a taxi, but I was lying because I had my own car parked in a lot just across the street. I didn't want you to see my car and I thought you would leave. I told you I would meet you elsewhere. Yet you said, "I see your car," and you waited for me as I drove my old '87 Chevy Celebrity out of the parking lot.

You appeared wary.

We drove to a historical building, like a mansion or farmhouse or museum, surrounded by park-like gardens. Some people were selling books and souvenirs outside. We kneeled to look at books and artwork displayed on the ground. You pointed out the books you had read, then you proceeded to tell me all about them. We were very close, our bodies touching at knees, shoulders, and arms. I felt powerfully passionate and rested my head against your head and shoulder. I could feel your long and silky dark hair against my skin.

We stood up and made our way to the historical building. This is what we saw: dozens of rooms decorated in an earlier era, and a tall-ceilinged, light-filled kitchen where women were baking.

I looked up at you. You appeared to be the age I last saw you, about age twenty-four, but your hair was quite short. You told me, "I have put on weight and most of it is in my butt." I complained about putting on more weight than you. You assured me, "Women have more padding on their bodies than men."

We left the building, went outside, and saw animals in the gardens. We fed them live grasshoppers, which were on sale for feed. I went to feed a grasshopper to an animal who didn't like it. It acted predatory, as if it wanted to eat me.

I think the dream is a riddle or a puzzle of memories. In the dream you were handsome and gentle in movement and spirit. What I felt later was shame because I have judged you and advised you about how to get your life together. I was blunt and may have hurt your feelings.

Maggie

November 23, 1998

Dear Julius,

I'm sending you this article about wild turkeys in Connecticut to prove we have them here. Also, here is my drawing and my rendition of a wild turkey. Maybe it's a little scrawny.

I haven't heard from you recently. I wonder if we are still corresponding. I've come to feel disheartened about relationships because there are so many problems and so many break-ups. Is there something wrong with me? It looks as if I am in the dark about the proper chemical formula. Every time I step into the lab, it explodes.

I have called you several times. Your mother says she will tell you I've called. Nevertheless, I do not hear from you. I am going to stop. Perhaps you don't want to talk to me. I'm beginning to feel a little stupid and my stupidity appears incurable. That's all for now.

Happy Holidays, Maggie

December 1, 1998

Dear Maggie,

Thank you for the Connecticut turkey. Being thin and wild it must have realized California offered opportunities. The last time I saw it, it was headed south with an odd assortment of birds. Hmm ... a Connecticut Yankee bird in Hollywood?

I think that you should step out of the lab; don't worry about any formulas. Concentrate on you and your family's well-being and pursue interests that are achievable on your own. A sense of mental and physical well-being and achievement in personal and social activities may lead to the formula you are looking for. If you don't find it, you may be in a better position to recover when the lab blows up.

I find your letters and you interesting. Maybe you feel that I am sending you a message by not returning your calls or by not writing. Don't try to read too much into it! I'm a little shy of long-distance communication. A big block of information needed for rational decision making is missing. I really don't write or call any of my distant friends much, but I don't feel that it has been a problem for me. If I do make contact, it seems that we pick up where we left off without much trouble. I'll try to be more punctual in returning your communications. Thank you for calling and writing, Maggie.

You seem to be available to me as a friend right now, but I understand you may need someone who can meet your needs in a personal, not abstract, way. As far as women go, if they are not available, I don't worry about it. I'm happy for anyone who finds someone, and hope that the formula is stable. If not, I think maybe we may meet again (we have met again) and circle around a common beaker, our chemicals in hand, putting them one by one (you put one in, I put one in, we each have many) into the common beaker, hoping there is not a blow up. Or, maybe we put our chemicals on the floor and walk away (together?) as friends and maybe more.

Maggie, I'm happy we have rekindled our friendship. I think I need to realize, as you pointed out, it's time for me to tie up my loose ends and get my shit together, somewhere (job, apartment, car, etc.). It may be an interesting transition. I think it might be best for me to maintain my independence, at least until I'm on my feet. In the meantime, meet my social needs through friendships and dating.

And yet, it seems I'm not sure what I say is right. In terms of how it affects my future (our future). Thank you for writing, returning your letter is helping me define and deal with the issues.

Merry Xmas and Happy New Year,
Your friend, Julius

December 15, 1998

Dear Julius,

Julius, I, too, have been happy to rekindle our friendship. I've read encouragement into your words and, therefore, I've felt at ease telling you I like you. But now I feel bad. I've stolen your kindness and charitable nature.

Abstract reasoning and psychotherapeutic interpretations I'll avoid. Analyzing is futile. Life is fine; it's really okay. And it's temporary anyway.

Maggie

February 9, 1999

Dear Julius,

I found this poem among my files of every memento I've saved and everything I've written. I had forgotten about this poem. I wrote it when I was sixteen. It is a poem about you and me. I never gave it to you because I was too shy back then. You may have it now. Ironic, isn't it?

Daily, I am finding dormant anger and fear beneath my mortal exterior. I have always been reckless and I've felt death and disaster circling around me when I feel alone. I'm wanting to connect with something bigger, such as compassion for everything living, as everything living is connected to me and to each and every other living creature. I want to retrieve the guts of life I first knew as a young child.

Julius, you possess wonderment of all life. You did when I met you and you still have it.

Maggie

AND THEN THEY MET

With a fragrance of sweet perfume,
A tilt to her head and a shine on her nose,
This girl of rare hidden beauty arose.
Born from the streams; living in caves,
Having no sense of direction, she wanders the mind –
Turning up her nose to some and loving eyes to the blind.

A potential of love and a mind of wisdom,
With a body of bronze his brown eyes searched.
A man made of the mountains need not rehearse.
For he lives for the moment and has gifts for the loved.
Needing no one and no one needing him; he began to sigh –
For his life was missing something; he dared not cry.
With a look of delight and a cry of wonder
They met while walking on the water.
Beauty and strength had found one another.
Slowly and lightly they met a caress,

And rolling in moments they knew they would miss –
They started and ended their friendship with a kiss.

By Maggie Mayes

March 24, 1999

Dear Maggie,

Well, I had a pretty good winter. I didn't get wet or cold all that many times, and there were some truly beautiful days with mild weather and great skies. I like rediscovering the beach after a big storm, when the sand is without a footprint and the surf is playing with two-ton logs like toothpicks. This last week I've been getting into looking for pretty rocks. I've been focusing on ones that I can see light through.

I'm still living with my parents and not working. My plan is to try to get it together somewhere after May, when the rain stops. In fact, I am very much looking forward to getting out on my own. You are right, it's for my own self-esteem and freedom. A job and the money should do the trick. We'll see. I'll keep you posted. In the meantime, I'm valuing my free time. I know how dear it is, once you enter the 9-5 world.

My friends sent me bus money for a trip to Cambria, California, as a Christmas present. I had a good time. We went on some nice bike rides and sat around and talked a lot.

Then, on Valentine's weekend I got a ride to SF with my friends, and I spent Friday night with them in their hotel room. The next day we toured North Beach, Chinatown, Top of the Mark, Borders Bookstore in Union Square, on to Virgin Records on Market, and eventually to the Mission District for dinner with friends. You know what? The Mission was a real dive for a long time. Remember? Now, all these houses are renovated. Noteworthy restaurants are springing up everywhere. Afterwards, I went back to my friends' hotel room for my stuff and on to visit another friend for Saturday night and yet another friend Sunday night. In the end, I took an overnight bus home on Monday night.

The bummer for me was how alone I felt. All my friends

had relationships and I was a third party. I guess when I am hanging out by myself, I don't realize how important it can be to have someone who wants to be with you.

So your letter and the poem you included got to me at an interesting time. Thank you for sharing with me and caring for me then and now! Of course, your poem about us affected me in the most personal way.

I cannot say I've got a handle on relationships at all. I can tell you I have learned to value people, though, and I value your friendship. Listen. Let's pretend. I am going to focus on this dot • and try to put into it a post-Valentine hug. You were brave to tell me that sometimes you just want to be held. Well, there are times when I just want to be held, too.

Hope this letter finds you and your family warm and well.

Your friend, Julius

April 15, 1999

Dear Maggie,

Thank you for your call. I hope you enjoyed your trip to California, but I know there's no place like home and am sure you were happy to get back to your children and pets. I'm sending you an agate I found in the sand at the beach.

Julius

May 5, 1999

Julius,

Sadly, the letter you sent had a slight mishap, an unfortunate misadventure, a suspicious disaster. A corner of both the envelope and the plastic bag inside were ripped. The poor little agate had fallen out. I wonder who has it.

Thank you, Julius, for thinking of me. You are always sending me interesting items. A wildflower, a book, your life history in papers, an agate. What might be next?

Do you ever read *Newsweek* magazine? I'm reading an article in the April 26th issue titled, "Who Were the First Americans?" If you can get your hands on it, read it. Or, I may send it to you. It made me examine the premise: Maybe Native Americans and the migrating Asians were more than the original natives of North America. Further this out: What if, after archeologists dig as far back as possible, it is discovered the first Americans were Adam and Eve? What do you think of this premise? Wouldn't that be wild? I think there is a good story brewing somewhere.

Hey! I have a favorite movie now: *Practical Magic*. I rented it last week from the library and watched it twice. It is about modern-day witches. I want to be like the characters. Maybe I could conjure up some of my own spells.

Another little piece of me leaves Connecticut and heads to California via this letter. California! The land of memories, dreams, and craziness. I'm over the edge.

Maggie

June 7, 1999

Dear Maggie,

Sorry about the agate. Oh well. Hmm ... Adam and Eve. If you wrote a story about that, it could be interesting. How would they feel about themselves, each other? What would the garden be like? How would you deal with the forbidden fruit? Or would you? Go for it, Maggie. It sounds like fun!

You know, I wish you had given me a little more warning about your trip to California in April. You called from Anne's house and you were already there. Maybe you could have disengaged from Anne and company for a while. We could have had a mini-adventure together in San Francisco. But, alas, it didn't happen. Your itinerary seemed set and not wanting to complicate things, I decided to chill.

Who knows, maybe sometime I'll be in your area, without forewarning, and I'll want to be able to call just on the chance that you'd be available.

As you can see, I'm sending you more mementos. I was going to junk these Paly class of '69 reunion scrapbooks, but remembered that you know quite a few people in my class. So I thought you'd get a kick out of looking through them. They are yours now.

You know, Olin has the largest collection of my artwork of anyone. I was so impressed that he kept some drawings I gave him in the '70s that I sent him representative pieces of my college work. He calls me each year at Christmastime. I haven't seen him in person since the mid-'80s. I think he's also divorced and has at least one kid. You might get a kick out of talking with him. After all, he introduced us.

Maggie, in my '89 reunion scrapbook statement, I said, "I'd get a kick out of someone making contact with me." You are the only one who I'd lost contact with who DID!

Thank you!

Your friend, Julius xo

June 13, 1999

Dear Julius,

Thank you a million times over for sending me your Paly reunion scrapbooks. What great masterpieces of nostalgia. I recognized several people from the past and greatly enjoyed learning where they had gone, what gems they had to offer in the way of piecing together their physical and spiritual travels, and, of course, what they look like. What a trip!

Also, thank you for sending photos of yourself. A few years older, yes, but you look happy, handsome, and healthy as always. Might I be so brave as to send you some photos of me?

Well, as you discovered, I was in California visiting Anne. I didn't warn you ahead of time for fear you might feel pressured. I was hoping to see you, but I began to feel guilty about asking for time away when I was there.

On another note ... might you really come to my area? With or without forewarning, you are welcome in my home. There is a world of fun over here to explore and to share with good friends. Anne and her son were here last year and we went to some of my faves: New York City, the local lake (we call it Great Pond), exploring our little town's Main Street, and an over-decorated restaurant called Texas Taco. It is owned by a little woman with purple hair and tons of makeup who I call The Taco Nazi—after Seinfeld's Soup Nazi. She refuses to alter any item on the menu. She has a monkey in a cage outdoors and a talking parrot inside who talks while you eat.

Summer weather has arrived with much gardening needed. Much too much to make it to look manicured, but this is Connecticut. The woods and the wildlife are just that— WILD. I garden and do housework when it fits in. Working full time and taking care of a home and children reminds me of pioneer women flung out on the prairie, meeting everyday survival challenges. My challenges are modern day. Money and the lack of it are ever on my mind. Debt piles up, I get tired, I question my ability to make ends meet, I go a little crazy, and I question my sanity. I wonder if I will be successful at raising my kids. As they get older, I feel they don't like me anymore. They are pushing for their independence and I am not sure how to give it to them. Three of them. One of me.

More disturbing, I question my emotional stability and how honest I am with myself and others. I wish life were easier. The more I wish it, the more questions I have. On the outside, most people see me as a laid-back, hard-working person. Is that a mask or is that reality?

Bye for now, Maggie

December 7, 1999

Dear Maggie,

You sounded great on the phone. I liked the way you pronounced "book," with just the right sounding emphasis on the "k."

Your story about the summer day you spent at a Rhode Island beach sounded fun. "The soft, off-white and warm sand stretching off into the distance, inviting long walks. The warm summer water tempting frolics in the surf." I am glad that you enjoyed it.

Texas Taco's owner, the strange little woman with purple hair and tons of makeup who you call the Taco Nazi, is an image I like. Maybe it's the idea of the accepted eccentric. The weather here has been nice, when it's not raining. The grass is green and some flowers are still in bloom. It almost seems like a second spring, but I know there is cold in the future. On clear days, I can see the snow-capped distant mountains.

The holiday rush is kind of fun. I like that people are at least pretending to be friendly for a few days. I went to the mall to window shop. I looked to see how much the things I usually buy in a thrift store cost full price at the mall.

Oh! Thank you for bravely sending pictures of you and the Palo Alto girls, your long-time friends. You must have had a nice visit with them in California this past summer. Of course, I recognize them all. You look comfortable in Palo Alto's Lytton Plaza.

Yes, I do remember the anti-war protests there. You all look happy and basically look the same as I remember you. You and Anne look mutually supportive in your placement together in the photo.

I'm sure if I had floppy ears, they would be flattened down on my head in an affectionate, happy position as your dog Star's are with you in that picture of you and your daughter in your living room. I see all those trees you talk about in that picture through the plate-glass living-room window. Are the leaves off the trees in your neighborhood now?

I admire the pictures of your children. They are each in such different stages in their progression towards independence. It seems like yesterday that we were young adults.

Your Friend, Julius

p.s. Did you get the Pushcart stories I sent you? I had just started reading the 1999 edition and decided to send you a copy. I am on page 79. I hope you (we) enjoy it.

January 1, 2000

Dear Julius,

This is my first letter dated 2000. It is winter, New England style. Unpredictable. You asked if the leaves are off the trees. Yes, they are. No snow yet except for an occasional flurry and there's a little ice, but it is cold. When I say cold, I mean the highs are 35 degrees and the lows are 16 degrees. On the other hand, last week we had a warm spell of 58 degrees for three days. I wrote a small poem about a winter night when I was sleepless.

The winter death goddess
One diamond symphony
Soars over man
Windy knife
Blowing light and time
Wants only sleepy worship

Thank you for the Pushcart Prize book. At this time I am also up to page 79. What a coincidence!

My first and foremost hobby is reading. It is a passive hobby and maybe a poor excuse for one. Like, if I chose rock climbing or skiing, I'd be more popular.

I have some sad news to tell you and I've been avoiding it. My mother died last year on November 15th. She had been in a steady decline due to a bad case of shingles that left her unable to walk. In 1997, she decided she couldn't live independently and moved into a nursing home. She rapidly declined. I never saw her smile again. Two years later she stopped eating and drinking. Then she died.

I spent eight days in Des Moines dealing with the funeral and legal business. My aunt was my right arm getting that in order. Don't think I've told you that my mother left Palo Alto and moved to Des Moines in 1981. Iowa is where she spent the first twenty-four years of her life. She was close to family, old friends, and had an active social life with new friends.

I find it difficult to explain what her death means to me. Outwardly, I drift between solitude and hanging out with friends. Inwardly, my memory is not good and I'm nostalgic for the Palo Alto days. I want my past to become my future. The mother I knew is gone. No more phone calls to get a recipe from her or comfort one another. Thank goodness my journey is still continuing, yet I have a burning passion to flee the mainstream, suburban lifestyle I lead here in Connecticut.

Love, Maggie

January 8, 2000

Dear Maggie,

Connecticut winter sounds cold! Thank you for sharing your poem. I'm glad that you are enjoying some of the selections in the '99 Pushcart Prize stories. It's one area I know we have in common.

Thank you for sharing some of your feelings in regards to your mom. I enjoyed my visits with her.

Moving towards the journey's end with people and art and a love of nature. It is a good way to live and leads toward rebirth through enlightenment and flowers our paths in life's struggle.

God bless those who have come before us and gone. God be with us on our paths towards the journey's end.

Your Friend Always, Julius

April 16, 2000

Dear Maggie,

I hope that these boots I'm sending fit you. Also, I hope these little bars of soap bring you some pleasure. In my explorations around town, I often find items I think you might like.

I look forward to visiting with you, maybe some time in CT or CA in the summer of 2001.

I enjoyed our last conversation on the phone. I enjoyed hearing about your friends: Pat, Pam, and Phil. We talked about yoga and myths. What a complex person you are, we are.

Hope you are enjoying the spring.

Love, Your Friend, Julius

June 8, 2000

Dear Maggie,

Well this is the orange agate with the black pedestal I told you I would send you one day. It is the only one I've found this year. It's to make up for the agate lost in the mail. I hope you like it.

I enjoyed talking with you last weekend.

Take Care.

Your Friend, Julius

September 12, 2000

Dear Maggie,

Thanks for the birthday card and note you sent me on my birthday in late June. Sorry I did not thank you earlier. It's nice to know someone out there thinks of me.

Your Friend, Julius

September 27, 2000

Dear Julius,

You are the safest person to whom I express myself. So, what does today's letter have in store? I don't know yet. I'll just ramble along and see where the ramble takes me. Since I talked to you last, these things have happened:

My oldest daughter came home from college in May and worked at a bank for the summer as a teller. She has a boyfriend who lives in Maryland and they visited back and forth. In September she went back as a sophomore. She still likes science and math, but is also taking a religion class and computer science class.

My son turned fifteen this month. He went to a sea kayak

class, babysat, did yard work at our house and another house, played his electric guitar, stayed up until 3:00 a.m., and woke up at 1:00 p.m. every day this summer. He started his first year of high school.

My youngest daughter went to tennis camp, took viola lessons, read, and slept late. She is in seventh grade at the middle school.

I took almost every Friday and Monday off this summer as vacation days at work. I wanted to do stuff with the kids and also sleep in late! We went to Rhode Island three different weekends and stayed in hotels on the beach. You can look at your map now to see where we stayed: Watch Hill; Narragansett; and Misquamicut. I like sitting on the sand near dark listening to the waves and near sunrise drinking a cup of coffee.

The weather in New England was rather cool and rainy for a majority of the summer. The deer ignored the coyote urine I sprayed and ate almost every flowering plant. I put together an album of old family photos. I painted my oldest daughter's room.

I have a new boss and our working relationship is great. She and I think alike, have similar values, and complement each other working on community health projects. I got appointed to a board that oversees the mental health facilities in the area. It is a new requirement at work that I represent our town. It's hard work learning something new.

How was your 50th birthday? Where do you go from here? What do you see and feel when you look at the stars? Remember what the Chambers Brothers said in 1968: "Time has come today"?

Take it easy. Love, Maggie

October 24, 2000

Dear Maggie,

I think I've found somethings that we have in common. An apprication of the pleasures that can come from nature (emerchion in nature). I also like the night. When I lived in

San Jose, I worked nights for 2-1/2 years. The 2 p.m.–10:30 p.m. shift. I worked out on North 1st Street and lived two blocks north of the heart of downtown for 10-1/2 years. It was cool, I'd ride my bike out 1st Street the two or three miles to my job and then at night I'd ride home through the resadenturl neighborhoods. Almost everyone would be inside and the smells from their flowers hung in the air for me to enjoy. San Jose's night sky was just this red glow of the city lights reflecting off the sky. The night here on the northern California coast is much more a thing of stars when it's clear. Sometimes an owl will cruze alone along the highway, maybe looking for prey. Do the headlights of the cars help it hunt in some way?

And I like to look out across the bay and see the lights of Acata and Eureka reflecting on the water. Sometimes I'll hear birds flying over head and I'll see the lights of ocassional farm house and off in the distance the sweep of the beacon light on Trinidad head. The whole sweep of nature. It's funny I'm more drawn to the bay then the ocean. It's calmer and there's a majac that can be with it sometimes. Of course I like eversthing and everywhere in away. I'm really a big city guy as well. I just try to stay centered and go with the flow up and down with my emotions and health.

Speaking of health sorry to hear about your back and knee – believe me I and identify. It days or weeks. I'll be verily moving with back sezorics that can and have taken me to the floor in a second and made me have to use very crutch to get up and the walls to stay up. Bummer! I don't know why my knees are blown but getting up after kneeling down can be a painfull experience as well.

I'm not hearing as well as I used to eather. I was hiking with some friends and they asked me if I knew what kind of bug was making that noise. I said what noise? They said: You can't hear it? There must be thousands of them. They've been making the sound all along. I said: Must be above my range. Oh well. Rock and Roll was fun… but in retospeck maybe…

Oh my right sholder is worn out. The Doctor said if it realy gets bad in the future they can operate. O.K. This summer I had a operation on my tummy (umbilical hernia) and a operation on the top of my right ear I had a groth they thought might be skin cancer. Any way they cut whatever it was off and said if they didn't call me in 2 weeks it was benine. The 2 weeks passed but it still hurt.

Last Halloween I whent out to a club in Arcata. Café Tomo to dance and check out the costumes. It was a DJ night that night and the guy cranked it up full volume, but I was in one of those moods (careless moods) and didn't stuff some paper in my ears – well the next day I heard ringing in my ears and it has never gone away. Next Tuesday Holloween 2000 will be my first anaversity of life without true quite. The noise is comming from my own head! The list goes on....I'm 250 lbs. and my stomack is out farther then my chest and my overall muscle tone is out of tone. I've spent to much time reading and not anuf time physically moving. Next year I'm going to try to be more active all around (balanced) and try to get back in touch with being a physical animal. I think getting back into condition will make me fill better in both boty and sole although I still whant to continue to read. I going to look for more balance.

Art is on hold untill I get independant. Living with my parents is not the right environment for working on my art.

My future: I'd like to find a job somewhere and settle down and work for the next 5 years then take a year off then work 5 years and retire at 67. Years off: 2006 and 2012. 15 work years to go! So for me it will be 15 on, 15 off, 15 on and then off for good. I do whant to work on my art in the future as well as travel, cook, garden, fish, swim, and the list goes on. I'm sure of one thing. I'm into life, and to the best of my abilities I'll live it to the fullest for as long as I'm around. I'm sure I have more interests than I have time in this life to enjoy them all. But I'll try.

Speaking of jobs – I'm very happy for you. Haveing a boss you can work with is so important. When I start working I hope more then anything that I enjoy working with my coworkers as well as the work.

Well today was one of those blustery days, strong south

winds (the storm direction) with a partly cloudy sky. I let the wind push me across the costal plain on my bicycle which was a few miles detor on my way to town. Then, made it to town just as it started to rain. Lucky for me. I don't like getting wet on the way in, but don't care (even like it) on the way home.

I like the ocean beaches best in the winter on the North Coast. The wild surf, the cleaned sand and the piles of debrie for each combing and of course – no fog! The trout fishing thing just didn't happen for me this summer but I'm ready for next summer. I did catch a nice costal cut trouth 12" a couple of weeks ago in a stream (little river) about 8 miles north of Arcata and there's a chance I'll catch some still head there or in the mad river this winter.

But I like summer fishing the best. No possibility of realy inclement wheather – I like the sun and heat. I remember you told me in one of your letters that you like the winter. My best whishes for a warm and comfortable home life and safe forests outside this winter.

On the reading front I read Carl Jung's autobiography this summer and am reading Blue Highways and an excellent anthology of contempory litature. Oh, I read the 2000 pushcart prize, but only liked a few of the stories. I'm thinking of reading Gertas Foust 1 and 2 next (maybe). It looks a little heavy for me but maybe I can get into it.

Movies: I whant to recommend a movie one of my friends turned me on to. It's a Canadian movie from a few years ago called Medicine River. You can rent it at the vidio store. It's listed under (Drama). Low key, good humor, excellent scenery.

Maggie thanks for your letters.

Love,

Your Friend

Julius

"Boo" for Halloween and Best whishes for the comming holidays. Good night. xxoo

November 20, 2000

Dear Julius,

I found this funny card and hope it suits your sense of humor. The turkeys sitting round the platter of pilgrims suited my mood. Happy Thanksgiving to you and your family.

A little off the subject of Thanksgiving ... thinking about you a lot after your last letter. It was a nice long letter! Thank you! How are you doing? For some reason I am concerned.

It's probably nothing ... just a vibe. I noticed your spelling was not its usual perfection. Hopefully we can talk on the phone after the first of the year. I want to run something by you. Strange things are happening in my house. Like in Palo Alto. Music plays at night from somewhere in the house. A black presence stood over me one night when I was in bed. My daughter said someone came into her room at night. I'm scared, Julius.

All my best, Maggie

February 26, 2002

Dear Julius,

It's been such a long time since our letters and phone calls, which gave me such joy. I hope this winter finds you well. It is so ice cold and hostile outdoors. The only time we'll get outside today is to take the dog on a quick walk and maybe the kids and I will go to a movie if the roads aren't icy.

Whether you will read this card is a mystery to me. I don't know what has happened to you. I don't know where you are. Perhaps I have upset you for you to stop communicating. The last time I called, I got the impression from your father that you have left Arcata. He told me you do not wish to be located.

That was over six months ago, so there does not seem to be more that I can do. I don't want to bother you or your family. Whatever may be, whatever may come, you have been a good friend. Our friendship has brought me the kind of happiness I had as a young child, when I would pull a carrot out of the soil and eat it, heedless of a speck of dirt or two. Pure delight all mixed in my mouth. Straight out of my grandfather's garden.

Bye? Maggie

16 DIVERSIONS
Summer 2015

Maggie paces back and forth in the studio apartment, working up the courage to make a phone call.

"Hello?" a deep male voice answers.

"Hello. Is this Joel Brownell?"

"Uh, yeah, this is Joel."

"I'm an old friend of your brother, Julius. This is Margaret Mayes. You probably don't remember me."

"I'm not sure."

"I met Julius in 1968. In Palo Alto."

"Were you tall and slender? Did you have long brown hair? Did Julius call you Maggie?"

"Yes, that's me. Well, Joel, the reason I'm calling is that I am trying to locate your brother. I'm writing a book. I'm an author, you see, and the current book I'm writing is kind of about Palo Alto. And I need Julius to give his recollections of the town. And I can't find him."

"How did you find me?"

"The high school alumni book. You know … Paly. Oh, yes, and through the internet. You have a website and blog. About your—"

"Artwork. Yeah. I illustrate children's books. I do some writing, too."

"I love your illustrations."

"So, you want to talk to Julius, you say?"

"I'd love to talk to him while I'm visiting here in Palo Alto. I live in Oregon now, and I have to go home soon. I've asked his friends, but no one has heard from him in years."

Maggie is getting nervous. She's sweating and her mouth is dry. *God, Joel sounds just like Julius. Weird. I don't know what else I can tell him. Is he gonna tell me where Julius is now?*

"Let me think about it, Maggie," Joel finally replies. "Give me your phone number."

Maggie wipes the perspiration off her face and neck. She empties a tall glass of pink lemonade before she sits down on a green-padded, chrome stool at the kitchen counter of the studio apartment.

"What to do? What to do?" She rests one hand under her chin, elbow on the counter. With the other hand, she taps her fingers. *Olin. Olin said he knows something. She's sick and tired of waiting for him.*

Grabbing her phone, she enters his number. For once he answers without sounding as if he's half-stoned.

"Look, Olin. Just tell me."

"What do you mean, Maggie?"

"You know what."

"About Julius and his family?"

"Duh."

"I am convinced, by the way, that my mother gave me the right info. Maybe you don't know this, but I've known Julius since elementary school."

"True. Meaning, I don't know that. I don't remember that."

"He and his family moved to Palo Alto from Utah in about fourth grade, I think."

Maggie nodded to herself. "I remember his talking about Utah. How much he liked it. Right?"

"Yeah. That's it. Julius missed Utah. He told me about it every chance he got. At recess. In the bathroom. At the school library."

"Okay. Got it."

"My mom felt kind of sorry for Julius and his brothers and

his sister."

"Why?"

"She worried they were so thin. My mom went to the Brownells' house one day. After church, she said. Yeah. On a Sunday."

"And?"

"I think my mom was Mrs. Brownell's only friend."

"That's terrible. I mean terrible as in she had only one friend, not that's terrible as in your mom was her friend."

"Yeah. Pretty sad, huh?"

"Back to the beginning now. You say there's a secret."

"A big one. Do not tell anyone else or it'll be real embarrassing to me. Julius's parents are brother and sister."

"Holy shit."

"Yeah. I know."

"Come on … you can't be serious." Maggie looks around for a beer. "Wait. It's too early for a beer. Darn."

"Beer? Why are you talking about beer, honey?"

"I didn't say anything about beer." Maggie catches herself. *Did I say beer out loud?*

"Hey, let's talk later. This is a lot for you to take in. Seems that way to me, anyway."

Her fingertips trace the open bottle neck of a Saint Pauli Girl. "Nah. I'm sorry. I did say beer. And I am drinking one this early. Because I'm an adult woman and I can."

"Listen to something, Maggie … "

"No. I don't want to. You are lying about this. Or maybe the nicer thing to say is that it's unbelievable. Truly unbelievable." For a nanosecond Maggie considers saying goodbye. She knows she can't tell Olin about her conversation with Joel Brownell if he's going to make up shit like this.

Olin is adamant. "I'm deeply offended, Maggie. You think I would tell just anyone about this? Maybe I'll just keep stuff to myself. I mean, why would I lie to you?"

"Maybe for the same reason I haven't seen you yet. I think you might be lying about why. At least withholding info. Shit,

Olin. I've had enough. Goodbye."

"Wait, Maggie. I might have to go back to Boise real soon."

"Olin, what are you saying? I won't see you?"

"No, no, that's not what I'm saying."

Maggie is frustrated. "Olin, just do what's best for you."

"Thanks, honey. I'll try, I really will."

Maggie sits down on the wicker loveseat but something's poking her in the backside. She stands up and pulls her phone out of her back pocket, just as it rings.

It's Elizabeth. "Hey, I've got a great idea. Let's drive up to San Francisco. There's some kind of bus tour called 'The Magic Bus.' Like a replica of Ken Kesey's Merry Pranksters bus."

"Oh yeah?"

"Yeah. Like one of those psychedelic school buses converted for travelers."

"Don't think I paid much attention to Kesey until I moved to Oregon. I mean, I knew he was an author, but didn't know he had property in Oregon. Didn't he and his group drive from Kesey's place in Oregon down to San Francisco? And to Haight-Ashbury in particular?"

"That's the one. I think it was the original painted school bus, and eventually scads of hippies did the same conversion."

"Those were pretty cool. And yeah, I'd like to go. You're working now, right?"

"I am, but I can take time off tomorrow ... or the next day—Wednesday."

"Tomorrow's perfect."

"Great. I'll get the tickets. How about I try for the tour that starts at noon. Can you drive over to my house about 10:30 or so? You can leave your car at my house and I'll drive us to the city."

Maggie works on her novel for the rest of the day. By 10:30 the next morning, she is primed for an adventure. She decides not to tell Elizabeth what Olin said about Julius's parents. She doesn't know whether to believe Olin—not only about Julius but his suggestion he might return to Boise without seeing her. She also doesn't trust Elizabeth to keep any of this to herself.

Precisely at noon, Maggie boards the "Magic Bus" with Elizabeth and reality is suspended for the next few hours.

The tour guide is enthusiastic. "Folks. Listen up. Put those daisies in your hair and get ready. Life's not a tour. It's a trip. All aboard the Magic Bus."

The "Magic Bus" is equipped with speakers that play the music of Maggie's youth while touring key landmarks of San Francisco. Maggie can see that the clever entrepreneurs who came up with this idea are making a lot of money by capitalizing on San Francisco's historical past, but the music, videos, and light shows can't capture the truth. The last stop on the tour and the highlight, of course, is to drive into Haight-Ashbury and revisit the Summer of Love.

Once the bus turns the corner into "The Haight," Maggie and Elizabeth look at each other.

"Are you thinking what I'm thinking?"

"Cutting school."

"Going to Haight-Ashbury."

Spring 1967. Maggie, Elizabeth, Anne, and Deb were eighth-graders at Jordan Junior High School. One morning they dressed for school as usual, wearing the required skirts or dresses. They changed into jeans and stashed their school clothes in lockers. They took a Palo Alto city bus from the school to the Greyhound terminal in downtown Palo Alto, where they boarded a Greyhound to San Francisco. Their parents had no idea their daughters had ditched school to have fun in San Francisco.

It was bitchen.

Maggie had grown up accompanying her grandmother as she traveled throughout the city, so she knew her way around San Francisco. Grandmommy had taught Maggie everything, including how to be bold and aggressive on public transportation.

Grandmommy had lived in two apartments. In the 1950s she lived on Cole Street near the corner of Haight. In earlier days the area was a packed neighborhood of small homes, apartments, and retail shops for the locals.

Later, she moved a half-mile away from the heart of Haight-Ashbury, where there were always "hippies smoking something on the streets," to an apartment on Shrader Street, where she lived until 1973.

Maggie knew the area very well.

The dry goods stores, pharmacies, butcher shops, toy stores, and cobblers that Grandmommy had taken her to when she was younger had been converted to head shops and music and jewelry stores. The girls wandered among hippies and marijuana-draped streets on and around the notorious sacred grounds at the intersection of Haight and Ashbury streets. Maggie had to watch herself. She was so happy as she listened to the music blaring from every storefront that she was afraid she might look like a tourist. She inhaled the heady, dark waft of patchouli oil and felt at peace.

Despite their parents' dire warnings about what happens at Haight-Ashbury (girls being kidnapped, drugged, forced into prostitution, and who knows what else), the girls made it back alive. Nobody stole them or drugged them. No one influenced them to run away. Their parents had been wrong.

After their modern day "Magic Bus" tour, Maggie and Elizabeth head for Chinatown for dim sum at City View Restaurant. Chinese servers quietly scurry about, pushing metal carts laden with colorful food items on very small plates. Elizabeth and Maggie eagerly sample several dishes, laughing at themselves, overeating, and politely thanking the waitstaff.

They follow up with foot massages at Foo Song Massage on Kearney Street. ("When are we ever gonna have this opportunity again?")

Still, Maggie has not told Elizabeth what Olin said.

In the car Maggie gazes out the passenger-side window as they drive south, heading back to Elizabeth's house. She is half-listening to Elizabeth's family stories while she's mesmerized by the sprawling new tech buildings that have been built next to Route 101–Bayshore Freeway. *What kind of friend am I? Why am I cutting her out of this alleged secret? What does this say about me?*

Deb and Anne are sitting on Elizabeth's front doorstep when they arrive, so Maggie puts any thought of sharing Olin's comments with Elizabeth out of her mind. She's had enough one-on-one time with Elizabeth anyway. Deb wants a cigarette and a beer. Anne is playing Words with Friends on her phone. Elizabeth is going to take a bath, then barbeque chicken for the gang, but Maggie is ready to do something else now.

"Think I'll go to Rhonda's house. Don is there. Haven't seen him in years."

The car stereo is blasting Prince's music as Maggie drives to Rhonda's house. Through the open car window she can smell the spicy eucalyptus.

"I feel so free," she says out loud. "So me. At home. Really at home."

Rhonda and Don are sipping milkshakes when she breezes in. Don is smiling, and if Maggie squints her eyes, she can almost see the three of them as teenagers. Not wrinkled. Not overweight. Just her first real crush and her teenage girlfriend.

Rhonda brings out a jug of red wine and they head out to the back patio. Don sticks with his milkshake.

"I don't drink anymore. And I gave up smoking years ago. I have COPD. Got more than a few pounds to shed."

"See, that's why I worry about you. Does my cigarette smoke bother you?" Rhonda hesitates before lighting up.

"Nah, it's okay." Don's still the same happy, easygoing guy.

After several days of being stuck in the house, laid up with a strained back, Rhonda is keeping a bad bond with despair. She's badmouthing some neighbors. She's trashing her kids. The wine isn't mellowing her.

Judging by Don's restless facial expressions, he's getting fed up, Maggie concludes, so she tries to cheer Rhonda up with a few jokes and compliments about the lush citrus trees in her back yard.

I want her to be happy. She's got just as much right as anyone else to a calmer life.

It works. Rhonda loves compliments.

"When we're all done here, I'll drive us to this family-run Mexican restaurant in San Jose," Don offers. "It's cozy."

As they're set to leave, however, Rhonda stops in the middle of her oil-stained, gray cement driveway. Her eyes are downcast, but she has a wry smile on her face that Maggie recognizes. She's seen that familiar, sly look many times since they were kids.

"Do you all want to see my terrier? I froze him for all eternity and he is in a freezer in the garage."

"Holy shit! No!" says Don.

"Holy shit, yes!" Maggie counters. "How many times am I ever going to get this experience?"

They trot back to the garage. Rhonda opens the freezer, takes a plastic bag out, and places it on a nearby table.

"Isn't he beautiful? Look at his eyes. Shut just perfectly," boasts Rhonda as she closes her own eyes.

Maggie and Don are silent as they stare at the dog encased in the thick plastic bag. It's a bit hard to see through the cloudy plastic, but Maggie decides he looks as if he is curled up sleeping and dreaming before a comfy fireplace.

Finally, Maggie speaks up.

"Did you have this done professionally, Rhonda?"

"No. No. Don't ask her that question," protests Don, his voice rising. "Don't encourage her. I know what the answer is!"

"No, I did not have him done professionally. I did it myself. He looks precious, doesn't he?"

Don says, "My god. Now I'll think of this dog every time I eat an enchilada."

"I kind of like it," says Maggie.

"You would," he retorts.

After such a long day spent with her friends, Maggie is more than ready to be alone. Back at her studio, she craves a long walk. Rambling around the neighborhood, she devotes her legs to a whole-bodied gait. She imagines people would think—if they were watching her—that she has a curious canter; something very horse-like. The type of gait one sees in the very young, very old, or very stoned. But this night she doesn't feel the need for drugs or alcohol. The walk does her good. She sleeps well with the TV volume on low.

17 THE MIGHT OF CHILDREN
AND GRIZZLY BEARS
September 2015

Anne wants to get together with her about six. "I'll pick you up. We'll go downtown."

"Sounds good, Anne. It's my treat."

Today there will be no waiting around for Olin and Steve. No waiting for Julius to call. No wasting the day in a wine-and-marijuana-induced la land. Her month-long visit is going by fast, so today is for researching the history of Palo Alto and writing. Focus, Maggie tells herself throughout the day. And she does.

By three o' clock, her body is stiff from sitting for so long. She stands and feels the blood rush from head to toe. Rustling through a box of miscellaneous manuscripts, letters, and poetry, she mutters to herself. "I don't remember packing all this. Huh. My first California poems."

She pulls several poems out of the box. All are handwritten.

"I remember now. I was eighteen and just graduated from high school. In June of '71. I wrote California poems for eight years. Scads and scads of poems until 1979, the year I moved to the East Coast."

She takes them outside and reads them as she walks back and forth to get her blood circulating again.

"Hey, these are fun. I'm gonna do it again."
She retrieves her laptop from the studio and settles into a lawn chair, letting a stream of consciousness take over.

Perfumed plant life has an aroma of childhood. Palo Alto aroma better than other towns. If the verdure of hometown had a face, it would look affectionate as a mama. My mama? Warm and secure. Agreeable. Fragrances exclusive to home.

Sharp, spice-scented, motley Juniper shrubs and eucalyptus. Aromatic, sugary roses. The sweet and savory kaleidoscope of misty elms, mighty oaks, and white magnolia.

Jammy loquat, gingko, apricot, persimmon, fuchsia, and fig.

Mine. All mine.

New construction. Swank alterations. Changing this town. Everywhere. They come in waves of expansion with the evolution of moneyed folks.

Variegated colors and aromas remain unchanged. But so many dollar signs. Insignias? Prestige everywhere. Are they inanimate?

So many gardeners. Can no one do it themselves?

Replacements: a modest home on a small lot scratched. Thrown away. Traded for a colossal house on a small lot. Is this wealth or progress?

Colossal homes resemble popular, rich kids: the ones who think they are at the top of high school's caste system.

You know who you are.

Bay Area economy is on steroids.

Historically, technology runs through here, seeds here, and grows. Grows thick, quick roots in the 1980s. Frantic high pressure. Even the valley gets a new name: Silicon Valley.

New families move into the area, taking on crushing mortgages.

Commuters spend hours on the road twisting their guts from the rat maze of competition.

No time to enjoy the parks, cultural offerings, tree-lined

streets, libraries, bike paths, and that musty, late-summer, unobtrusive, calm quiet air.
No time to mow and sit down and admire the green aroma.

Maggie stops and gets up to move about. Some stretches. Some food.

An hour passes. "Now I can work on the novel. Maybe weave in some poetry."

First, for the setting: Made-up name of a town. One old, retired teacher tells the mayor in private how angry he feels about changes in town. *"Hell, this is all from the influx of money from China. Asians with lots of money who want to live here. Real estate is skyrocketing. The natives say ... (yeah, now we're natives—ha!). The natives say we can sell our houses, our properties and make millions. I'm tellin' ya, Mayor, I have Asian friends who were born here and they tell me they hate this new culture of working to reach the top. Pushing, pushing, pushing. It's just way out of hand. Listen, Mayor. I'm not making stereotypes. This is just the truth."*

Maggie cannot stop writing even though her muscles are aching from a stooped-over position. Eventually the bathroom calls.

Later she finds some online news clippings about youth culture. She reads about the disturbing trend of self-harm and suicide among the youth. Depression, stress, and anxiety—a Medusa-like tangle of destruction.

I used to make bad decisions because my frontal lobe was undeveloped and my hormones were in a frenzy, Maggie acknowledges. *Craziness. Carelessness. I'm lucky to be alive today.*

She reads articles about mental health professionals who conclude Palo Alto students are tragically groomed to triumph at all cost. She agrees with one journalist who writes about how the money culture breeds a shroud of illusion, concluding that materialism is the be-all, end-all. To achieve the monetary goals set by the culture, a student must focus on enhancing a resume with a high GPA, extracurriculars, learning second and third languages, and community volunteerism. Who has time for random joy? Some cannot cope. Maggie reads about kids from her old high school—her beloved Paly—and neighboring Gunn High School, who have thrown themselves in front of trains. Guards now patrol the railroad crossings, and complex barriers have been erected in an attempt to thwart suicides. Maggie is horrified that the same railroad tracks where she and her friends once strolled so freely, smoking cigarettes, are now hosting a rash of teen suicides.

The Santa Clara Valley Transit Authority announces a new project to improve safety, Maggie discovers as she peruses the online news.

The railroad crossings at four Palo Alto locations need enhanced safety features, such as fences and guard rails, because kids are lying down on the tracks near Paly and Gunn high schools.

Maggie counts eleven suicides by train in a twelve-year time period. So much death under Palo Alto's sunny skies. And that doesn't include the suicides that have taken place using other methods, like guns, drugs, or jumping into traffic. Why so many? She feels herself slipping into a dark place and knows she needs to shake off this sense of doom and helplessness.

Finally, it's a quarter to six and Anne arrives.

"Well, Maggie, are you ready for an evening of martinis and appetizers?"

"Hey, Anne. How come Deb doesn't want to go with us?"

"She went to meet some other friends for dinner."

"What? Other friends? She has friends other than us? Oh, ho!" Maggie laughs. "On another note, I don't think we're going to see Olin or Steve."

"Yeah, Olin's been calling me and Deb. Deb, mostly. I don't really wanna talk about him. Let's just have fun now. Oh, look! A parking space!"

They make their way to one of the swanky bars and restaurants along University Avenue. There is outdoor seating available alongside the sidewalk, and they are soon settled in some comfy rattan chairs with bright orange cushions.

"Hey, these cushions match my T-shirt. Plus they're my favorite color."

"You look good in orange, Anne."

"And, you're wearing my other favorite color. Love that purple scarf, Maggie."

They chat about fashion and decorating for a few minutes until the server arrives. Anne orders a dirty martini and Maggie, a gin and vermouth. Maggie is finished with small talk. A question has been on her mind for hours.

"Anne, do you remember kids offing themselves when we were living here?"

"Offing? Well, that's a bit crude, even for you, Maggie."

"Drink up, Annie. You won't mind me so much after a martini or two."

"I think suicides were uncommon then. There was that one girl in the early 1970s who had gone to our school. She just lay down on the railroad tracks one day. And then there was that boy who I went out with a couple of times who hung himself. I think it was two years after graduation."

"Yeah, I remember now. And then there were those two best friends we knew. They were a grade ahead of us. They went to Vietnam and when they were discharged, they came back to the Bay Area and shot themselves. One played Russian roulette with a pistol and the other used a rifle on himself six months after his best buddy died."

"What did Vietnam do to those guys?" Anne queried. "Imagine having the nerve to blow their heads apart."

"There you go, Anne. Relaxed enough to be morbid. Seems the martini has taken hold."

Maggie looked away for a minute or two, remembering her own darkness. Red wine and sleeping pills. It was so long ago and she had been so young. Only twenty-two. She wills herself not to go there and looks back at Anne, who is wiping away a tear.

"Maggie, I know what you're contemplating. It's alright. Let it go. You were another person."

"Yeah. I was another person. You were the only friend I told, Anne."

Maggie starts rifling through her purse and pulls out a piece of paper. "On another note, look! I brought a copy of this article for you to read."

She gives Anne a moment to scan an article about Palo Alto being selected as "the most popular place to live."

"I'm going to write about this fictitious town in my novel, you know, and fashion it after Palo Alto. Listen ... " Maggie reads a few paragraphs out loud.

In the beginning, the story goes, the little California town was populated by indigenous people. The native communities were forced out by Spaniards and Mexicans. By 1810 vast-acre ranches and land ownership were created from stolen land.

This lush land was home to the grizzly bear. In the 1830s there were two to three thousand grizzlies. They lived in the hills during the rancho days of dons, Spanish land grants, and Mexican rancheros.

But the Gold Rush brought a swarm to California, and less than seventy-five years after the discovery of gold, almost every grizzly bear in California had been tracked down and killed. Humans played roulette with nature, and northern California grizzlies lost their land.

The little town was built in a wheat field, but it thrived and became a symbol of success in the worlds of business, academia, medicine, and architecture.

"That's good, Maggie. I'm so proud of you being an author and all."

"Thanks, Anne."

"So here we are in our old hometown. Still you and me, Maggie. Feels like the old town. Swensen's Ice Cream Parlour is still here, across the street. But the tech world is all around us."

"You know, those tech giants have historical landmarks here. The garage where William Hewlett and David Packard experimented with electronics. Voila! Hewlett-Packard. And the garage where Steve Jobs and his pal put together the boards of their first computer in 1976. They hired neighborhood kids to help. Another voila! Apple!"

The waiter is approaching, so Maggie pauses.

Anne gives one of her sunny, California-girl smiles to the waiter as she orders another drink.

Maggie orders another gin and vermouth, then gets serious. "So, Anne, I gotta tell you. I'm not happy at home. You know, my husband's an alcoholic. I just don't drink that much anymore."

"We did drink a lot when we were in high school and college, didn't we? I guess I should just speak about myself. I drank a lot more."

"But the novelty of drinking to get drunk disappeared."

"You remember my first husband, Maggie? He was a terrible alcoholic."

"Ah, he's got nothin' over mine. Mine gets mean and says hurtful things."

"Well, you joined a twelve-step group, right? Does that help?"

"Yeah. It's starting to help. It's all about taking better care of me. We'll see. What about you? Let's talk about you. And your volunteer job."

"God, I just love it. Probably more than the pottery. There's always a story with the folks at the nursing home. They love to talk. Especially the five-hundred-pound guy."

"Holy moly! He's hefty," laughs Maggie.

Anne shrugs. "But he's a sweet guy. Used to sing opera."

Maggie nursed her drink. "You know, Leland Stanford, the founder and president of Stanford University, was a teetotaler. Palo Alto used to be a dry town."

"Yeah, I remember. And that section of Palo Alto around California Avenue used to be called Mayfield. A separate town altogether. It had a ton of saloons."

A man in a brown sweatshirt and black swim trunks stumbles barefoot past them, a glass bottle of vodka to his lips. The bottle slips from his mouth and shatters on the sidewalk.

"Watch out, sir!" Anne stands up so quickly, she knocks over her chair. "The glass!"

Three servers run out of the restaurant. One has a broom,

another a dust bin, and the third a cell phone. He says, "I'm calling 911. This is ridiculous!"

"Well, Maggie, I guess this town is too hoity-toity for vagrancy."

"It seems to be everywhere."

"Sir? Sir, are you alright?" Anne asks.

"Ma'am, it's okay," one of the servers assures her. "We'll take care of him."

Maggie sniffs. "Hoity-toity is right on, Anne. Did you know that in Palo Alto, home prices in 1925 were only four to five thousand dollars. The house my parents moved into in 1955 cost them nineteen thousand dollars. That same house is worth a million bucks now. A million bucks! That's insane."

Anne is only half-listening. "I'm worried about that man. There's a guy who needs some help. This state has an epidemic of homelessness. There are just too many homeless people out there, Maggie."

"Yeah. Probably because California has too many people. You know, there's thirty-nine million people livin' here."

Anne gets up. "I'm going to the restroom. Let's get out of here when I get back."

Maggie pays the tab and waits on the sidewalk for Anne.

"The guy with the vodka ran off while you were in the bathroom. His foot was cut."

"Yeah, I see blood on the sidewalk."

They stroll downtown. The faces they see are so different from those of 1968. Now everyone looks so serious. Plain faces on women in heels with French manicures. Dapper beards on men talking into a Bluetooth about tech trends and shares of stock.

"Everybody looks the same," says Maggie.

"Yeah, they're all doppelgängers," says Anne. "Hey, look, a new wine bar. Let's stop in."

On the land where Native women once gathered acorns in Palo Alto, ultra-upscale shops like Neiman-Marcus, Bloomingdales, Stella McCartney, and Tiffany's now reside. Native men once brought home venison after a long day of hunting. Now grocery stores sell free-range, hormone-free beef. Fresh stream water has turned into wine bars.

As they are walking back to the car, Maggie says to no one in particular, "The dollar sign. Let me introduce you to the almighty, her majesty."

"Oh, dear, Maggie," sighs Anne. "Are you done yet?"

"No. Oh, well then, yes." Maggie curtsies. "For you I will shut up."

Almost sober, Maggie is watching television, wrapped in a cotton blanket. It's about nine o'clock and Anne is spending the night with her in the studio apartment. In fact, Anne is already asleep on the fold-out couch.

Maggie's cell phone rings. She doesn't recognize the number, but the area code is local.

"Hello?"

"Maggie?"

"Julius? Julius!" She sits up straight. Anne stirs but doesn't awaken.

"Hi, Maggie."

"Oh, Julius, thank you. Thank you for calling." Maggie hears a weak cough.

"Maggie, I have to say upfront that I don't know how long I can talk." A sigh.

"Julius, I'm just happy to hear from you."

"What? Oh, wait." He sounds distracted. A few seconds later he adds, "I can't talk now, Maggie. She's home."

"Who's home, Julius?"

"My girlfriend. Later, okay?" The call ends abruptly.

18 MARY JANE AND ME
September 1968

Maggie believes everything she could ever need is in San Francisco and Palo Alto. She revels in the unconventional standards, the aura of pizzazz, the cultural sophistication, and the pop culture.

Enormous pride is what she feels most.

She wants to express herself, but it is difficult to put into words what she wants people to understand. She notices her peers rush to complete sentences for others so they can jump into another subject. So many short subjects with little depth. Too many interruptions. Just shootin' the shit. Patience is a casualty.

There are some opportunities for her to express herself in one particular environment: a gathering of fellow marijuana smokers. She appreciates how they use great detail to express themselves. Dope is a great fuel to expand the mind. She is able to find the perfect words with like-minded friends. She loves their colorful conversations.

Like the deep revelations she shares with Julius one day, sitting on the grass in a pocket park near Lytton Avenue.

Julius smiles affectionately, stroking her hair. "I see what you mean, Maggie. Swear to god I see in front of me The Pinnacles. I see myself like I'm lookin' at a movie screen."

"What pinnacles?"

"Ha, ha. I love how you say Pinnacles. It's a national park."

"Where is it? Close by? I never heard of it."

Julius can't sit still. He jumps up from the lawn. "Okay. Now imagine: You are in a car on Bayshore Freeway, 101. You are traveling south toward San Jose. And you get to this town called Gilroy. And another one, Hollister. I've never driven a car there myself, but I guess it takes a couple hours to get there from Palo Alto. But that's not the important thing.

"Eventually, you see these massive granite columns. And there you are. The Pinnacles themselves are crystals rising up from molten lava. Volcanos. And there's granite right under those crystals turned stone. Massive I tell you. Massive."

"Whoa." Maggie stands up with Julius. "There you are. I can see you climbing."

"That's it. Like you said … all this nature … "

"… to fall in love with." She wants to get back to their walk. "We can talk and walk at the same time, right? I mean … is anyone gonna know we are stoned?"

"Look at the trees lining the street here on University. They're so symmetrical. Look. Look at the stonework on this building, this store. It's like you say … We have everything here in Palo Alto."

"There's a crowd at Lytton Plaza. They've got signs."

"Yeah. They're a-carryin' signs."

"They better stop. Listen. Ha ha. Hey. Anne and I are gonna go to a free Be-In next Sunday. It's pretty close to your house. Over at the ballpark on El Camino." Maggie skips in front of him.

"Watch out, Maggie. You're skippin' backwards into some people."

"I think it's the best thing. The coolest ever. To say, 'I was born in San Francisco.' That's like saying, 'I was born in Paris.' You were born in California, right?"

"Born in Paris is exactly the same as S.F. It's like you were reincarnated from, say, a tribe of exalted natives. And you were the queen. Was only natural you would eventually wind up in San Francisco. Like where else? And no to your other question. Born in Utah."

"I went through Utah on a family trip. My dad was driving the Pontiac. Utah means you are a mountain man born from thousands of years of mountain people."

"Yeah. I can feel it in my blood. So true, man."

It's everywhere. Maggie sees marijuana everywhere, especially at concerts. It's very blasé.

What do our parents know? What do they get?

Anne and Maggie go to the Be-In at the baseball field on Sunday afternoon.

This Palo Alto Be-In is a rejoinder to Golden Gate Park's Be-Ins in San Francisco. Free, live music from local bands plays all day. No authoritarian adults.

Today's Be-In is loud. Joints and pipes are passed around willy-nilly, and barefoot dancers swoop around with long, gauzy streamers. A guy and a girl are making love on the lawn, their bodies barely covered with a sleeping bag. The only order of the day is to get high and listen to music.

When Anne and Maggie have their fill of marijuana and hot sun, they leave the festival and stroll towards downtown, passing the El Palo Alto, a very tall redwood tree that is the city's first landmark. It is surrounded by its own park, El Palo Alto Park, located on the northern boundary of the city near the shade of the San Francisquito Creek's trees.

They head toward the city buses at the station on Alma Street to wait for the number thirty-six bus to take them home. On the way, they see one of Julius's brothers, nine-year-old Stanley, standing on a street corner. He's grinning, drooling, and making music with empty Coke cans. Clink clang, clink clang.

"Stanley. Hi! Making music?"

"Yesh," he replies.

"Right on."

"Do I know you people?"

"Kinda. We're friends with your brother, Julius."

"Yesh."

Maggie laughs, but Anne frowns.

"I wanna work with kids like Stanley someday," Anne tells Maggie in a disapproving tone.

Maggie spends the rest of the summer swigging the bourbon and vodka her friends steal from their parents' stashes of liquor. She sneaks out at night to run the streets in her stocking feet. She lurks with her friends outside boys' houses in the dark. She plays "spin the bottle" and sits on a boy's lap for the first time. She crosses narrow train trestles over the San Francisco Bay with Olin and Chris to see where they fish for baby sharks.

Summer is flying by, and high school is starting soon.

There is one more outdoor concert at the Grass Steps before school begins. Julius asks her to go with him. Eric Burden and War, Elvin Bishop, and New Riders of the Purple Sage are the headliners.

"Yes. I'll ride over and meet you."

"Far out, Maggie. It's a date. I'll walk over or take the bus and meet you at noon at the ticket booth."

Maggie talks to her mom while she's making an apricot pie. She leans into the kitchen counter and watches her knead the pie crust, remarking, "Yum. My favorite."

Her mom looks pleased. "I know. It'll be ready for dessert tonight."

"I'm going over to Elizabeth's house, Mom. Then we're going swimming at another girl's house."

"Can you be home before dark?"

"Sure. See you for dinner, okay?"

She plays it safe, lying to her mother for fear the truth will only cause worry; worse yet, she might say no. She bikes alone out to the Grass Steps, aka Frost Amphitheater. She is unafraid because she has such a curious, independent nature. She learned early in life that an only child needs to find her own entertainment.

Riding her bicycle up the familiar oaks that encircle Frost's open-air amphitheater, she notes that the trees camouflage the outdoor theater from the rest of the world.

Even from the ticket booth outside the amphitheater, all is hidden.

There's Julius, waving and jumping. "Over here! Lock your bike. I got tickets."

Maggie gives him a smile and he gives her a hug. They walk up a steep path to the top of the venue and look down at a forest enchantment: a bowl-shaped theater and the grass steps lead down to the concrete stage.

Frost is its own biosphere. For the flower children, this once was a blessed, forested play-scape where a kid could hide and climb, get dirty, and run alongside nameless kids on the wooded, oak-shaded paths. Maggie loved the feeling of being unleashed.

These days, those same children smuggle dope and booze into the venue. Some get stoned and sit in trees, or tumble down dusty brush and knolls, or dance by the stage. They are adorned in open, fringed, suede vests; peasant blouses; silver and turquoise bracelets; garlands of flowers; and cut-off jeans. They are always barefoot.

Julius has a doobie. They get a good high. Acapulco Gold is a smooth high, eventually turning the music to bells and crystals ringing out in her head. No bummers. Only euphoric contentment.

Seated so close together, Julius can smell the sweat at the nape of her neck. He kisses her there and she's so hot.

"You're cute, ya know it? Maggie oh Maggie ... Hey Maggie, I really had fun at your house the other morning when your mom made those Danish pancakes. What are they called?"

"Aebleskivers."

"What? Say it again? How do you pronounce it?"

"Sounds kind of like *ev-el-skeever*. She's showed me how to make them in that special cast-iron pan with the hollows where the flour mixture settles in lots of butter to heat up, then they get flipped over, and there you go. A round ball instead of a flat pancake. I especially like to stuff jam into its little pocket."

"Yeah, well. It was nice she made those for your friends. I think your mom is the only mom who likes us."

"Thanks, Julius. I'll tell her you like her."

Musicians fill every pocket of space. They laugh. They sway.

Songs about love, the Vietnam War, and freedom. Spiritual guides floating lyrics out to their eyes.

Maggie suddenly needs to find a bathroom. The outhouses have such long lines. She is too paranoid now to face the crowd behind her so Julius walks her to the bathroom and waits.

At concert's end Julius guides her with his arm around her waist. He watches Maggie ride her bike until he can see her no more.

"There goes my baby."

In 1898, the year it was founded, Palo Alto High School was the only secondary school between the peninsula towns of San Mateo to the north and San Jose to the south. The school was originally located on Channing Street in the central part of town. Stanford University sold a thirty-acre site to the town to build another public high school for one dollar an acre. It moved to its new location across the street from Stanford in 1918. A beige, two-story stucco building with a red, clay-tile, Spanish roof, it was designed to resemble an early-California Spanish mission, complete with bell tower.

Two days before the start of school, Maggie organizes the first week's worth of outfits and school supplies. Her shoes, purses, and miniskirts, plus her binder, class list, and map of the school grounds—they will make her or break her.

Wednesday, September 4th, is the big day. The first day of high school for Maggie and her girlfriends.

Maggie rides with Anne and Deb in Chris's car.

"Thank you, Chris. Riding the bus on the first day of high school is embarrassing."

"Eight o' clock and here we are. The back of the school is student parking." The girls listen carefully as Chris gives them some pointers.

"Deb, you can smoke in this lot here if you watch out for teachers.

"Maggie, act like you know what you're doing. Not too much eye contact. Don't go all gaga-puppy-eyes over Olin in the hallways.

"Don't eat in the cafeteria on the first day of school, Annie. That's gonna peg you right off the bat. Meet me at the library and we'll go get something from the deli at Town and Country shopping center across the street."

"I won't be hungry. I've got a nest of hornets in my stomach."

"Don't be worried, Annie. Ol' Chris here will protect you. Plus, there's lots of other food places over there in the shopping center."

"Maybe."

Maggie finds her locker near the library and fiddles with the combination to make sure it works. She's wearing a cute brown and pink, empire-waist minidress. Her mom and dad let her spend a little extra for it at Joseph P. Magnin, one of the ritzier clothing stores. Her pink leather shoes match the pink in the dress.

The school halls are swarming with hundreds of kids. Maggie compares herself to the other girls.

Uh oh. There's that junior girl—Steve's girlfriend. Wouldn't you know it? Crafty are her eyes! So much mascara and black eyeliner.

The girl sees Maggie staring, so she stares back and shakes her head.

"No, no, no, no. I'm not gonna let her bug me," Maggie mutters as she makes her way to her first class of the day, World History.

It's gonna be a day, for certain.

19 DON'T HAVE A COW, MAN
September-December 1968

e hasn't liked me from the start. Mr. Esse and his dumb suit and tie and crewcut. I can't stand his pitted, pink-tinted face or his plastic, black-framed glasses. Look how he holds that stupid yardstick in one hand and chalk in the other. He knows I'm struggling, but he just sneers and turns away.

Geometry is a difficult class for Maggie. Math in general is one of her weaknesses. Her brain understands words, not numbers. But here she is, assigned to Mr. Esse's geometry class to start off her sophomore year at Paly.

Maggie takes the humiliation from Mr. Esse personally. A voice in her head says, "He doesn't care if your grades slip."

Maggie can immediately sense if a man is nice. Nice men smile and talk low and slow; their eyes kind of sparkle. Mean men scare her right from the get-go. She knows they have no respect for women or girls. It's not the first time she's felt singled out. Her fourth-grade teacher, Mr. Silver, would pick on her in front of the entire class when she made a mistake. She kept this to herself.

In junior high at Jordan, Maggie thrived in Spanish because her teacher, Mr. Bernal, was a kind man. She was top of the class, straight As all the way. That's how she achieved most of her good grades—from a teacher's praise.

Math has always been confusing. She wants to fly into a raging tantrum to expel the mess from her mind. Women teachers keep her calm. *Why can't they all be like Miss Kintz from ninth-grade algebra? This Mr. Esse worries me. Geometry makes me ill. I just don't get it.*

Mr. Esse isn't the only mean one. Her third-period Spanish teacher, Mr. McCormick, is another one who likes to sneer. He has the same crewcut and glasses as Mr. Esse. He's already singled her out, too. "Excuse me, daydream girl. On the board—yes, on the board and not out the window—you'll see what we're studying today. Please give me and the class the past tense for all verbs listed."

One gray, cold November day, Mr. Esse sends her to the dean's office right in the middle of a test because she is dressed "inappropriately."

"You know what the dress code says. No pants. So you just take yourself right down to the dean's office and report to him. Come back tomorrow with a signed note from the dean and a parent. Dress in appropriate attire."

"Yeah, sure, asshole," she says to herself as she heads out the door. "You're just gonna ignore the four other girls in jeans today? At least I've got nice slacks on. Sayonara, I'm never coming back to your stupid class. Humiliate me and that's the last you'll see of me. I'm dropping geometry. So go screw yourself, Mr. Esse."

As she leaves the outdoor math and science building, cold air stings her cheeks, already red from embarrassment and anger. She's scowling as she enters the building that houses the administrative offices.

Just this morning I was admiring this old building. I was in love with its wide hallways, those soaring ceilings that are two stories tall, and that cool bell tower. Now it's all shit.

A little spark of joy lightens her mood when she sees who is waiting in the foyer outside the dean's office. *Randy!* It's a sophomore kid she knows. She's always thought he was pretty darn cute. She walks through the glass double doors, smiling as she sits down on the wooden bench next to him.

"Hey, Maggie. Are you here to see the dean? What did you do?"

"Pants. What about you?"

"Kissing my girlfriend in the hall outside the library."

"Shame, shame," they both laugh.

Randy has the cutest smile of all time. Maggie feels a little tingle in her nether regions, but what can she do about it? Boys her age wear their hearts on their sleeves, so desperate to proclaim their love. She needs a man, not a boy.

Maggie dislikes school when her grades aren't As or Bs. She doesn't know who to ask for help. If she saw her guidance counselor, what would she say?

Being at home isn't appealing, either. At times her mother seems supportive, offering a comforting shoulder to cry on as Maggie shares her anxiety, her anger over her father's alcoholism, and her sexual confusion. Weeks later, though, she inevitably regrets confiding in her mother, as sympathy is replaced by lectures—especially lectures about sex. Maggie feels ashamed and betrayed.

Where do I fit in at Paly? Well, I feel good with my girlfriends and my guy friends. Where else?

Even in junior high she couldn't get her foot in the door with the popular kids. She sure doesn't expect to be able to do it in high school. She's not a cheerleader, she's not in the math club, she's not in the theater department. She likes watching *General Hospital* after school, smoking weed with Anne, and dancing to Jimi Hendrix and the Chambers Brothers. She feels safe confiding in Anne.

"Do your parents give you advice about life, or anything?" Maggie asks her friend.

"Sometimes they talk about college. Both my mom and her mom went to college. My dad is pretty quiet. We spend time in his darkroom where he teaches me about developing film. But I don't know what else. Stay away from boys, they kind of imply."

"My dad likes to tell me about World War II," Maggie says. "He won't let any black kids in our house. My mom says I should go to secretarial school like she did. I don't think they ever help me much when I'm in a bad mood. Except for my mom. She distracts me by getting us to cook or garden together. So I don't know if I'm in a bad mood because I'm a teenager or if I'm possessed by something, like ... well, I don't know what."

"I think you're overreacting. Seriously, Maggie?"

"Have I involved a demon or the devil? Well, there are ghosts in my house. And they mess with me. Making things move. Clutching my hand in the dark. Pushing over my tower of books by my bed. Sitting on my bed. Looking at me, like a dark human shadow."

"Life sure is a rollercoaster for you, Maggie."

Maggie spends more and more time with Julius. Now that she's at Paly, she can see that he's more than just a free-spirited surfer. He's on the varsity football team and he's well-liked by everyone. And he's respectful toward her in a way that the popular boys are not. She watches them at school, how aggressively they act, even when they're flirting. She'd rather hang out with Julius or double-date with Anne and Chris or another couple from Paly.

Julius doesn't know that she also likes to spend time alone with Olin. With Olin there's a stronger sexual attraction. He looks as though he just stepped out of a cigarette commercial and she's attracted to his bad boy image. Olin doesn't know Maggie's seeing Julius as often as she is. She feels no need to volunteer anything. Why not keep her options open?

Maggie attends a few of Julius's home games and imagines herself as his silent cheerleader. The pompom girls make football-shaped posters and tape them above the school lockers. Maggie seizes a few for keepsakes: "Beat 'em Brownell!" "Break 'em Brownell!" "Jump 'em Julius!"

"Hey! Maggie!" says Olin one day. "I gave Julius a tab of acid that he took before school let out and before football practice. I was watchin' practice from the bleachers. When it kicked in, Julius slowly dropped to his back on the field and stayed there during the scrimmage. He didn't move. The coach let it go on for, I swear, fifteen minutes, before he yanked Julius up. Didn't say a word to him other than 'hit the showers.'"

Whenever they go to movies, drive to the beach or a park where they might get stoned and hike the trails, Julius never drives. No one knows if he has a driver's license, but it's obvious he doesn't have his own car.

He is a sweet guy, completely trustworthy because he is consistently transparent. He is a white orb of warm affection, exposed and radiant. Comical and silly, he makes everyone laugh. Guileless, he is above suspicion. And he's a brilliant conversationalist.

Olin, on the other hand, is moody and dramatic. Maggie is thrilled when he offers to walk her to her classroom, when he asks her out on a date, and when he pulls her towards him and plants a long kiss on her lips.

He's unpredictable, but it's this very challenge that makes her tingle with a charge that runs through her veins.

She is wounded when he flirts with other girls, but that doesn't stop her from writing love poems about him and crying over songs on the radio.

Since January Maggie has had three bouts of tonsillitis. When the third one occurs in November, her mother has a ridiculous recommendation.

"You can have them out during the upcoming Christmas break and not miss any school."

"Nah. I'll have them out when school is in session. I'm not missing hanging out with friends over the winter holiday."

"No siree, Bob! Your grades aren't good enough to take time off from school. If those infected tonsils are bothering you so much, get them out over Christmas."

"No way. I'm just gonna live with them if that's how you are going to play this."

"Fine. If you prefer chronic tonsillitis, it's your pain. That's your choice."

"How in the hell can you put me in this position? School breaks during holidays are for having fun. I will be sixteen before Christmas and I've got plans!" She doesn't tell her mother she'll be spending New Year's Eve alone with Olin.

"I don't like your tone, missy. You're not getting around me this time. Now go find something else to do. Like homework."

All tonsil talk is dropped. Maggie turns sweet sixteen. Sweet is a term Olin uses for her. She can think of nothing else lately. On Christmas Eve, millions are enthralled by the American astronauts who orbit the moon ten times and send pictures back to earth. It's the first time humans see the far side of the moon. And the first time Earth is photographed from space.

But Maggie is only enthralled by Olin. She asks her mom if it's okay for him to come over and watch the countdown to the New Year on TV. Her mom wants her to stay home that night anyway, so a deal is made and they both win. Her parents conveniently stay in the back bedrooms with the doors ajar.

In the living room the floor-to-ceiling turquoise drapes are closed. One table lamp is on. The light brown wooden walls and the red-bricked fireplace, with a Presto log burning, create a cave-like atmosphere. Olin and Maggie lie as quiet as can be on the carpeted floor, making out.

The musical guests on the New Year's Eve show are serenading them at 10:30 p.m. when the kitchen phone rings.

Maggie jumps up to answer. A male voice asks to speak to Olin. *Strange*, she thinks, as she hands him the receiver. Chewing on her fingernails, Maggie watches him as he speaks briefly, then listens for what seems like forever.

Finally, he says, "Okay" and hangs up.

Avoiding eye contact, he tells her that was his brother calling on behalf of their mother. Her first language is Spanish and when she is anxious, she cannot remember her English words so she asks family members to place calls. Once Olin was on the line, his brother turned over the phone to their mother, who spoke to him in Spanish.

"My mother wants me home now. She doesn't mean to be impolite. She wants me to choose."

"Choose?" Maggie questions.

"Yeah. It's hard to explain to you what she means. But if I

don't go home, as she asks, I will be in big trouble. She is mad at me now for … oh god, just trust me. I have to go home. I'll phone you later, if I can."

He doesn't call. Maggie's nerves are shredding. One by one they fall into a puddle of self-hatred. She doesn't get it. Did he really go home or was he just trying to get away from her? She blames herself. New Year's Eve, 1968, has been destroyed. She has to know if he's lying, so just before midnight she calls him at home. He answers the phone, but insists he can't talk.

In her room she listens to KYA on her transistor radio as they play a countdown of the Top 100 Songs of 1968. She hopes number one is "Revolution," by The Beatles, but it's "Hey Jude." Nothing is going her way tonight. Her girlfriends are partying with some senior boys from Cubberly High School over at Stanford while she's in her room with her parents hovering outside her closed door. Why would a tough guy like Olin let his mother just command him to come home like that?

The adoration seventeen-year-old Olin has for his mother cannot be easily explained to anyone, especially Maggie Mayes. Trying to be a tough guy on the outside and being a softie on the inside is damned hard.

His mother is a feisty Columbian woman who adopted him and loves him with all her heart.

His mother tells him often to respect the girls.

"Olin, elegir a tu vestido! El corazón es difícil. Tanto dolor! Ser de honor para su familia, a ti mismo y a una chica y a su familia."

"Yes, Mama. I will try to choose my sweetheart. I don't want to dishonor the family. Any girl? But really! Did you have to search for me? Did you have to call me at Maggie's house?"

"You are my boy. Mi hijo. Ser un man."

The next day Olin comes clean.

"Look, Maggie. My mother really wanted me home on New Year's. Really. I would have been grounded if I didn't go home. I think you sounded sad and I don't want to make you sad. When you called me before midnight, my mother almost wouldn't let me answer the phone. But see! I was at home after I left your house. It's complicated. She talks about respect and honor and I was raised in this culture where I must respect her. I'm sorry. She may not speak great English, but she's full-blooded mama bear.

"Listen. Do you want to go to see the Steve Miller Band at the Avalon Ballroom in a few weeks? It'll be a gas. Please, please go with me. I've got some good weed to take with us."

Maggie is torn. She wants to resolve the unhappiness she felt last night after Olin left but how can he go from hurting her to asking her out on a date?

I can't skip so easily over the betrayal I felt when he left me sitting in the cozy living room to jumping with excitement over going to a concert. But I gotta go with Olin. If I don't, he might ask some other girl. Bury it. Bury it all. Bury my instincts.

163

20 MAGGIE AND OLIN
Winter 1968

The New Year's debacle has smoothed over. It was in Maggie's self-interest to tell her parents the truth. Olin's mother wanted him to come home and he obeyed her. The truth worked. Her parents looked happier. It would be easier now for her to date Olin.

It's the night of the Steve Miller Blues Band concert in San Francisco at the Avalon Ballroom. Another couple is going with Olin and Maggie, but she tells her mom and dad that the four of them are going out to dinner in Palo Alto and then to a late double feature.

They smile and nod with parental approval. "We want to meet them, please."

Maggie calls Olin. "Heads up. I lied to my parents. Told them we're going to dinner and the movies. I can't risk telling them we are going up to the city for a concert. Please tell your friends my mom wants to meet them. And they gotta know about my lie."

She is beside herself with delight and nervous primping and pacing in anticipation of going out with Olin. She didn't get enough of him on New Year's Eve.

The San Francisco music scene is exploding with big name bands of the '60s. Several musicians have emerged who are from Palo Alto and some have attended her high school: the

Grateful Dead's drummer, Pig Pen, lived in Palo Alto; Joan Baez graduated from Paly; Jefferson Airplane's vocalist, Grace Slick, lived in Palo Alto.

Janis Joplin got her start in a little bar in San Francisco's North Beach area, where she stood on a table top, wailing her bluesy songs.

San Francisco is a landing strip for the psychedelic, rock and roll, folksy musicians. They often play in large concert halls, two in particular: Fillmore West and Avalon Ballroom.

Maggie thinks lying to her parents is partly their own fault. She wants them to let go of her and they stubbornly hang on. She pushes away a nagging voice. *You know they worry. If you were a parent, you would, too.*

But the other voice in her head—a much louder one—says, *This is a once-in-a-lifetime opportunity. GO!*

The sun has set and a black, cold sky dresses the night as Olin, Maggie, and the other couple travel up Highway 101 to San Francisco. Olin and Maggie sit in the back seat. He rolls joints and the four of them smoke number after number, hyping on music, schoolyard rumors, and anti-war sentiments.

In the front passenger seat, the other girl warns her boyfriend, "Be careful driving. We don't want to get busted."

Exiting the highway, they find Avalon and park on a darkly lit side street. Winded in their excitement, they scurry across the narrow sidewalks, searching for the entrance. There it is. The Avalon Ballroom.

Waiting in line, Maggie feels like a kid waiting for an E-ticket ride at Disneyland. All along the line, young people spontaneously improvise comedic jives and jokes, sending spasmodic tentacles of laughter through the crowd. There is a dreamlike aura to the low-lying swirls of Pacific Ocean fog that darken the storefronts. Ahead of Maggie and Olin, the couple they came with pays the entrance fee and strolls through the front door with nary a glance backwards.

"How old are you?" asks the man who seems to be both bouncer and ticket-taker.

"Eighteen," says Olin matter-of-factly.

"Sixteen," says Maggie.

"Sorry. You can't go in. You have to be eighteen. Notice the rules here on this sign? Eighteen."

Maggie is devastated. Jesus H. Christ! How could she not have seen the sign? Why didn't anyone tell her? Now they can't get into the Avalon Ballroom because she is not eighteen!

Olin's face looks ghastly and his eyes are doing this crazy dance between Maggie and the bouncer. He isn't eighteen either, but at least he seems to know the score.

Back to the cold car they trudge and Maggie keeps her head down. As has become her habit, she takes the blame and is horribly embarrassed.

"I'm sorry. I'm sorry. I'm really, really sorry."

"It's not your fault. We thought you knew ahead of time you had to be eighteen to get in. That's why I lied. Didn't you notice?"

"No."

"Didn't I tell you?"

"No."

"I'm sorry, Maggie."

Is he sincere? Does he mean it? I am SUCH a doofus.

They get in the car. Olin rests his head against the headrest, closes his eyes, and sighs. Maggie is mortified. Olin takes her chilled hands in his and blows on them. He finally talks to her.

"Hey, it's okay. So, do you know how the Avalon came to be? It was a ballroom before the 1950s. When you get inside, you'll see how it looks all Victorian and everything."

"Olin, you said when I get inside. You think we'll really get in there?"

"Yeah, sure, kiddo. And then you can see all the light shows on the walls."

"Well, I've seen light shows before."

"Yeah? Where?"

"Like at the Fillmore. I saw It's a Beautiful Day there."

"Hey! You never told me you went to the Fillmore. How come?"

"I don't know. Anyway, it doesn't look Victorian or anything. It's decorated like an outdoor Mexican plaza. It's got all these stucco-arched doorways and balconies. They show light shows on the ceiling there."

"Yeah, Maggie, I've been there. Do you know the history of the place?" He's frowning.

"Kind of ... Are you mad at me?"

"I just thought I was taking you to your first San Francisco concert. Now I find out you've gone to one without me. That's all."

"It's okay. Don't worry. I do know that Phil Graham is this guy who owns the Fillmore East in New York. And he bought this old building here and called it Fillmore West." Maggie flashes Olin a conciliatory smile.

"Oh, god. It's so hard to be mad at you when you look so cute. Anyway ... righto, kiddo. It used to be a dance hall. A ballroom, I guess. Like, it's real old. Built in the early 1900s. Think it was even a roller rink at some point. Ya know what kind of music was playing there in the '50s?"

"No."

"Rock and blues. I heard that James Brown and B.B. King played there."

"Cool. Olin. What are we gonna do now?"

"Like you just told me, it's okay. Don't worry. Here, let's listen to the radio."

And they do, for what seems like hours.

Thirty minutes later, Olin says, "Okay, let's try to get in again."

There's the forbidding entrance. From the other side of the dark front doors, Maggie can hear the din of voices.

"Two tickets, please," says Olin.

"How old are you?" the bouncer asks.

"Eighteen," says Olin.

"Eighteen," says Maggie.

He eyes them suspiciously. "Weren't you guys here before?"

"No." Olin replies.

Maggie doesn't hesitate. "No," she says firmly.

Olin pays for the tickets, the bouncer lets them in, and they enter a parlor filled with old Victorian velvet couches and lamps. They pass through an arched doorway supported by large, round, white columns on either side. Revolving above the doorway is a strobe light. Olin and Maggie hold hands and stand in the darkened chamber. For Maggie, every movement freezes in time.

As they step into the concert area, the gleaming designs on the walls and the audience's white clothing shine even whiter from black lights in every corner. Even their teeth glow.

The ballroom is the size of a skating rink. In one corner is a raised stage for the band. A couple dozen people are in the balcony opposite the stage. Otherwise, everyone else is on the floor.

"Look, Maggie, the light show." Olin points all around them at the soaring walls. Maggie is pulled to swirling colors, pulsating to the music.

"These walls look as tall as a four-story building," she responds.

"Do you know how the lights are made that way?"

"Yeah. Oil and water, mixed together on glass surfaces and displayed through a projector."

"Maggie Mayes, you're the sweetest and smartest girl I know."

Maggie and Olin spot their friends and must wind through the bodies on the floor to reach them. The foursome shares a doobie and Steve Miller plays Maggie's favorite song, "Living in the USA." The crowd hollers. Olin reaches for Maggie's shoulders and pulls her back to rest against his chest.

Maggie is in heaven.

21 MAGGIE AND JULIUS
Spring 1969

It is still winter when spring starts showing its face in the Bay Area because the daffodils always come up in February. It is the time of year that reminds Maggie her mood swings will soon be cured by the sun. While Maggie's mood swings soften, spring's mood swings are just beginning. One day it's sporadic rain, followed by the sun and early morning flowers opening, followed by torrential downpours.

March and April arrive with the fresh ache of hormonal joy and yearning. Maggie has an itching restlessness, especially while sitting in a classroom learning nonsense like conjugating sentences in Spanish or examining the topographic map of Asia.

Outside the classroom window, the sky is sunny. Sweetly wafting yellow Lady Banks roses climb the side of the building. Through the open window they smell aromatically wet.

Hypnotizing songbirds and bees vibrate and a breeze caresses Maggie's cheeks and hair.

"Miss Mayes. You haven't answered my question. You don't have the answer, do you?"

Realizing Mr. Donkey Face Spanish Teacher has caught her off guard, Maggie blushes and says nothing. Once again, he has humiliated her.

I gotta get out of this place.

Her mother knows her grades have slipped from As and Bs to Cs and Ds. She used to be brilliant in Spanish. When she was flunking algebra in junior high, her parents switched her to a slower-paced algebra teacher and her grades soared.

Look at me now. I've dropped geometry and I'm getting Ds in Spanish.

Drugs and alcohol make her feel good and forget her struggles. She cannot imagine herself living without them.

Her other escape is taking solitary bike rides in the spring around the vast acres of Stanford University property.

Starting from her neighborhood of newer homes, she is soon transported to wide boulevards shaded by wizened, giant trees. They match the beautiful older homes, which are mostly made of adobe, stucco, brick, or dark wood. The lawns look soft and dewy like northern-growing, green-shaded moss.

Closer to the university, narrow streets twist and bend past bungalows where former college professors lived in the early 1900s. Pink and white magnolia petals fall and carpet the streets.

Once on campus, Maggie rides past grassy fields and eucalyptus groves on narrow, winding paths. One such path leads to the white-washed and massively columned Stanford Museum, housing Palo Alto's history.

She sets her bicycle aside and sprawls on the lawn. She doesn't want to go into the museum. She prefers the shady spots of turf and drops of dew. Traipsing barefoot through the lawn, she takes time to notice the fresh smell of the spongy grass wetting her toes.

Then it's a quick ride over to the Stanford family's mausoleum, hunkered beneath great oak tree canopies. The white stone mausoleum contains the coffins of Mr. and Mrs. Leland Stanford and their son, Leland, Jr. It is guarded by two stone sphinx statues, one on either side of marble front steps.

The mausoleum and its surrounding lawn are completely shaded by the massive oak limbs that stretch for yards, some twisting among themselves. It is a quiet place.

She likes to sit on top of the sphinxes. After climbing up one of the statues, she leans back against the building and watches people as they stroll or hurry along the dirt paths that surround the mausoleum. Students walk by, carrying textbooks. Couples link arms or drape them across each other's shoulders.

Maggie feels a twinge of jealousy as she watches the loving couples. In the months since her perfect date with Olin at the Avalon Ballroom, her feelings have changed. She is growing tired of Olin's fickleness and beginning to appreciate Julius's unwavering loyalty.

She pulls tiny yellow petals off a dandelion and swings her legs in their bell-bottom jeans. After a time she grows restless, jumps off the sphinx, and roams an earthy boulevard until it leads to a cactus garden.

"Look! It's you!" She whirls around at the sound of a familiar voice.

It's Julius. He's got one of those cute, laid-back surfer-guy smiles on his face.

"Hey, man, whatcha doin', Maggie?"

"Hey! Hi Julius. What a trip to see you. I'm just on my own today. Seems everyone was busy. So I rode my bike all over. How did you get over here?"

"I walked. First went to the shopping center. Had a sundae and then came over this direction hunting for the mausoleum cuz I wanted to lay on the grass under the trees."

Getting close to her, he takes her shoulders gently, pulls her closer, and bends down for a kiss.

She kisses his freckled, peeling nose.

"You went surfing this weekend, didn't you?"

"I did. Oh, man! The waves were so fine. Danny drove us over Friday night and we stayed at his family's beach house. Saturday, all day, the waves were a gas."

"Come with me. I want to tell you something," Maggie says as she pulls him by the hand.

They swing their arms and skip a little on down a path. With Julius skipping feels natural. He is just that childlike and playful.

On the lawn by the mausoleum, Julius and Maggie sit cross-legged, facing each other.

"So, here's the deal. Anne's parents are going away one night in late June. They have to go see her mom's mother. They say I can stay over with Anne and keep her company, and my mom said it is okay with her. Did Chris tell you?"

"No. My family didn't say anything about him calling me or coming over when I was at the beach."

"Oh," she says. "Okay, well, you see, Chris is gonna try to stay over there at Anne's all night. Like go over after dark and crawl through a side window so the neighbors don't see because they would tell Anne's mom."

"Oh, ho! Well, jeez, what do ya think? I can maybe stay over, too. We've never done that, Maggie. Stay all night together. I mean, can we?"

He rocks back and forth a little.

"Oh, yeah, we can." Maggie doesn't even hesitate.

22 SHOULD WE STAY OR
SHOULD WE GO
September 2015

I t's been a full day and a half since Julius returned Maggie's call, then abruptly hung up when his girlfriend came home.

Maybe Julius won't call back. And Olin is ignoring her. In her studio apartment, Maggie is growing increasingly anxious. She begins muttering to herself as she paces back and forth.

"Not sure what to do. It might be one of those days I need some recreational goodies to get rid of this pounding in my chest and calm down." Maggie takes a pain pill, swallowing it with a swig of beer.

Outside she eases herself onto a chaise lounge on the patio and watches black squirrels balance on top of the fence, chattering at her and each other, jumping up the sides of the elms and redwoods. Her laptop computer is balanced on her knees; hopefully, she can focus on gathering some more information.

The midmorning sun feels good. Her earbuds are in and her iPod is playing a collection of funk and soul. She ponders what Olin told her about Julius's parents. Could it be true? Brother and sister?

She turns to Google to search for articles about inherited

conditions among families when siblings have babies. Genetic disorders in siblings will increase the probability that their children will carry the disorders, she reads. Such as developmental delay.

"That might be why those kids were a little whacked out," Maggie mutters. She catches herself for being insensitive, then says out loud, "Shit! No one's listening. I can talk freely to myself. They *were* whacked out."

Before long she turns her attention back to the online vault of articles about Palo Alto youth—and some of their obituaries. The suicides. How did the teens feel the moment they lay down on the tracks, turned their heads to the oncoming trains, and surrendered?

She knows she's being morbid.

Her tongue is stuck to the roof of her mouth and her throat is sore and swollen. She trudges into the studio, sun-parched and scorched. A Saint Pauli Girl calls from the fridge.

Beer in hand, she rummages through the books on the coffee table, looking for a passage she read the other day about Palo Alto history. *Aha, here it is.*

Where are the nine-league ranches of the native Californians?
They have been swindled out of them.
Where are the grizzly bears and coyotes?
They have been killed off.
Where are the endless herds of cattle?
Butchered for the San Francisco market.
Who cut down the magnificent trees that once stood here?
The Pikes. *

The passage was written by a Pennsylvania journalist named Baylord Taylor, who had visited California during the Gold Rush. When he returned a decade later, in 1859, he was astounded by the changes that had taken place in the area between San Francisco and San Jose.

"Pikes" was the derogatory term used for immigrants from the Midwest.

Maggie is relieved she found what she was looking for, but she realizes she needs to focus. Her cell phone buzzes, notifying her of a new text. Actually, she has three new texts. Her husband wants to know when she is coming home. *And aren't you a little selfish to be gone so long?* he texts. Irritated, Maggie decides not to respond. He agreed to this trip of hers beforehand. He has no right to complain now.

The second text and third texts are from her daughters. Both are worried about money. *What should I do?* one asks. *Can I live with you?* the other wants to know.

Maggie is mad. This is not what she wants to deal with today.

Maggie forgets about Baylord Taylor and the book it had been so important to locate. Her discomfort shifts to obsession over Julius. She grabs another beer and reads through letters the two of them exchanged in the late '90s. She's already read them many times.

It's all in the letters—his reluctance, his pulling away, and his reaching out to her.

How could I be so blind? I see it now. Throughout his letters.

He was cautious. I was pushy. Selfish is what I was.

His philosophy was to stick to the present and be realistic. She put a veil over the fear she had felt after another divorce, another failure. She had no philosophy or plan, only a need to quash loneliness by reaching out to Julius.

It was all right there, staring her in the face. She had been manipulative, sending him embellished poems, suggesting she still adored him. She had pried into his life and tried to force her version of independence on him, suggesting he leave his parents when she knew how cautious he was. She had taken offense when he pushed back against her, then tried to draw him back in by apologizing. She had been too self-absorbed to notice that in some letters he was suggesting, in his cautious and subtle way, that they might get back together in the future.

And that last letter from him, that damned last letter. All the uncharacteristic misspellings. It almost appeared to be written by a child. She had been so determined to bring a man to her emotional rescue that she hadn't seen that her old friend was drowning.

Didn't he warn her? "A big block of information needed for rational decision making is missing from me."

Maggie hates the guilt she's feeling. She works on her novel, but there's no substance. Everything in her mind is shit. She pops two more opiates and waits for the float into detachment, sitting in one spot for an hour, waiting for peace. The disjointed jumps from subject to subject—sibling marriage, suicides, the Gold Rush, her family, Julius's letters—have ceased. Tears wet her cheeks and neck. It is almost dark. To keep the numbing effect, she rolls a joint, smokes in the yard, and then paces the neighborhood until it is a black, moonless night. Her senses are heightened. She hears every sigh of the brindle foxtail. Time is multi-dimensional. This is her peace and serenity. This is her high. It's been this way forever.

Maggie is awakened by the ringtone of her cell phone. She sits up in her bed, confused. The last thing she remembers is walking around the neighborhood. She had an epiphany, but she can't remember what it was. Shit. She grabs her phone from the nightstand.

"Hello?"

"Maggie! Right on! It's Olin! That other secret. The one I kept from you. I worked undercover for the government on a consulting basis. If you ever tried to get a hold of me, even a couple of years ago, I was away. Far away. Sometimes I had to leave for months. I couldn't tell anyone where I was going or what I was doing."

Maggie isn't paying attention. She's noticing the bottle of Xanax on the night stand, pills spilling out of it, and she's remembering the other drugs she took.

"Holy shit! I'm lucky to be alive."

"Yes, you are, Maggie. You are lucky to be alive. I am

lucky, too, because soon I get to see you. All of you."
Maggie tries to focus. "Really?"
"Yes, Maggie, really."
Olin can't see her as she shrugs.
"Okay, Olin." Maybe later she'll feel something.

23 HE SPEAKS
September 2015

Maggie sits on a sun-warmed bench with a cigarette in one hand, cell phone in the other, and mug of hot coffee at her side. She is about to call her Al-Anon sponsor, but her mind is a chalkboard that has been wiped clean. She cannot remember what she wants to say. She only knows she needs help.

The pocket park three blocks from her rental studio is practically deserted. The lawns are more brown than green due to California's perpetual drought. Picnic tables and barbeques to the left, playground and tennis courts behind her. The men who practice tai chi early every morning are long gone. The basketball court is empty of their graceful moves.

Three landscapers wearing khakis and holding clipboards scratch their heads as a fourth leans over a sprinkler head. Their polo shirts read "City of Palo Alto Parks Maintenance."

A yellow Labrador retriever and a woman in black and turquoise spandex jog past Maggie. Maggie takes one more drag on her cigarette before she calls her Al-Anon sponsor, Peg.

"Maggie, how are you? Are you still in California?"

"Yes, I am. I'm doing pretty good, Peg. Been writing. Seen a few friends."

"So what's on your mind today? Are you in a good place to talk about it?"

"You know me, Peg. Just when I'm ready to tell you something, all that something floats away. Here I am trying to get it all back."

"When you're ready then."

"I had a rough night last night. Not sure how to explain it." Peg has been in Al-Anon for fifteen years. She has been living with recovering and actively drinking alcoholics even longer. She has been helpful in getting Maggie to take time for self-care while living with an alcoholic. Maggie wants to tell her about her own substance abuse, but she's hesitant.

"Hold on, Peg. I just need a sec to light my cigarette." She lights up another cigarette and notices her bad breath when she exhales. "Thanks, Peg. I'm back."

"I didn't know you smoked cigarettes, Maggie. Not that I'm judging. Just commenting."

"I need to talk to somebody. An objective somebody."

"Glad you called."

"Peg, as my sponsor, you should know I'm smoking marijuana every day lately. And that's not all. I'm taking opiates and benzos." She pauses. "And the occasional drink. Okay, maybe more than occasional. I just keep wondering ... How long can I get away with this?"

"I thought you told me most of your alcohol and marijuana days were back in high school and then later, in your twenties?"

"Yeah, but I'm at it again. I've been pretty good at hiding it. I'm sure nobody knows."

"Let me ask you this: Are the benzos and opiates your prescriptions?"

"Yeah. Well ... the benzos are. For panic attacks."

"Where'd the opiates come from? And what kind?"

"The opiates are a prescription. Not my prescription. Someone else's." *I'm spillin' the beans now, Maggie thinks. Too late to take it back.*

"Maggie, a couple of minutes ago you asked a good question. Maybe it was rhetorical, but ... I wonder if you really *want* to get away with this?"

"No. I don't know. I'm scared, Peg."

"Have you asked for guidance from your higher power?"

"I forgot about that."

"Let's sort this out. Do you have some time?"

Thirty minutes later Maggie slowly leaves the park. She looks back and admires its neatness. She glances down at her feet and remembers the rule: *Step on a crack, break your mother's back.* She's careful to walk along the sidewalk as she has always done before, stepping carefully to stay within the squares.

A few minutes later she's back at the yellow farmhouse. She notices the two gingko trees on the lawn across from the front porch are shedding their bulbous, mottled, and orangey fruit. The foul, rotting smell reminds her of vomit.

Some fool doesn't know their gingko rules. Obviously, these are female trees and they all have the stinky fruit. Only an idiot would plant trees before doing the research. Male gingkoes don't produce fruit. Those are the ones you plant.

She makes her way around the side of the house to the attached studio apartment. Once inside she's eager to journal her conversation with Peg but is interrupted by her cell phone's ringtone. She recognizes the number Julius called from the other day.

Before she answers, she takes the half-full pack of cigarettes out of her pocket and throws it in the trash. A question races through her brain: *What do I want from Julius? Do I even know?*

"Hello?" Her voice sounds breathless and she feels her cheeks flushing.

Julius doesn't take time to identify himself. "Hello, Maggie. First, I'm sorry I hung up on you the other day. I'll explain in a minute. And, second, I'm sorry I disappeared out of your life. I'm going to tell you why. Are you still there?"

Listen to him, Maggie. Don't interrupt. Let him tell it his way.

"Yes, Julius, I'm still here. I'm really glad you called back."

"Wait a minute, Maggie. My throat is so dry. I feel like I can't breathe. Oh, there's my water." Maggie can hear choir music playing in the background. "Now, I'm gonna sit down," Julius says. "Much better. Water is the source of life, you know. Right? Rhetorical question, Maggie. I don't expect you want to talk about water. When I called you that day, I was all ready to talk. Not nervous. Then my girlfriend walked in the house. She works until six and rarely comes home for lunch. But, on the other hand, she can surprise. Wants to make sure I'm alright."

He has a girlfriend?

"Sounds to me like she cares about you, Julius. Should she worry you're not alright?" Maggie catches herself too late. *Let him talk.*

"She's super. I've had troubles, Maggie. Needed a legal guardian. My family can't or won't help, but she's nice. Though she's kind of a jealous person."

"Somehow I can't picture you with a jealous woman, Julius. You were always so independent."

"Oh, no, it's not so bad. She's a caring person. You'd like her."

I don't know about that. Not if you can't talk on the phone freely ...

Maggie listens patiently as Julius talks at length about how he met his girlfriend. How she was a waitress in a sushi restaurant about thirteen miles south of San Francisco. How he remembers the name of the restaurant was The Happy Eel. How he started calling her his "old lady" right away. How she loves astrology. How she did his chart.

"She saw me once at an ecstatic dance near Half Moon Bay," he says. "It was one of those clubs, and the dance floor was surrounded by windows that hang over the beach. An ecstatic dance is where people follow a beat of their own to live or piped-in music. Sometimes the people go into a trance. Well, almost a trance."

"Yeah, I know ecstatic dances," Maggie says. "We have

them in Oregon, too. 'Piped in' ... now there's a term I haven't heard in a long, long time."

"Ha! Yeah. Remember? We called prerecorded music played through loudspeakers 'piped in'? Guess my lingo hasn't caught up to DJ."

"The ever-changing language we create. Yeah, Julius, I'm with you on that one."

He tells her how they bonded over dancing. He took her to Humboldt, California, where he showed her where he went to college and lived with his parents. *He sounds so young*, Maggie thinks. *Like he's stuck. What happened?* She's not sure what to say.

"Julius, I'm glad you have someone. It sounds like you're happy."

"Yeah, well, I guess I should tell you why I disappeared back in 2000. I'm sorry. I couldn't write to anyone. I couldn't talk.

"I lost my mind, Maggie. I started seeing red everywhere I looked. I broke down—way beyond a run-of-the mill nervous breakdown. Faces were distorted. Lost my hearing. I was an animal but not human."

"Christ, Julius! Were you possessed?"

"What, you mean like *The Exorcist?* Are you Catholic?"

"No. Maybe that sounded kinda dumb." She wasn't sure what she could say that wouldn't sound dumb.

"It's okay. The thing is, I was locked up for a few days in a place for the criminally insane."

Maggie is speechless.

"Hey, Maggie. Are you still there? You're quiet."

She doesn't know what to make of "criminally" insane. Did he commit a drug crime?

She doesn't want to push him, but she has to ask. "Are you still doing drugs? Like, I heard you and Anne's old boyfriend Chris got arrested for heroin somewhere in the central valley."

"Nah, man, they were messing me up. I quit way back when, after the Navy. That heroin deal was all on Chris. What about you, Maggie? Still doing drugs?"

"No," she said. "I'm on a cleanse."

"A cleanse? Okay, that's interesting. For how long?"

"Today's the first day."

"Ha! Figs! You gotta eat figs." He elaborated on the health benefits of figs for several minutes. "Yeah, your nervous system, muscle function, heart health ... and your mind, Maggie. Keeps your mind healthy."

"I love 'em, Julius. Maybe I've been craving them for a reason."

"Hey, Maggie, I got an idea. I have a fig tree at my house. Full of figs right now. Come over and get some. I mean if you want. Tomorrow?"

Maggie hesitates. Is she ready to see him face to face? Does she really want to solve the mystery after all?

"Okay, Julius," she says. "I'd love to get some figs tomorrow."

"Cool," Julius says, " ... and Maggie ... We won't talk about exorcist stuff, okay?"

24 SCHOOL'S A DRAG
June 1969

Tenth grade is almost over and to Maggie, it seems like boys are dropping from the sky.

Community dances, parties at kids' houses when parents are out of town, school sporting events, and friends of friends of friends. There is a faction of senior boys at Paly who seem appealing, but all they want is sex and they are willing to go to great lengths to get it.

Her wild friend Skipper has been hanging out with boys who attend Cubberley, the high school across town. "Hey, I found some more guys you have to meet," she tells the girls. "They've got fake IDs. They know where to buy beer and they always have grass."

At first Maggie isn't interested. She doesn't trust Skipper, for one thing. But the other girls want to meet the guys, so before she knows it, she's moving on to Cubberly parties and Cubberly boys.

Her suspicions fade away when she realizes the middle-class Cubberly boys are a refreshing change from the upper middle-class Paly guys. They have smaller egos and seem humbler than the Paly jocks and rich kids. And they're never stingy with their motorcycles and cars.

Best of all, though—they are respectful. They don't use drugs and alcohol as an avenue to get into her pants.

At one of the Cubberley parties, Maggie chats with Deb on

the patio as a couple dozen kids mill about. "On the plus side," Deb points out, "It doesn't hurt to look at their faces." She follows this appraisal with a low whistle.

One boy in particular catches Maggie's attention. He's one of the cutest senior Cubberly guys, and he does most of the driving. His family's hand-me-down pink Rambler station wagon is as big as a boat and fits lots of kids. Every time Maggie gets into the Rambler, she asks him to put on one of his four-track Grass Roots tapes.

"You always ask for that one, Maggie," he says as he smiles at her. Her heart melts.

He has a signature call when he's had a few beers: "Zooties!"

Maggie doesn't know what "zooties" means, but she laughs at his antics.

God, how I love his blonde hair and how it falls over his brow and into his deep-set, brown eyes. And his light-brown skin. I love his long, dark, sturdy arms. He has this smile and straight white teeth. How badly I want to kiss his lips.

And, before long, she did.

Maggie likes to prank her friends. She does not mean to hurt them; she just sees an opportunity and cannot resist. Anything for a laugh.

One day she shoves Deb toward a bank of school lockers. Unfortunately, Deb loses her balance and falls on the floor. Her books scatter and her miniskirt ends up hiked up to her waist, exposing her blue-and-yellow-flowered bikini underwear.

Once Maggie pushes Skipper into a pond at a miniature golf course. Skipper never sees it coming as she squats at the pond's edge to retrieve a wayward golf ball. Maggie's infectious, loud, and hearty laugh causes Skipper to laugh so uncontrollably that she pees in her pants.

Then there's the night Maggie and Elizabeth ride in the back seat of Elizabeth's brother's Corvair while he drives up and down University Avenue. With the windows rolled down, the girls crouch down low on the floorboards, screaming like apes in hopes people on the street will think Elizabeth's brother is crazy.

Maggie is motivated to feel better, not to do better. Academically, she is still struggling. She soothes her pain and anger with a joint or a beer, but she is careful to stay in control of her body. She is still a virgin.

When she is not high, there are some lonely nights when she bursts into tears for no apparent reason. Her dad is still so sickly and reclusive in the back bedroom. The house feels too tight and oppressive. She flees to the library when she can't breathe in her own house. Not to study but to watch everyone. The younger kids like to flirt. Who is sitting with whom? Who is smoking outside? Who's on that bike? Is it a Kawasaki? A Triumph?

Maggie thrives on the liveliness even if she is not a participant. They seem so innocent compared to how she feels these days. She leaves the library one night and as she rounds the corner of the building, she sees two teenage boys furtively fumbling with something.

"Stop it."

"No."

"Stop!"

"I'm not doing anything!"

"You're walkin' back and forth."

"So."

"Stay still, someone will notice us."

"Shut up."

"Shit. Really, stop it."

"What for?"

"I said, someone will see you. See us."

"Doin' what, candy ass?"

"Fuck you."

"Gimme a cigarette."

"Then stand still."

Maggie's heart feels as if it will fall out of her body.

25 MAGGIE AND JULIUS
Summer 1969

Maggie studies the little astrology booklet she picked up at the drugstore. Every day she reads it, along with other horoscope books she's borrowed from the library.

The fact that Mars is stationed in Sagittarius over the next six months will incline you to give much more positive expression to your emotional and sexual urges. Thus, you will be particularly ardent in your love-making; your sex appeal will be stimulated and because of this you'll have much to do with the opposite sex ...

It makes sense. Next Saturday is when Anne's parents are going out of town and leaving her at home. They even said Maggie could stay over and keep her company. Can't they see how untrustworthy Anne is? Put her with Maggie and what do they expect. Anne says, "We've got to be real careful and not get caught."

Maggie looks forward to spending that night with Julius and his sensual and rosy lips. He wears T-shirts and shorts during the summer, and when they sit close together, she can feel the muscles and tendons of his long, suntanned arms. His legs feel so warm. These are the first boy's legs she has ever felt. Olin always wear long pants.

Julius glances out his living room window to make sure his younger siblings aren't getting into trouble. His long, brown arms are crossed over his chest, his bare feet planted solidly on the worn carpet.

His mother plods past him, going out the front door to the wooden porch. She's laughing.

"For the love of god! What are you doin' out there, kids?"

She is all of thirty-nine years old yet looks twenty years older. Her hair is wispy and fully gray, her large breasts are barely contained by her housecoat, which is covered in bluebells and daisies. Blue varicose veins are visible on her bare calves. She shakes out a dust mop on the wooden front porch and when done, she points the mop at the twins.

The boys are about eight years old. Julius keeps forgetting their exact age. He watches them as they stand near the curb, shaking soda cans filled with pebbles as they do a little dance.

Julius can't figure the twins out, just as he can't figure his mother out. She never looks the same; her facial expressions change by the hour so drastically that she looks like another woman altogether. Sometimes she laughs, sometimes she seems confused by everything.

She tries to keep house the best she can, but she never touches the yard. No gardens grow in the dusty front and back yards. Such a contrast to Julius's friends' homes. Sometimes his mother forgets to cook and on those days, dinner is a free-for-all. Whatever is in the kitchen is fair game.

"I don't think she's cooking tonight," Julius's younger sister tells him.

"So what do you want to eat?"

She doesn't reply. His sister is about a year younger than the twins. At seven, she is already having mood swings like their mother. She's looking at Julius with dark brown eyes, devoid of expression. Suddenly, she turns her attention to the kitchen sink and the flies that are landing on the dirty dishes. Then, she looks back to him, spits at him, and screams. All he knows to do is offer his hands, his arms. She takes them and he hugs her ever so lightly while she sobs.

"Let me make you a sandwich now. Before I leave the house."

Even after high school graduation, Julius continues living at home. He faces uncertain adulthood responsibilities. If he gets drafted, next stop, Vietnam. His draft number is not too low, but low enough that he has an appointment at the Army Recruitment Center in November. In the meantime, he knows there is no money for college, where he could avoid the draft.

His morals lead him to oppose war of all kinds. If he wanted to, he could register as a conscientious objector or he could move to Canada.

Slathering strawberry jam on a creamy peanut butter sandwich, he contemplates how just last spring he was so verbal in his opposition to the war. At Paly they had suspended regular classes to devote an entire school day to Vietnam. He had sat in the packed auditorium, listening to the debates about the war.

Ha! There I was, listening to this bullshit from General So-and-So as he spouted patriotism. I was about to blow. Then I did. I stood up on my seat and shouted at that general. I shut him up good. I was so worked up, I ran from the auditorium. On the way out, though, I caught a glimpse of Maggie in one of the seats. She was clapping and smiling at me.

I think she was proud of me. I was proud of me. But now I've got an appointment for a physical and an interview at the Army Recruitment Center. Shit! I'm moving onward into a life unscripted by me. But what's even more weird is this: I'm wondering if maybe the Navy is the place for me after all. I could get away from home.

After making his sister a sandwich, Julius helps his mother get the twins out of the yard and into the bath. They splash around and his mom smiles.

"You got it from here, Ma? I kind of want to take off for the rest of the day."

"Yes. Thank you, Julius. They can color after their bath."

"Great. Okay. Get them dressed, too. Ma, ask Dad to help with dinner."

"Dinner?"

"Yeah. Remember to ask Dad for help."

"I don't know if he'll help."

"I'll leave him a note and call him later." Julius scoots out of the bathroom.

Enjoyment and embarrassment. His life is a dichotomy. Joy resides in the breathtaking wonders outside his house—in nature, friends, and books. But inside the family's rundown house, it is a stark circus. The house is far too small for his five younger siblings and his parents; and his family is mostly mentally deficient. He wonders if they inherited this from his mother. His father, the scientist, appears fairly normal. His father works full time at a laboratory and tinkers in the shed, inventing shit after dark. And his high-school-age brother, with the 4.0 grade point average and a part-time job, seems okay, too. But the fifth younger sibling is completely insane and lives at a state hospital. Julius considers himself somewhere in the middle of those two—not an honors student but also not a nutcase.

Booking out the front door, Julius heads toward Olin's house just a few blocks away. He strides barefoot under the cool shade trees. His blue jeans drag on pavement, fraying the hems even further. Hopefully, Olin is home. Julius wants to talk about his family and Olin is one of the few people he can trust.

It was Olin who suggested, when they were both in the fourth grade, that he stop bringing friends over to his house after school. He told Julius the other kids laughed about him behind his back. It was Julius's first experience with feeling ashamed. He took Olin's advice and stopped inviting anyone to his house.

Years later, he still keeps visitors waiting on the porch, so they won't see the shabby, worn furniture, the odd things his siblings have done to the rooms, and most importantly, the way they act around strangers. He loves his family with all his heart but is afraid of their outbursts of gibberish, their lack of boundaries, their disrespect of personal space. Keeping people away is the easiest way for him to feel normal.

Julius spent much of his early youth at Olin's house. Olin's mom loved to feed him. He would sit at a large table in the center of the kitchen, with its old appliances and black-and-white checkered floor. It was one of Julius's happy places. His heart was full and he easily cried when he felt the affection of Olin's family. Sometimes his little sister and brothers sat silently around that kitchen table, waiting for Olin's mom to serve them a hot meal.

In spite of it all, Julius found making friends easy by the time he got to high school. Playing varsity football helped smooth his way socially. If he heard guys talking about surfing near Santa Cruz beaches, he asked to join them. They generously taught him to surf. He was so fearless that strangers on the beach asked him to teach them.

"Jules, you're a natural. Here's to some bitchen waves. Hang ten," wrote a friend on a full page in their yearbook that was devoted to a picture of Julius surfing.

His talent as an artist garnered him many admirers during the three years he took art classes at Paly. To keep his drawings safe from his destructive siblings, he stored them at Olin's house. He didn't tell anyone he was usually high when he was drawing.

It only takes a few minutes to reach Olin's house. He bounds up the front steps and opens the front door.

"Olin. Hey. You home?"

"Yeah, Jules. Come in. On the phone with Maggie. Be right there."

Maggie? He's on the phone with Maggie? He spent an evening at her house only the other day listening to music and playing Canasta. I doubt Maggie tells him when we're together. What are they talking about?

Julius puts a Velvet Underground album on the stereo and sprawls out on the couch in Olin's living room, waiting for him to get off the phone. "Maggie-isms" fill his brain: her pretty smile, her warm, taffy-like sighs; that skipping thing she does on the foggy beach; and her sweet, minty kisses. Not an hour goes by that he does not think about her.

This kind of friendship is new. The double dates they go on give him a chance to let down his guard and be vulnerable.

And it's usually double dates since he doesn't have a car. Maggie doesn't complain and she even drives sometimes. Julius shrugs off his lack of a vehicle and laughs about the symbiotic relationship between high school guys and their cars.

Sometimes Maggie and Julius fool around in the back seat of Chris's Volvo while Chris and Anne fool around in the front seat. They park in the hills overlooking the lights of the Bay Area. He is still a virgin. Virginity is awkward, but the road to nonvirginity is equally awkward. A lot of guys he knows brag about sex, but he approaches sex carefully, especially with Maggie. He takes nothing for granted with her and it's a cinch treating her nice. He even gave her some Chanel No. 5 on Valentine's Day this year. It smells good on her; especially when they fool around.

Julius likes the way things are going. He doesn't need to go steady. He is prone to disappearing for days when he hikes the Sierras at Lake Tahoe and surfs up and down the coast. When he returns, it seems as if Maggie has an air of fairy newts. Like an angel, she saves him from something scary in his home life.

He suspects he is poles apart from other guys she knows. He pretends not to know she sees anyone else, but of course he knows. Outwardly, he clings to his nonchalance. Hey, it's all good, man.

He likes going to her house and talking with Mrs. Mayes about everything from music to politics while Maggie laughs affectionately. Last month, over a large slice of homemade apricot pie and a glass of milk, they talked about Gore Vidal and William F. Buckley, Jr.

Julius is growing restless. *Why are Olin and Maggie on the phone so long?* Julius bites his nails and sweat drips off his neck. A horrific thought enters his mind. *Is she going to tell Olin what I said to her the one time we spent the night together?*

Anne's parents were out of town for the weekend, so he and Chris snuck in after dark. Maggie and Julius slept in the same bed overnight, a big step up from the back seat of a car.

The closest they got to going all the way was when, partially clothed, he positioned himself on top of her. They moved around and around and suddenly he came all over his boxer shorts and her pink baby doll PJs.

"One of us just had a baby!" he exclaimed, humiliated and at a loss for words. *Maggie would never share that with Olin, would she?*

He's getting tired of waiting for Olin. He turns the Velvet Underground album over to side two, then fishes a piece of paper from his pocket. He reads what he wrote just a few days ago.

Have you ever woken up at eight in the morning on a Saturday and were not able to go back to sleep, no matter how tired you were because you felt so lonely and your heart was breaking? Did you ever feel that you needed someone to fill that emptiness and hold you and make you feel wanted? Unfortunately, the one person you really wanted is the very person you are lonely for. And did you start crying at eight in the morning on a Saturday?

26 SEARCHING FOR HER IRRECONCILABLE SELF
September 2015

So much for the cleanse. At four o'clock Maggie is sitting outside a wine bar in downtown Palo Alto, sharing a couple bottles of dark red Malbec with Deb, Rhonda, and Anne.

Lost in the thought of seeing Julius, she pulls one of her ruminations out of the air. "Love felt like a frontier in 1968. Unknown limits. Sweet fruit grew everywhere. The world was not flat and that was all the truth we needed to navigate the wild, wonderful world of the opposite sex."

She hears a whistle of wings above her, followed by a soft call: "Coo. Coo. Coo." Four mourning doves swoop past.

"Do you see that? The doves?" She puts on her sunglasses and looks again at the sky.

"No."

"No."

"No, where?" Deb asks, then coos for effect. "Maggie, I just love the way you see things. And the way you describe our past."

"Opposite sex. Well, yeah, we dated a lot," muses Anne. "Every day, week, month, and year that followed 1968. Plenty of guys."

Maggie sighs. "I figured it out last night. I'm needy.

Acting all independent and everything. I rarely flew solo. I was lonely."

Rhonda takes a healthy swig of her wine. "I could have told you that."

"But you were always going places alone or reading. It seemed you were good at being alone," says Deb.

"Well, that was different, Deb. That's about being an only child. I had to make my own kind of entertainment. Annie gets it. She's an only child, too."

"Yep." Anne nods.

"Annie and Mags. You both had guy after guy after guy. No breaks in between. Pour me a little more. I'll be right back." Rhonda goes outside, a block away, to smoke a cigarette. She turns her head to look at them; her waist-length brown hair swishes around her. She waves and giggles.

They cannot hear her giggle, but they recognize her expression.

Maggie studies Anne, still mostly blonde and in trim shape; and Deb, hair faded from red to almost blonde. *She looks a lot shorter.*

"Deb, your eyes hold a mystery. Don't they?"

"What do you mean, Maggie? Wait, tell me when I get back. I'm gonna go have a cigarette with Rhonda."

Anne starts whispering, even though she and Maggie are alone. "Okay, now they are both gone, I want to remind you how lonely I was over my divorce." She raises her voice as Deb moves out of earshot. "I had no idea he was contemplating divorcing me. First chance I got, I looked up old boyfriends. Met new ones. Anything to feel better. You remember."

"You told me about panic attacks. I know something about panic attacks, Anne. What did yours feel like?"

"I thought I might have a heart attack. My heart thumped into my belly. Arrhythmia. That's what I thought was happening."

"Once I thought I was having a heart attack, too. I was in a meeting at work. I remained calm and waited to fall on the floor. Another time, I was driving and I got so afraid. Just out of nowhere. Dread knotted in my belly. About a month later, I had a seizure. A real seizure. Doctor couldn't find anything. Eventually said it was maybe a fluke, due to stress."

Anne brings her wine glass up to Maggie's. "Cheers to that business. Once I got in my car and drove over to this guy's house when my kids were in school. We met at work and kinda hit it off. I don't know what I expected, but there I was. At his door. Knocked. He answered. And he had a woman with him. So stupid. I had to talk my way out of that one. Stop." She lowers her voice again. "Rhonda and Deb. Coming up behind you."

"What are you two whispering about? Mysteries of the universe?" Deb moans as she sits down. "My goddamn hip."

"Are you drunk?" asks Rhonda. "You kinda look it. Deb and I were talking about the guys. Maggie, when are you gonna see Olin? And what's up with Julius?"

She picks out the cashews from the bowl of mixed nuts on the table. "I remember your mom's voice as clear as day, Maggie. She would say, 'I'm telling you, you're running off half-cocked and burning the candle at both ends.' Is that what you're doing with Julius and Olin? Weird undertaking. That's what it is. Why it should matter where Julius is? It seems obvious he doesn't want to be found and Olin is getting off on stringing you along. Just like always."

Maggie looks down at her drink as Rhonda continues.

"I don't really get it, Maggie. You keep every memento and dwell on the past. I don't know anybody who saves letters from years ago. What made you keep those letters from Julius? It's just a little strange. But I have no opinion either way. I'll help you any way I can."

Maggie has always admired Rhonda for being blunt, even when it stings. "Okay, Rhonda. You got a point. Maybe I'll forget about it and go home."

"No, no, no. I don't want you to go home, Maggie. I like hanging out with you. Just forget what I said."

"I know how pitiful I must look to you, Rhonda. But hold on a minute and let me tell you. I talked to Julius on the phone today."

"Wow."

"Huh?"

"When were you gonna tell us?"

"I'm tellin' you now. Not only that. I'm going to his house."

"He's here?"

"Where?"

"Just south of San Francisco." Maggie takes another drink of wine. "So the mystery will soon be solved."

Maggie stands on the sidewalk across from Julius's house. She tried to leave her nerves in the car.

It's a white, stucco bungalow with a sky-blue front door. A stand of eucalyptus trees lines the driveway to the right of the bungalow, which leads back to a detached, one-car garage. A ten-speed bike is locked to a rack beside the trees.

Julius is on the other side of that door.

She knocks, then rings the doorbell for good measure.

The door opens and Julius Brownell stands in front of her, dressed in brown, corduroy cut-offs and a navy T-shirt that says "I'm Passing This Way Again."

"God in heaven. It's you, Julius."

"Holy mackerel, Maggie."

"What do you think 'holy mackerel' means? I haven't heard that one in ages."

"It means Maggie Mayes is standing at my door. Come in. Come in. Yeah. Come on in."

Amid hugs and laughter, Maggie takes in Julius's surfer tan, freckled nose, and rosy lips. *I swear, he looks nineteen again. The same innocent dark eyes.*

"So you're a blonde, Maggie! Blond-ish with some brown. And what's that? Some white? Some beautiful white hair, yes. You look the same, yet more womanly."

"That's generous. Well, then, Julius. You are manlier."

"This blows my mind. I need to sit down." He points to a sofa by the front window. "I'll sit in this chair. It's my favorite chair. It's my mom's."

As soon as he sits down, he pops back up. "Tea! I bet you'd like some tea. Jasmine?"

"Sure. I can help you with it."

The kitchen is in the back of the house. Julius fumbles with the boxes of tea. Maggie saunters over to the enormous window over the white porcelain sink. Crystals hang down from fishing lines from the ceiling, turning and catching the light.

"Deb has crystals hanging in front of a window in her house. Just like yours."

"Deb? Where does she live? Are you still friends? What a trip."

"Yes, we are still friends. Best of friends. She lives in Oregon. I live in Oregon now, too."

"Not Connecticut?"

"Some things change, Julius. Others, not so much."

Beyond the window are dozens of rose bushes. All different shades of pink. In the middle of the rose bushes stands a fig tree.

"Come. Sit outside on the patio. That's where I relax. There's a table for our teacups. And look, the fig tree I was telling you about on the phone."

Maggie is surprised by how relaxed Julius seems to be. He asks about all their friends and she fills him in on what everyone is doing now. Eventually the conversation runs dry and she waits, sipping her tea. After a few minutes of silence, Julius begins to speak.

"It started when my sister came over. You remember my sister, don't you, Maggie?"

She nods. Julius looks off into the distance while he tells her the story.

It happened in December 2000. His sister came over to the house in northern California where Julius was living with his parents. She was there all morning, agitated, fussing with their mother's crocheted doilies and blankets in the front room. Complaining about what she called a silly hobby.

"She started spitting out curse words at our mother and

saying, 'You made my childhood hell.' I didn't know what brought this on." Julius shudders at the memory. "I chased her out the front door. When I went back inside, I found my father pounding on the bathroom door, yelling, 'Get out of there, you bitch.'

"Maggie, my mother hadn't even locked the door. I pushed past my father and went inside the bathroom and there she sat. On the toilet. Curled over her knees. Singing a church song. I think it was 'Onward Christian Soldiers.' Her hands were covering her ears."

His father came in and carried on where his daughter had left off. Shouting in his wife's face, he yanked her hands off her ears and told her what a witch she was. A witch who puts spells on the family. He said she destroyed the family and demanded that she keep her mouth shut. Then he started hitting her, repeatedly smashing his fist into her face.

Julius lost it.

A neighbor heard the ruckus and called the police. According to the police report, Julius tried to kill his father. The police pulled his hands off his father's neck. The paramedics took him to the psych ward at the hospital for observation, where he went into shock. He was catatonic.

"I didn't remember anything for a long time."

His parents also went to the hospital. His mother needed stitches for the injuries to her face. She was eventually taken to a woman's shelter. His father's neck was so bruised and swollen, the doctors wondered how he survived the strangulation. He was charged with assault and wound up in jail.

"Mom didn't want to press charges," Julius said, but it was out of her hands. She was persuaded not to bail her husband out or pay for a lawyer, so he remained in jail for six months until his trial. He decided to act as his own attorney, was put on probation and performed community service, cleaning bathrooms in the city parks.

In the meantime Julius was so out of his mind, a string of psychiatrists said he was unfit for a trial and needed psychiatric care. The judge ordered him to a VA hospital, where he remained for three years.

"Otherwise, Maggie, I would have been tried for assault with the intent of murder. The real sad thing is, my parents got back together again. I stayed away as best I could."

"So your father was abusive, your sister was abusive, and you, dear Julius, went haywire." Maggie pauses. "Julius, can I ask you ... Why was your father so angry with your mother? Why was he telling her to keep her mouth shut?"

Julius looks away again. "Maggie, I don't think I can tell you. Doesn't everyone have at least one secret they keep to themselves? Don't you have one?"

Maggie nods. "Yeah, I have some stuff I don't tell anyone."

"Then we're even, right? We'll each keep a secret to ourselves."

"Okay, Julius. I won't ask anything else. I'm just so glad you recovered."

"Yeah, I got some good rehab through the VA. Made it back out into the community. Can't work anymore, though. It's just too stressful."

He smiles at her. "But I got VA benefits, disability, and ... I can't remember what all I get. My girlfriend is my guardian, so she'd be the one to ask."

"Julius, I'm not going to stay long enough to ask your girlfriend any questions. I just wanted to make sure you were okay. I need to leave soon." Maggie is suddenly very, very tired.

"Well, wait. Before you go, tell me about you. I'm tired of talking about myself. What are you doing here?"

"I'm actually writing a book. I write mystery novels."

Julius smiles wistfully. "Goddamn. You did it. You became a writer. You know, I've always loved your poems."

"Thanks. That means a lot to me. I'm using Palo Alto as an inspiration for the book. Feels good to be here."

"What's the mystery about?"

"To quote your own words: 'I don't think I can tell you.' Besides, I'm superstitious about revealing too much."

Julius looks pensive. "After what I told you, do you think I am a horrible person?"

"I can't judge you."

He stands up and walks over to the fig tree. "Can we reminisce for a while? And then I'll get the figs I promised you."

"You bet."

"Remember the concerts at the Grass Steps?"

"I'll never forget them. Remember the Poppycock and its jukebox?" They both laugh as they revisit the days that seem so incredibly innocent now.

Before leaving, Maggie gives Julius her home address and phone number.

"So we'll keep in touch, right, Julius?"

"No promises. I'm worried I'll disappoint you, Maggie. Again."

"Well, then, Julius, let's just do what feels comfortable."

"I'm grateful for your friendship." Tears cloud his tortoise-shell glasses. "But I've got to tell you that in 1968 I wanted to be your boyfriend something fierce. And you dumped me. You never talked to me about it. You just dumped me.

"The years we wrote letters when you were in Connecticut … I didn't trust you. Not really, Maggie. I asked myself why you'd want to rekindle a relationship when we hadn't seen each other in decades. We lived so far apart. I asked myself what kind of frame of mind were you in that you wanted us together?

"I tried to slow it all down, but you ignored my words. You pushed me, Maggie."

Maggie can't defend herself. He's right, after all. She puts her arms around him and hopes he feels her regret.

"Goodbye, Julius."

"Let's take good care of ourselves. Whatever that means to you, Maggie. Be gentle with me and especially with yourself. I won't tell you not to write me, but if you do, write sparingly."

"I will."

27 TIME HAS COME AT LAST
August 1969

"When I came home from the lake with Olin, my mom looked at me with that mean face." Maggie is recounting her story as she and Anne sit on her bedroom floor. "We should have trucked right out of there, but we started making milkshakes."

"Those rocky toad milkshakes?" Anne asks.

"Yeah. Those milkshakes we invented last summer with Rocky Road ice cream. We had the munchies because we got really stoned at the lake and then messed around a little on a blanket in the dark. I got a little weirded out because Olin wanted to go all the way. I don't want him to be my first. I don't want to get hurt if he thinks I'm a slut. What if he dumps me after?"

"Yeah, that's risky business with that fella! I'm so glad my first time was with Chris. He has been so sweet to me ever since. I think because he felt like kind of a heel when I started crying after we did it."

"So cool, Anne. You have a tender heart. He loves you so much."

A hush grows between them. They look at each other and Maggie can see the tears streaming down Anne's cheeks. Her mascara is running, and when she wipes her face with the sleeve of her peasant blouse, her eye makeup smears even more.

"I'm a mess!" she complains.

"Chris is so cute," remarks Maggie.

"I know! I mean, everybody thinks he's kind of a badass ... " Anne sniffles, "but he's a softie inside. Just like Jim, Deb's boyfriend, on that Harley of his. He wears leathers and kinda sneers like a tough guy. And then on the inside he has a heart of gold. Doesn't talk much, but when he does, he's soft spoken." Anne pauses. "Jim kinda feels like a brother to me. It seems like he wants to protect me. Not like a boyfriend or anything even close to that."

Maggie is silent. She wants what Anne and Chris and Deb and Jim have. She wants to possess and be possessed in that way that is undeniably flesh, bone, and body bound. She stands up and puts another record on the stereo. The Velvet Underground breaks the silence like a burp right out loud.

Anne has recovered from her emotional confession. "Okay, Maggie, so back at the ranch. What happened with you and Olin and your mom and the rocky toad milkshakes?"

On the floor Maggie crosses her legs. Her skin-tight jeans make it a little uncomfortable to sit this way.

"Yeah, so then, all of a sudden my mom comes out of nowhere, kind of like Norman Bates, all psycho and wild-haired and mad-faced. All five foot two of her, blue eyes blazing, and she whips out the baggie of grass I left in my jacket pocket that I wore to the lake. Stupid me! Then she hauls off and slaps me in the face! In front of Olin!

"I can barely remember the rest. Olin left pretty fast. I don't know what happened and in what order, but the next morning she told me she burned the grass in the backyard."

"Burned it? In the backyard? That sixteen-dollar lid of Acapulco Gold that we split? Do you believe her? Do you think she got high? Man, oh man!"

"Speaking of munchies, I've invented a tasty snack. Come out to the kitchen with me."

Anne follows Maggie. She takes a spoon that Maggie hands her and watches her take a Hershey's chocolate syrup can out of the fridge. Next, she grabs a Jiff creamy peanut butter jar from a cabinet and a spoon for herself.

"Okay, now take a spoonful of peanut butter and then hold your spoon over the sink and do what I do," says Maggie. She drizzles chocolate syrup over the spoon, watching the extra syrup threads drip into the stainless steel sink. Plink, plink. They are eating the gooey mess over the sink when they look up to see Chris and Julius through the window.

Anne screams, "Holy cow!" as she and Maggie try to wipe off the peanut butter and chocolate syrup off their faces.

The boys let themselves in the front door and meet the girls in the kitchen. Chris snatches Anne and puts her in an embrace. He playfully licks a stray dab of chocolate off her face.

Julius stands in the doorway between the foyer and the kitchen, howling like a rogue. Maggie can't help but notice how his tall, lanky body looks so fine today.

"Hey! Get this," he says after he settles down.

"Chris's madre isn't going to be home tonight. We have a place to go instead of the car on the side of a road in the hills," he tells Maggie. "And I've got some good dope."

28 LOVE
August 25, 1969

Sagittarius Horoscope for Monday, August 25th
Romance–A date at a very fashionable
rendezvous is in the cards.

Chris, Anne, Julius, and Maggie have come up with a plan for tonight's rendezvous. When Maggie emerges from her room at six o'clock, showered, hair brushed, and with the palest of lip gloss, her mother says, "Have a good evening at Tressider Union with Anne."

"Thanks. Yeah, we're going to bowl and play pool. Hopefully, Anne's cousin will meet us there. She's got the Stanford student ID to get us in," Maggie lies. "She said she'd bring her roommate so we can all bowl together."

"Who's driving, Maggie?"

"Um, Anne is. Oh, I hear her VW now."

"Home at eleven."

"Sure, Mom." Maggie waves as she heads out the door, avoiding eye contact. She hustles down the driveway and jumps into the car. "Hit it," she tells Anne.

Anne fills her in as she pulls away from the curb. "Okay, here's the plan. Meet the guys at Foothill Park. Get stoned. Make an appearance at Tressider so we don't feel too deceptive. Eat with the guys at the Union. Then head to Chris's house. Sheez! So much to think of," laughs Anne.

Driving east up Oregon Expressway, they cross El Camino

and the expressway changes to Page Mill Road. From there they hit the hills, climbing steadily up curving Page Mill Road to Foothill Park. Anne shifts her Bug around the corners of the two-lane country road and up the hill to the gate of the park. If they had driven past the park, a twisting, two-lane road would have taken them up to Skyline Boulevard at the crest of the Santa Cruz Mountains, offering a sweeping panoramic view of San Francisco Bay and the surrounding Bay Area.

Foothill Park is accessible to Palo Alto residents and their guests only. The 1,400-acre Foothills Park is a nature lover's paradise. Fifteen miles of trails provide access through rugged chaparral, woodlands, fields, and streams. In the middle of the park sits a small lake. Fishing and motorized boats are not permitted.

Anne shows the park attendant her driver's license for entry into the park. The guys are waiting, reclining on the lawn.

"Good gracious!" says Julius, as he watches the girls mosey up to them. "You look worried, Maggie. Are you okay?"

"Hell, yes!" says Maggie. "I just need a minute to unwind is all."

"Doobie time!" laughs Chris. "Light it up, Jules. We got a date with a joint."

"This is primo stuff," smiles Julius. "It's such a bummer that your mom took away your Acapulco Gold and burned it in the backyard, so I scored some for us tonight."

Their knees touch as they sit in their circle amidst a fragrant drift of grass. Eight deeply suntanned arms lift and pass the joint as if they are slowly flying and hovering. Chris and Anne fall back on the lawn in an embrace and he tickles her. She wriggles and arches her back to escape his torture. Maggie feels that creeping flush of warmth between her legs and stands up quickly to quell it.

"We better go, guys!" she says. Julius pulls her back down to him and swiftly she is kissing him, her tongue finding his. They can barely part.

"Hey! Hey!" she pants. "We gotta make it to Tressider for something to eat. I've got the super-munchies!"

They all admit they're hungry. Besides, curfew is eleven o'clock and they have business to get down to.

"Monkey business," says Anne.

"Show business," laughs Maggie. "Anne, are you okay to drive?"

"I hope so. I'll go slow and steady, Freddy." They boogie on out of there in two cars and get a quick snack at Stanford University's outdoor café at the Tressider Student Union.

Now, to the den of iniquity—Chris's house, sans family. His parents are divorced, and while it is rumored his dad is a drunk living in a dump of a house in Redwood City, his hard-working mom rents a modest three-bedroom apartment wedged in between statuesque, early 1900-era homes and other apartment buildings in the heart of downtown Palo Alto. Their mother's job at a local catering company doesn't pay much, so Chris and his older sister both work to help with expenses. After high school graduation, Chris got a job working at a gas station. His sister does clerical work.

Their home is sparse of decoration, but the living room is furnished with purple, velvet-covered club chairs and a large matching sofa. Chris says the furniture belonged to his late grandmother.

Daylight is fading, so Chris lights some candles. He puts some Chambers Brothers on the turntable and mixes a vodka Collins for everyone. The mood shifts. The music ends. It doesn't take long before they head into Chris's darkened bedroom furnished with twin beds. Another stereo sits atop the nightstand that separates the two beds. Chris puts some Hendrix on and closes the door, leaving the lights off.

Anne and Chris are on one twin bed. Maggie and Julius are on the other.

Maggie feels more determined than nervous. *I know it. This is it. I'm going through with this for the first time. We're going all the way. Sweet Julius. No fumbling in cars. No stopping us now.*

207

29 I DON'T WANT TO SEE YOU ANYMORE, BABY
September 1969

Maggie sits sideways on Julius's lap, her legs draped over the curved arm of the club chair. Julius's arms are around her. They laugh and whisper.

"No, really, Maggie. I can't be the first guy you've done it with. You and Olin, right? I just assumed."

"No! No way. Never. We didn't. Tonight, with you, is the first time for me."

She is starting to feel the throbbing again.

"Wow, man." Julius smiles and says, "Let's go do it again."

They return to the dark little bedroom. Hendrix's "Crosstown Traffic" plays while both couples move quietly on the twin beds.

Maggie's father continues to neglect his health and disobey doctor's orders. One day he falls deathly ill while he and Maggie are alone in the house. She calls her mother at work.

"You need to drive him to the hospital," her mother says.

Everything is a blur to Maggie. She remembers her father moaning in the car and how the sound makes her sick. She remembers very little about the hospital. Or his death.

She can only remember how glad she is that he's gone.

A horde of her father's relatives arrive for the funeral. There's an emptiness to the service. None of Maggie's girlfriends are in attendance. She is surprised and gratified when her former boyfriend Chuck and his brother Don—her former crush—come to the service, along with their mother. For another month, right up through September of her junior year, Maggie and Julius are an intimate couple. Intimate in a sweet way. There's no opportunity to go all the way again, due to her father's death, but Maggie is happy that Julius was her first. She's not in love with him, but she can trust him.

She cannot imagine her social life beyond where it is right now, but something unexpected happens in late September. A couple she knows tells her about their friend, who just graduated from Cubberley High School. "We think you two will really hit it off. C'mon. Give him a try. We'll go along, too."

She agrees to a blind date. A double date is easier, she reasons, if it turns out she doesn't like him.

But she does. Right away she's smitten by his foxy smile and long eyelashes. The four of them listen to Santana, drink beer, and talk about astrology. Her friends are right. So absolutely right. Something in her expands like a well filling up after a wild rainstorm. His eyes. That smile. They hit it off, alright. He asks her out for the following Saturday night.

Maggie is so blown away, she can't get to sleep until three in the morning.

After just four hours' sleep, Maggie is exhausted and anxious. She wants to go out with this boy again, but she'll have to cancel her date with Julius. She's torn. It's been good with Julius. She's not unhappy, it's just that this new guy seems to have it all together: junior college, job, van ... Plus he's athletic, self-assured, and assertive. Maggie is swept off her feet.

She cancels the date with Julius over the phone. She tries to think up a good reason, but fumbles so much that he is suspicious. Finally, she admits the truth about the other guy.

Julius hangs up. Maggie returns the phone receiver to its cradle and stares at it.

"I've done this all wrong. This just does not feel good."

Somewhere inside she knows this is cruel, but another part of her doesn't care.

Julius takes out his anger on the telephone, slamming the receiver into the cradle as he starts to cry and shake. He rarely expresses such rage, but he can't help himself. He feels like something has snapped in him.

"I've got to get out of town. I'm gonna go nuts otherwise."

He grabs his jacket, wallet, and sunglasses before walking out of his family's small house. He practically runs the few blocks between his house and the Greyhound Bus Station. He's just in time to catch the next bus into San Francisco, where he knows he can find some really fine weed.

30 JIGSAW PUZZLE
September 2015

Maggie's on the phone with Olin.
"I'm telling you, Maggie. Julius's parents were brother and sister. I suppose they are dead now and so it doesn't really matter if I tell you."

"Did Julius tell you this?"

"Nah. My mother did because Julius's mother told her. She trusted my mother and had no other friends."

"And they got married? What minister or justice of the peace would marry them?"

"Well, I don't know about that. They came from Utah, though."

"Yeah, I remember Julius told me he was born in Utah."

"If you ever see Julius, you can't tell him you know this." Maggie is silent. For some reason she doesn't want to tell him she already saw Julius.

"The girls are coming over tomorrow, Olin. It's probably the last chance we're going to have for that reunion before Deb, Anne, and I have to leave. Are you and Steve coming or not?"

"Sure, we'll be there," Olin says. "In fact, we'll bring breakfast."

Maggie gets Deb and Anne on a conference call. She tells them Olin and Steve will be coming tomorrow and Olin has a secret he's ready to share about Julius.

"Do you know the secret?" Deb demands.

"Yeah, I actually do," Maggie admits.

"I want to know the secret before I come over. That's what I want," says Anne.

Maggie understands their curiosity. She sighs. Might as well tell them. "He says Julius's parents were brother and sister. And I didn't tell you yet, but I saw Julius yesterday. I found his brother's contact information and he let Julius know I was looking for him. He called. I went to see him. He's been through some horrible shit but he's getting better. He has a girlfriend."

Deb and Anne have a million questions, but it's getting late and Maggie still needs to call Rhonda. "Look, let's talk more in the morning," she tells them.

Her conversation with Rhonda is brief. Rhonda bluntly uses the "R-word" when talking about Julius's family. "The whole family was freaky," she adds. "And about Olin, I don't expect much from him. He had a big ol' freakin' crush on me, too, you know, Maggie, back in '68. He asked me to sing in the band he had with Steve, and I was tempted because Steve was so good-looking, but I thought Olin was kind of gross. Sorry, I know you liked him."

Good old Rhonda. Still as opinionated and outspoken as she was in 1968. Maggie smiles as she says goodbye.

The next morning, Anne and Deb arrive at eight-thirty. "Wake up, Maggie. You scoundrel," says Anne as Maggie opens the studio door.

"I'm awake. I'm awake. And even dressed."

"Well," asks Deb. "Aren't Olin and Steve supposed to be here by now?"

"In an hour or so. Listen, I know you're mad. Does it help for me to say I didn't want to let it all out until I had some proof Olin was right?"

"Tell us more about seeing Julius." Anne wants to get to the point. "Tell us if the secret is true."

Maggie has had a lot of time to think about exactly what Julius said, but she keeps her answer brief.

"Well, I already told you pretty much everything. Julius did allude to some awful family stuff, but I didn't try to pry it out of him. I just couldn't. So I don't know the truth. He was sick for a while, but like I said, he's getting his life back together."

Fiddling with a glass of water in the kitchen, Deb says she will stay just to give Olin hell. Anne says she wants to see Steve.

"C'mon, girls," Maggie says as she motions toward the door. "Let's sit outdoors. I feel too cooped up inside. Rhonda will get here soon, I think."

"What about Elizabeth?" Deb and Anne ask in unison.

"She's at work. She'll come over later this afternoon if the guys are still here."

It's close to ten o'clock when Rhonda arrives. "Oh, my god! There you all are. Where are the guys?"

"No idea," Maggie says. "Probably more car trouble … wasn't that their excuse last time?"

Rhonda scowls. "Car trouble, cell phone trouble … Olin isn't very creative, is he? Got any coffee while we wait, Maggie?"

Maggie walks briskly down the street, heading in the direction of the little community park she has visited so often during the past four weeks. The squirrels scatter as she invades their territory, striding down the dirt path that winds through the park. In the morning the old men practice tai chi on the basketball court, but it is late afternoon and the court has been taken over by boys practicing their three-pointers and slam-dunks.

When she reaches the other side of the park, she walks about a mile down Louis Street. Soon the architecture of the neighborhood changes to a cluster of small tract homes that were built in the mid-1950s by Joseph Eichler. Intrigued by the modernist designs of Frank Lloyd Wright, Eichler emphasized bold, buoyant design through indoor-outdoor living, atriums, radiant-heat floors, walls of glass, and ceiling beams that extended outside.

Within minutes Maggie finds herself standing in front of the Eichler house where she grew up. Not long after Maggie was born in San Francisco, John and Greta Mayes made the decision to move to suburbia and they purchased their Eichler tract house in Palo Alto.

It's been quite a few years since Maggie has seen her old house. The last time she was here, she felt a roller-coaster of emotions. Too many memories to process. She had pictured herself and all her friends roaming around from room to room, those ghostly teenagers who have never left her mind or her heart.

This time she doesn't feel the same sense of nostalgia, and she's not sure why. The house looks run down and rather lonely, as if it's been waiting for her to return. How could you leave me behind? She hears the words in her head and is not surprised. This house tried to communicate with her from a very young age, sometimes in otherworldly ways.

There were secrets in this house, she always suspected. She always wanted to know the truth, but it eluded her. She's at peace with that now, since she finally understands that sometimes secrets should never be shared.

Like the secret of why Julius lost his mind. When she visited him, he had told her about the horrific fight with his father, but he had not told her everything. Julius had not told her that when his father was screaming at him, he had learned for the first time that he was the child of a brother and sister. That was the secret that had broken Julius's mind for so many months. He had grown up with his strange family but had never known the full truth about his parents until that violent day. To his credit, Olin had never told his good friend what Mrs. Brownell had confessed to Olin's mother.

It didn't take long for Maggie to figure out what must have happened in the Brownell house that day. After all, she was a mystery writer.

Maggie walks a little farther down Louis Street. She doesn't want to attract the attention of any of the neighbors by standing too long in front of her old house. She notices yet another Eichler house has been torn down and replaced by a new structure and curses under her breath. *What are they doing to this historical neighborhood? It's a crime to destroy these iconic homes. Joseph Eichler built and sold his homes to people of all races. His work was a retort to homeowners who wanted to keep their neighborhoods white. Ashamed and defeated, those white folks backed down. Don't people have any sense of history anymore?*

Maggie recalls the day the girls arrived to visit her at the studio apartment, when they wanted to know everything about her visit with Julius. She had been cagey, and now she understands why. She was being protective of him.

She could not betray Julius again. It was bad enough that she had treated him carelessly. It was bad enough that Olin had blurted out the truth about his parents and she had shared it. She did not have to take the next step and describe the reasons for his breakdown, or how he tried to kill his father, or his struggles to stay sane.

She could be a good person.

Maggie turns around and walks past her house again as she heads back toward the community park. She ignores the urge to gaze upon it one more time.

Her thoughts turn back to the other day, when Elizabeth finally arrived at the studio apartment in the afternoon. Anne, Deb, Maggie, and Rhonda were all laughing and drinking outside on the patio.

"Hey, looks like I've been missing a great party. So where are the guys?" she said.

The girls just looked at each other and burst out laughing again.

"Olin called," Deb said. "You know, he's been staying with his niece in San Jose, right? Well, he said he walked to the donut shop on the corner to buy a bunch of donuts and pastries to bring to us and who do you think he ran into? One of his old girlfriends from Paly! So he told Steve he wanted to catch up with her and could Steve pick him up later than planned, and then he and Steve got into an argument and, well, you know, the whole thing just fell apart."

"You're kidding!" Elizabeth said. "That jerk. So we're not

going to see them after all?"

"Guess not," Maggie said. "No boys of summer this time. Hey, do you want something cold to drink?"

The ageless sound of the laughter of girls soon filled the air again.

31 PURPOSE
September 2015

Maggie bends over and snaps another dead flower from the planter outside her studio apartment door. She has watered the flowers faithfully, but they are dying. It's this damn drought, she decides. Why, then, is the fig tree bursting with figs and the ginko tree still producing its stinky fruit? It's spooky, that's what it is.

All her friends have gone back to their own lives. Promises to write, text, or call are exchanged. They all wish Maggie well with her book. She's certainly gotten enough material from her visit to be able to finish her novel, but somehow the drive is no longer there. A week without distractions should have been the perfect time to write. *What did I do all week? It's kind of a blur.* Maybe when she gets home, she'll be motivated.

She heads inside to finish packing for the drive back to Oregon tomorrow. File folders stuffed with notes and manuscript drafts are still scattered around the room. On the desk sits a letter she finished writing a few hours ago. *Better go to the post office before I forget*, she decides. She picks up the letter and reads it one more time.

Dear Julius,
It is a challenge to live in the present. I focus so much on trying to control the future, trying to force joy to last forever,

that I find myself shoving momentary joy away. As far as loving myself, I see a cycle. I love myself, get hurt by other people, hate myself, spend time with myself, and then I love myself all over again. There is always someone waiting with a quip and then I feel betrayed. Again. Joy and a blow and a bandage. A cycle.

My teenage years brought rapid cycles of emotions. I had my opportunity on the timeline to be lithe, pretty, and full of smiles and big dreams. I loved how I moved, sang, danced, and flirted. I relived life in the way I did my little-girl dances in front of a round mirror attached to an art deco dressing table: scarves draped on my body, dancing to Frank Sinatra and American folk songs. Flirting with myself in the mirror.

Dangers and betrayals visited me but did not limit my expansion of horizons. I was a mouse on the edge of one field, waiting to scurry across pavement headed for another field. Barn owls swept down to carry me off in their talons. The pain accumulated. I found bandages. I sometimes used substances to numb the pain, and I shoved pain into those locked rooms in my brain.

I love the girl I've brought along with me all these years. With all the beautiful memories for which I am so grateful. I'm also grateful that I'm a flirt. I accept and embrace my boys of summer. The boys who live in my mind always. I love them most and always will. I don't know if I'll ever stop looking for them.

In hindsight, it doesn't matter who asked the questions. It doesn't matter who lied. It could have been anybody. I understand it's quite possible to like someone and maybe even love someone who has unbecoming personality traits. It's possible to encourage the real person beneath. I can't say a person is born bad; perhaps an angry or frightened person appears bad because they had to use survival tools just to make it. I think we are all villains and saviors.

I am sorry I did anything to you or anyone else that caused sadness. I want epiphanies to show me my footsteps from behind and in front of me. I need to believe that I can live in the present while still seeking answers. They can co-exist. I want to be shocked by electrical sparks from within to see and understand myself in three-dimensional decades of floating colors. I will swaddle my little abandoned self until she is ready to stand up. She always stands alone yet always needing an angel, a wise confidante, a psychic, a medium, and lifelong friends.

I want my mother, who has been dead now for sixteen years. I know now, as a mother and grandmother myself, that my mother knew me inside and out from the beginning. No matter what I did or said, she loved me anyway the best way she knew how. I wish she were here to talk to, for that kind swipe of my hair from my cheek, and a song while I tried to sleep. I must be looking for her in everyone I meet and if not for the moments I watched and wondered about you, I could not be writing this to you now. Hold me in your memories and smile, Julius. Your innocence has not left you.

Your friend, Maggie

Maggie addresses the letter to Julius and decides to walk to the post office instead of drive. She is oblivious to the cracks in the pavement, stepping carelessly wherever she pleases. Her usual languid stroll, absorbing the scents and sounds of Palo Alto, is replaced by a focused trek to mail her letter.

After the post office, Maggie heads to the Baskin-Robbins ice cream shop across the parking lot. She orders her favorite, a Triple Treat. Three scoops of ice cream, three toppings, nuts, and a cherry. She savors it on her walk back to the studio.

Once inside, she takes a bottle of Riesling out of the fridge and pours herself a generous glass. She turns on the TV, smokes a doobie, and finishes her wine. When the glass is empty, she pours another and takes it over to the bed. *I just need a little nap before I finish packing.* Fifteen minutes later she's still wide awake. *How can I be so awake yet so tired?* she wonders. She glances over at the nightstand, where her prescription Xanax and her stolen stash of opiates are still lined up, waiting to be packed in her toiletries bag. *These will help. Maybe not too many, though.*

Maggie falls asleep to the soft cooing of the doves.

ACKNOWLEDGMENTS

I would like to thank my husband, daughters, and grandson for their patience and encouragement. I am grateful for the friends who are also family to me. Their shenanigans inspired many stories.

The Coffee Talk writers' group was a mainstay of support during the process of writing this novel, as was the LPGC critique group. I also appreciate Carol Pound's time and care in reading the manuscript and giving me valuable feedback.

Finally, thank you to my diplomatic editor, Stephanie McMullen, who believed in me and turned me into a storyteller.

ABOUT THE AUTHOR

Jodi Lynn Threat has a degree in journalism and enjoys writing poetry. *Letters to Julius: Postmarked Palo Alto* is her first novel.

After living and working for many years on the East Coast, she moved to Oregon with her youngest daughter and their greyhound. It was there that she met her husband and then her cat, who sits on her lap while she writes.

Jodi is currently working on her second novel.

35687884R00129

Made in the USA
San Bernardino, CA
13 May 2019